PRAISE FOR THE NOVELS OF MARTA PERRY

"What a joy it is to read Marta Perry's novels! . . . Everything a reader could want—strong, well-defined characters; beautiful, realistic settings; and a thought-provoking plot. Readers of Amish fiction will surely be waiting anxiously for her next book."

—Shelley Shepard Gray, *New York Times* bestselling author of the Amish of Hart County series

"A born storyteller, Marta Perry skillfully weaves the past and present in a heart-stirring tale of love and forgiveness."

—Susan Meissner, author of *As Bright as Heaven*

"Sure to appeal to fans of Beverly Lewis."

—*Library Journal*

"Perry carefully balances the traditional life of the Amish with the contemporary world in an accessible, intriguing fashion."

—*Publishers Weekly* (starred review)

"Perry crafts characters with compassion yet with insecurities that make them relatable."

—RT Book Reviews

"[Perry] has once again captured my heart with the gentle wisdom and heartfelt faith of the Amish community."

—Fresh Fiction

Pleasant Valley Novels

LEAH'S CHOICE
RACHEL'S GARDEN
ANNA'S RETURN
SARAH'S GIFT
KATIE'S WAY
HANNAH'S JOY
NAOMI'S CHRISTMAS

The Lost Sisters of Pleasant Valley Novels

LYDIA'S HOPE
SUSANNA'S DREAM

Keepers of the Promise Novels

THE FORGIVEN
THE RESCUED
THE REBEL

SARAH'S GIFT

Pleasant Valley

BOOK FOUR

MARTA PERRY

BERKLEY
New York

BERKLEY
An imprint of Penguin Random House LLC
375 Hudson Street, New York, New York 10014

ISBN: 9780451491572

Berkley trade paperback edition / March 2011
Berkley mass-market edition / August 2018

Printed in the United States of America
1 3 5 7 9 10 8 6 4 2

Cover art by Shane Rebenschied
Cover design by Sarah Oberrender
Book design by Tiffany Estreicher

This story is dedicated to the memory of my parents, Joe and Florence Perry, and my grandmother Mattie Dovenberger.

Acknowledgments

I'd like to express my gratitude to those whose expertise, patience, and generosity helped me in the writing of this book: to Erik Wesner, whose *Amish America* newsletters are enormously helpful in visualizing aspects of daily life; to Donald Kraybill and John Hostetler, whose books are the definitive works on Amish life; to Louise Stoltzfus, Lovina Eicher, and numerous others who've shared what it means to be Amish; to Mary Hostetler, for her invaluable guidance as a midwife to the Plain People; and most of all to my family, for giving me a rich heritage upon which to draw.

Chapter One

The first step in Sarah Mast's new life didn't seem to be going quite the way she'd expected. She stood at the bus station in the village of Pleasant Valley, her plain dark suitcases by her feet, and pulled her black coat around her against the chilly November wind.

She could sense the curious glances of passersby, even though the brim of her bonnet cut them from view. Folks were probably used to seeing the Amish in this central Pennsylvania valley, but maybe not an Amish woman standing alone in so Englisch a place as a bus station.

She could see the clock above the counter through the plate glass window. Nearly a half hour past the time she'd told Aunt Emma the bus would arrive. Why was there no one here to meet her?

Doubt crept in, as it did so easily these days. Maybe this move had been a mistake. Maybe . . .

She pushed the weakening thoughts away. Aunt Emma's letter had offered her a chance she hadn't expected . . . a chance to start over in a new place where she was Sarah

Mast, midwife, a useful member of the community; not Sarah Mast, childless widow, an object of pity.

The creak of a buggy alerted her, and she turned to see an Amishman climb down. She let out a breath of relief and headed toward him, but when the man turned, Sarah saw he wasn't one of her cousins. She stopped, flushing when his startled gaze met hers.

Recognition seemed to grow in a strong-featured face that was vaguely familiar, even though she couldn't put a name to the man. He stopped, inclining his head slightly.

"You are Emma Stoltzfus's niece, ain't so?"

"Ja." She let out her breath in a sigh of relief. "Sarah Mast. I was afraid Aunt Emma had forgotten I was arriving today."

His dark eyebrows drew down over brown eyes as he seemed to assess her words. "You were expecting her to send someone to pick you up already?"

"I thought you—"

"I'm afraid not." He seemed to realize she wasn't sure who he was. "I'm Aaron Miller. My home and shop are just down the road from your aunt's."

"Of course. I should have remembered." She'd have met him the last time she was here, probably.

"I think it must be a good six or seven years since you visited Pleasant Valley. Long enough to forget a few names, ain't so?"

She nodded, but the memories had begun to come back now that she had a name to hang them on. Aaron was taller and broader than the boy he'd been then, but he hadn't changed all that much. He was clean-shaven, showing a strong, square jaw, which meant he wasn't married yet, and he had to be a year or two older than she was. That was unusual among the Amish, who married and started their families earlier than their Englisch neighbors.

The wind whipped around the corner of the building, and Sarah couldn't stop a shiver.

Aaron frowned, glancing up and down the street that

was lined with a mix of businesses, some Amish, some Englisch. "How long have you been waiting?"

"Half an hour. Maybe a bit more. I'm sure someone will be along soon . . ."

"There's been some mix-up—that's certain sure." Aaron bent and picked up her suitcases. "Let me stow these in the buggy and see if the part I expected came in on the bus. Then I'll take you to your aunt's place."

"I don't want to put you out." Though anything would be better than standing here in the cold.

"It makes no trouble. I'll be headed home anyway." He hefted her bags in easily and then took her arm to help her up to the high seat, closing the buggy door to cut off the wind. In a moment he had vanished into the bus station.

She settled on the seat of the closed buggy, tight muscles relaxing. Foolish, to be so stressed by the trip from Ohio, but what had been an adventure when she was an enthusiastic eighteen, out to spend the summer with a favorite aunt, had been a tiring ordeal this time. She looked back at the girl she'd been with a sense of amazement.

She'd been so sure then of the course her life would take. She'd be a midwife like Aunt Emma, delivering lots of babies. She'd marry the man she loved and have babies of her own.

She'd become a midwife. She'd married Levi. But the longed-for babies hadn't come, and eventually that seemed to taint everything else.

Aaron returned, shoving a cardboard box under the seat before he climbed up. He settled on the seat next to her and gave her a smile that brought her memories of him into sharper focus. "All set?"

"Ja, fine."

She slanted a glance at him as he picked up the lines and clucked to the horse. His face had always been strong, even as a teenager, with a gravity that seemed to say he took his responsibilities seriously. She waited until he'd moved into the stream of traffic before she spoke again.

"You had younger brothers, I remember. And a sister who was a bit younger than me."

"Molly." The gravity lightened at his sister's name. "She married last year. She's expecting a baby."

"That's wonderful news." Warmth filled her voice—the warmth she always felt at knowing a new life was coming into the world. She'd tried to never let her own childlessness affect that. "She must be so happy."

"Ja, and her husband, too. She married Jacob Peachey. He's a gut man."

"And your brothers?" They were on the edge of town in a matter of minutes. The traffic lessened, and his hands were relaxed on the lines.

"Nathan and Benjamin are still at home. They work with me doing carpentry and remodeling."

"That's gut, having them with you."

Aaron would be a fine older brother, she'd guess from the little she remembered of him. Patient, steady, soft-spoken, with a quick intelligence showing in even light conversation.

"I heard that your husband died. I am sorry for your loss."

She nodded in acknowledgment. "Denke, Aaron." She tried to stifle the pain that sympathy always brought on. Levi was gone, but his disappointment in her lingered. Maybe it always would.

Sarah. Barren, like Sarah in the Bible. The difference was that the Old Testament Sarah had eventually seen her dreams of a child come true. Of course that Sarah had waited until she was over eighty for God's gift. This one would rather have it a little sooner, if ever it should happen for her.

She took a deep breath, focusing on the road ahead. That wasn't part of her future, as she saw it now. Aunt Emma's need for help and Sarah's need for a new life came together in a way that had to be God's design for both of them, surely.

Aaron turned onto the narrow blacktop road that wound past farms and woodlots. The trees had lost their leaves already, and the corn had been cut for silage. Aunt Emma had written that autumn had turned cold quickly this year in Pleasant Valley. But the silos would be filled, and the Amish farmers ready for the quieter time of year—time to read, write letters, visit with family.

"Your aunt will be looking forward to your visit," Aaron said, as if he felt bound to make conversation with a visitor. "Especially now, since I hear her practice is closing."

Sarah swung toward him, shock ripping through her. "Closing?" For a moment she couldn't breathe. "No. The practice is not closing. That's why I am here, you see. I'm a midwife. I'll be helping her with the practice." All her hopes for the future seemed to fill the words.

She saw his face in the moment he processed her words. Saw it harden, turn tight with rejection of her, of her plans.

To Aaron Miller, at least, she wasn't welcome here.

Aaron didn't say much for the rest of the trip to Aunt Emma's. Maybe that was just as well. His unguarded reaction to her presence was enough for Sarah to handle.

"There's my place," he said.

Aaron jerked a nod. A white frame house stood well back from the road, with a small barn and a few other outbuildings behind it. A hand-lettered sign simply read, *Miller, Carpentry.*

Identification enough, she supposed. In a community like Pleasant Valley, everyone would know who did what.

"Is there enough work to keep you and your brothers busy, then?"

"There's always work for a carpenter." His face tightened slightly. "That's what I tell Nathan and Benjamin."

His expression seemed to add that his brothers didn't always agree.

"How old are they now? I've lost track."

"Nathan's nineteen. Settled in his work, he is. Starting to think of courting."

So it must be the other brother who needed reminding of the value of steady work. "And Benjamin?"

"Benj will soon turn sixteen." His mouth clamped shut on the words.

Maybe it was best not to ask more about Benjamin, who was probably like most almost-sixteen-year-old boys, eager to experience a bit of life before settling down.

And Aaron? She did some mental calculations. He must be nearing twenty-eight or twenty-nine, she'd think, some two or three years older than she was. She thought again how odd it was to find an Amishman that age who wasn't married.

They rounded a curve in the road, and Aunt Emma's house came into view. Sarah's heart gave a leap of pleasure. The frame farmhouse, its front porch sagging a little, was as welcoming now as it had been years ago, even though the flower beds looked sere and brown without their welcoming blaze of color, with only the dusky purple of the fall sedum to add a spark.

"I hope Aunt Emma is all right." The question of why no one had been sent to meet her demanded an answer. If her aunt were sick . . .

Aaron's broad shoulders moved under his black coat. "Seems like Emma's been a bit forgetful lately."

She bit back a retort. Aunt Emma had always been sharp-witted, as well as the strongest woman Sarah had ever known. Surely she couldn't just forget that her niece was arriving today.

There was no point in getting into an argument with Aaron about it. Besides, she'd know for herself in a moment. The buggy rolled up to the hitching post at the back door, and Aaron jumped down.

He pulled her bags out. She slid down easily, not waiting for his proffered hand. In a few steps she was at the door, opening it as familiarly as if she were in her own house.

"Aunt Emma? Aunt Emma, are you here?" Concern lent an edge to her voice.

Aunt Emma emerged from the living room, brushing a

strand of graying hair back under her kapp. "What . . . Sarah! What are you doing here today, child?" She rushed across the kitchen to envelop Sarah in a satisfying hug.

Sarah held on for a moment longer than necessary, blinking back tears. It was like hugging her mammi again, gone now nearly five years.

Aunt Emma pulled back, beaming, and patted Sarah's cheek. "Ser gut to see you. But you weren't coming until tomorrow."

"Today," she corrected gently.

Aunt Emma turned toward the calendar pinned to the kitchen wall, its photo of kittens in a basket the only picture in the room, of course. "Thursday, that's what you told me. See, I have it marked."

"Thursday." Her heart sank, and she would not look at Aaron to see his expression. "Today is Thursday."

"It is?" Aunt Emma's round cheeks paled. "Ach, I can't believe I made such a mistake. What will you think of me? Imagine you coming in on the bus and no one there to meet you."

"I'm fine." She hugged Aunt Emma again, wanting to wipe that expression from her face. "Aaron gave me a ride, so it all worked out."

"Aaron, that is ser gut of you." She seemed to notice Aaron for the first time, standing by the door with Sarah's bags in his hands. "Denke, denke."

"It makes no trouble." He set the bags down. "I'd best get along home." He nodded to Sarah. "Wilkom to Pleasant Valley, Sarah."

"Denke, Aaron." His words had sounded welcoming. But some shadow in his voice didn't.

Enough, she told herself as Aaron went out. What Aaron Miller thought of her presence didn't matter in the least. She was here now, ready to leave the past behind and begin her new life.

But even as she said the words to herself, she knew it wasn't her own reassurance she needed. It was Aunt Emma's.

"Komm, take your coat and bonnet off and warm up." Aunt Emma was already at the stove, putting a kettle on. "Sit, talk. You must be hungry after that long journey. It won't take a minute to hot up some vegetable beef soup."

"That sounds gut." And her stomach did seem to be flapping against her backbone about now. Maybe that was why she was letting doubts creep into her mind.

"How did you happen to find Aaron?"

Aunt Emma cut slices off a crusty loaf of bread, her movements sure. She sounded more like herself every moment, and the memory of the stricken look on her face when she'd realized she'd forgotten the day began to fade.

"He was picking up something for his business, I think, that had come in on the bus. He tells me the boys are working with him now. And that Molly is married and expecting a boppli."

"Ja." Aunt Emma turned, her face filled with the same joy Sarah felt at the news. "Imagine little Molly old enough to have kinder of her own."

"Not so little, surely. She's only a year or two younger than I am."

"That's so." Aunt Emma stirred the soup. "I didn't know how Aaron and the boys would get along without her when she married, especially since she's clear out in Indiana. But Aaron takes care of everything, just as he always did."

"What about his daad?" she inquired.

Aunt Emma shook her head. "Such a sad story. Poor man always did have a weakness for drink. Time and again the bishop and the ministers would try to get help for him, but . . ." She let that trail off. "He passed away two years ago. The young ones were fortunate to have a big brother like Aaron, that's certain sure. Their grandmother helped out as best she could, but she was never all that strong, so it fell on Aaron."

"It's odd Aaron never married. I'd think he'd want a woman's help with the younger ones."

Aunt Emma set bowls of steaming soup on the table and fetched the bread. "Folks always thought that, but Aaron never seemed to consider it. Maybe he felt the responsibility was his alone."

Sarah nodded, mulling over the idea. It fit with her impression of the man. Aunt Emma sat across from her, bowing her head for the silent prayer before eating.

Thank you, Father, for this new beginning.

Once Emma raised her head again, Sarah broke off a piece of bread and picked up her spoon. The first mouthful of soup sent warmth through her, chasing away what remained of her doubts.

"Wonderful gut soup." She smiled at her aunt. "I've been so eager to get here to see you."

"Ach, I feel the same." Aunt Emma reached across the table to clasp her hand. "I never thought to say this, but it gets lonely here in the evenings by myself. Maybe Jonas is right."

When she didn't continue, Sarah lifted her eyebrows. Jonas was her cousin, the oldest of Aunt Emma's three sons and the only one still living in Pleasant Valley. A gut man, but a little bossy.

"What might Jonas be right about?"

"Thinking I should move in with him and Mary, and sell this place."

The words shocked Sarah so that for a moment she couldn't speak. In all Aunt Emma's letters this possibility hadn't even been hinted at.

"But they live clear over near Fostertown. How would you tend to your patients from that far away? And what about your plans to build an addition for birthing rooms, so women can have their babies here if they want? I thought you'd started work on it back in the spring. It must be about done, ain't so?"

Something in Aunt Emma's expression warned her. Sarah stood, walked to the door that should lead to the new addition, and opened it. And stared, her heart sinking.

The foundation was completed—Aunt Emma had written about that. And the walls roughed out. But otherwise, it was just an empty, unfinished space.

Sarah turned, closing the door, feeling as if she were closing the door on her hopes. "Aunt Emma, what happened? You said it would be all ready by the time I arrived."

Aunt Emma drew back, lips pursing. "I thought it would. But Jonas felt it was a waste of money. He insists it's time for me to stop working so hard and just take it easy."

"But that's what we planned." Sarah was drowning in a tide of dismay. "What we talked about. That we'd be in practice together, working together the way we always wanted to."

"Ach, do you think I don't know that? It's what I always wanted, too. And I certain sure don't want to disappoint you."

Sarah took a steadying breath, trying to drown out all the voices that had insisted she was being foolish and headstrong to make this move to Pleasant Valley.

"Don't worry about me." It took an effort to say the words. "Or about what Jonas thinks. What do you want, Aunt Emma?"

Her aunt drew herself up, a flash of her usual determination in her face. "I want to go on delivering babies, just like always. I want to go ahead with the birthing rooms." She glanced toward the door. "Still, Jonas . . ."

She let that trail off, and Sarah thought she understood. Jonas was making difficulties about the money it would cost to finish the addition.

But Sarah had the answer to that, didn't she? If she really was committed to this move, maybe she had to be willing to take a risk.

She sat next to her aunt, clasping Emma's work-worn hand where it lay on the table. "Let me pay for the rest of the addition." She tightened her fingers when Aunt Emma seemed about to protest. "That's only fair. After all, if I'm going into practice with you, I should invest something, and I have the money from the sale of our share of the farm."

For a moment she could feel Aunt Emma's resistance. Then, slowly, it faded.

"You would do that?"

The money was all she had. But what was it for, if not to invest in her future?

"Nothing would make me happier."

Tears shimmered in Aunt Emma's faded hazel eyes, but her grasp was firm. "We will do it, then."

"We will do it," Sarah echoed. Come what may, she was committed now. There was no turning back.

Aaron walked into the carpentry shop, carrying the package he'd picked up at the bus station when he'd run into Sarah Mast.

Nathan looked up from the workbench where he was sanding a cabinet door. "Something wrong? You look like a thunderstorm."

"Nothing. Here's the new knobs for Mrs. Donohue's cabinets." He set the package on the workbench. "Maybe now we can get that job finished."

Nathan grinned. "If she doesn't change her mind again."

"Easier to work for Amish than Englisch." Aaron slit the tape on the box, checking to be sure the knobs were the ones they'd agreed on. "An Amish woman wouldn't be so worried about having the latest fashion in cabinet knobs. A knob's a knob, isn't it?"

Nathan shrugged. "She's the customer."

"She is." He shouldn't be taking his ill-humor out on Nathan, of all people. And his mood had little enough to do with Mrs. Donohue, with her constant chopping and changing. It was Sarah Mast's arrival that had him annoyed, and that was the truth of the matter.

He smoothed his hand down the cabinet door Nathan was working on, appreciating the fine grain of the wood they'd chosen. Then he glanced around the shop. "Where's Benjamin?"

"He saw you drive on by. I guess he thought that meant we were done for the day."

"That boy thinks anything is an excuse to quit work."

"He's not yet sixteen." Nathan's tone was indulgent. "A boy's mind is on everything but work at that age."

"Listen to you, sounding like a long-bearded elder."

Aaron clapped Nathan's shoulder, regaining some of his good humor. Nathan tended to take things as he found them, which made him a gut partner in the business. As for Benjamin—

Well, maybe Nathan was right, and the boy just needed to do a bit of growing up. But Nathan hadn't been so heedless at that age, and as for himself . . . well, he'd never had the chance to be that way with the younger ones to take care of.

Nathan smoothed a cloth over the door. "So, are you going to tell me what you were doing over at Emma Stoltzfus's place?"

"When I got to the bus station, I found Sarah Mast waiting there for a ride. You remember her? Emma's niece from Holmes County?"

Nathan looked thoughtful. "Can't say I remember her, but I knew Emma had kin there. So you brought her to Emma's."

"Ja." Aaron frowned. "It seems Emma forgot this was the day Sarah was coming and hadn't sent anyone to meet her."

"Lucky for her you happened to be there today. This niece came by herself?"

He nodded. "She's a widow."

He seemed to see Sarah the way he'd seen her in that first moment, standing alone, an isolated figure in black, out of place among the Englisch who brushed heedlessly past or stared at her with curiosity. And to see the smile that lit her green eyes when she thought he'd come to fetch her.

"So this Sarah's come for a visit to her aunt?"

Nathan sounded interested. Not surprising. The Amish of Pleasant Valley, Pennsylvania, were a little isolated themselves, living far from the heavily Amish areas like Lancaster County and Holmes County. A newcomer was always of interest.

"That's what I supposed." He felt the tension grip his jaw again. "But she says she's a midwife, come to join her aunt in her practice."

Nathan lifted an eyebrow. "I thought Jonas said his mother was closing down the midwife practice and moving in with them."

"It looks like Jonas was wrong." Or maybe Sarah was wrong, in which case she'd had a long trip for nothing.

"I guess you think that's too bad."

"It's nothing to me." He avoided looking at his brother. Whatever he felt about midwives . . . well, he was entitled to his opinion, but to share it smacked of speaking ill of a member of his congregation, and he would not do that.

"You've met this niece before, ain't so?" Nathan was obviously not done with the subject.

"She was here for a summer a while back. Maybe six or seven years ago."

If someone had asked him yesterday, he'd have had trouble recalling that fact. Now an image of the girl she'd been popped into his head, as clear as if it had been a week ago. She'd come to a singing with his sister, the two girls laughing and talking together as if they'd known each other forever.

That was their Molly, open and warm, quick to laugh, with a determined glint in her eyes when she thought he was being too bossy with her or the boys.

Next to her, Sarah had been quiet, even a little shy, but with a warm sparkle in her green eyes that reminded him of a stream bubbling over moss-covered rocks, and a reddish tint to her brown hair.

That glow was gone now. The Sarah he'd met today looked as if she'd been through some difficult times. Her oval face was thinner, and the eyes held wariness as well as maturity.

Well, not so surprising. She'd known sorrow all right, with her young husband dying that way. An accident of some sort, he thought, though if he'd heard the details, they'd been forgotten.

Nathan set the cabinet door upright and held one of the knobs against it to see how it looked. "Not bad. Maybe Mrs. Donohue was right."

"Maybe. I'll be glad to get the job finished."

"What do we have coming up next?"

Nathan was shaping up to be a fine carpenter, but he seemed to have little interest in the other side of the business—getting the work, keeping the records, paying the taxes.

"Nothing pressing. Bishop Mose was talking about having some new shelves put up in the harness shop, but that won't take long."

Business always slowed down this time of year, but this year seemed slower than usual.

Nathan shrugged, unperturbed. "Something will turn up."

The door rattled, letting in Benjamin and a blast of chilly air. The boy was sprouting out of his coat, it seemed, his sleeves showing bony wrists and the big hands he hadn't quite grown into yet. But he was closing in on them. He looked like Mammi, with those clear blue eyes and corn-silk hair, but he was going to have Daad's height.

Worry tightened inside Aaron. As long as that was all the boy inherited from their father.

"Where have you been?" The words came out a bit more sharply than he'd intended.

"Just took a little break." Benjamin was instantly defensive. "Nothing wrong with that, is there?"

Aaron forced his face to relax into a smile. He kept praying God would give him more patience with the boy, but he had to do his part.

"No, nothing wrong." He nodded toward the bundle clutched in Benjamin's hand. "Anything interesting in the mail?"

Benjamin grinned suddenly, looking about six again. "A letter from Molly. That interesting enough?"

"Molly?" Nathan grabbed for it, but Benjamin held it teasingly out of reach. "Komm, give it."

"Wouldn't you like to know what she says?" Benjamin ducked behind the workbench, grinning.

"Grab him, Aaron." Nathan dove toward his brother, and Aaron joined him in wrestling their little brother for the precious letter.

When Aaron stood, running a hand through his hair a couple of minutes later, whatever remained of his ill-humor had vanished. "What would Molly say if she caught us wrestling in the shop?"

"Stop that, you boys," Benjamin piped in a silly treble. "Read it, Aaron." He hoisted himself onto the worktable.

Aaron ripped the envelope open, scanning the pages quickly. "She says she's well, and Jacob has been busy with work. She says—"

Nathan took advantage of his stopping to snatch the letter from him. "You're too slow. She says . . . Ach, listen to this. 'Jacob's work crew is going out to Wisconsin on a job. I don't want to stay here by myself, so tell Benjamin to get out of my old room. I'm coming home to Pleasant Valley to have the boppli.' "

Nathan waved the letter, grinning. "Molly's coming home!"

Joy flooded Aaron's heart. His little sister would be with them again.

To give birth to her baby. He sobered. One thing was certain. If he had anything to say about it, Molly wouldn't be going to a midwife to have this baby.

Chapter Two

Sarah walked slowly around the outside of the addition to Aunt Emma's house, wrapping her shawl around her against the cool air. The late-November sunshine was weak in comparison to the chill, but it carried a welcome warmth. She tipped her face back, enjoying the touch of the sun on her skin, feeling as if she were waking from a long sleep.

Maybe she had been asleep, in a way . . . The sudden blow of Levi's death had been followed by what seemed a long period of inertia, when she'd been unable to move in any direction.

With Sarah's own mother gone, Aunt Emma, in the form of her constant letters, had carried Sarah through that time. Her proposal that Sarah come to share her practice had been the prod she needed to wake up. To seek a new direction—a new life.

Now that new life was starting, and if her arrival here had contained a bit of disappointment—Aunt Emma's failure to send someone to pick her up, the discovery that the birthing rooms weren't finished—at least she was here and ready to move forward.

The birthing rooms were a simple matter, ain't so? She'd talk to Aunt Emma about getting the carpenter back to work again.

She turned, glancing toward Aaron Miller's shop and house. Had he done the work? She'd have to find out.

She couldn't see the house from here, not with the stand of trees in the way. But a plume of smoke drifted above the woods, marking the place.

A pasture stretched from Aunt Emma's house toward the trees, fenced in for her buggy horse. The animal lifted its head to stare at Sarah when she moved, then dropped it again to crop at the browning grass. A few trees dotted the pasture, to provide shade in the summer, and a pond eliminated the need to carry water. Everything about Aunt Emma's place was as neat and tidy as ever—no doubt Jonas saw to that.

"Sarah?" Aunt Emma called from the doorway. "Komm, schnell, breakfast is ready."

With a last glance at the addition, Sarah obeyed. This was going to work out the way they'd planned. Of course it would.

She brushed the dampness from her shoes at the door and hung her shawl on a hook, following the aromas of coffee and breakfast bread to the kitchen.

"You didn't need to fix such a big breakfast for just the two of us." She picked up the coffeepot as Aunt Emma set a pan of cinnamon buns on the table.

"Ach, I must make up for forgetting the day yesterday. Such a wilkom that was for you." Aunt Emma pressed her cheek briefly against Sarah's, then sat down and bowed her head for the silent prayer. Sarah did the same. *Denke, Father. Thank you.*

"Eat, eat." Aunt Emma passed her a bowl of scrambled eggs. "You are too thin."

She accepted, knowing her aunt would only be happy if Sarah ate some of everything she'd set on the table.

"I was looking at the addition. You've made a gut start, ain't so? Will you let the carpenter know to start again?"

Aunt Emma frowned. "Sarah, are you certain sure you want to do this? I know you said you have the money from the farm, but—"

"I'm sure." She brushed away the faintest sliver of doubt. "The money is mine to do with as I want, and this is what I want to do."

It had been a battle of sorts, getting the money for Levi's share of the farm in a lump sum. His father and brother had not liked the idea, insisting she'd be better off to go on living with them, accepting small payments each month.

There'd be time enough to want the rest if she married again, which she might. A widower with children to raise would be a gut match, according to Levi's father.

Her lips tightened at the memory of that conversation.

"There was trouble with Levi's family over your selling his share of the farm, ja?"

Sarah hadn't mentioned that in her letters to Aunt Emma, but her aunt seemed to know anyway. "Ja." A small sigh escaped her. "I didn't wish to be at odds with them, but I could not fall in with their plans for me."

"Marrying a widower with kinder who needed a mammi." Aunt Emma had a twinkle in her eyes. "No, you didn't tell me so, but I know well enough how some people's minds work. Levi's father is a gut enough man, but not one to understand a woman wanting to go her own way."

"No, he's not. But Daadi talked to him with me." She felt a rush of gratitude for her father. He might not understand her moving so far away, but he had supported her decision.

Aunt Emma nodded. "Your maam did well when she settled on your daad. She could have had any of half a dozen boys, as lively and pretty as she was, but she never looked at anyone else."

"No, she didn't." Sarah's voice went soft. She knew how

devoted her parents had been. "I thought that Levi and I would be like that, but . . ." She let that die off, not wanting to sound disloyal to her husband.

"Levi couldn't deal with not having kinder of his own." Aunt Emma patted her hand. "He could not accept that it was God's will."

"No." Familiar guilt stirred at the thought.

When the doctor could find no reason why she hadn't become pregnant, Sarah had ventured to suggest once that Levi go to the doctor for testing, but his anger had shown her that it was better to accept the blame herself rather than persist.

"Well, now, we should talk about the clients who are coming in today." Aunt Emma seemed to understand that Sarah wasn't comfortable with the subject of her marriage. "I want both of them to meet you."

"There are just two?" That startled her a little. She could remember a time when Aunt Emma saw many more than that on her at-home days.

Her aunt stiffened. "Not so many as I once had. There is a new doctor in town, and some of our people are going to him. But things will pick up once we have the birthing rooms finished." She moved briskly as she spoke, bringing to the table the notebook in which she'd always kept her schedule. "You'll see."

Her confidence was a contrast to the doubts she'd expressed the day before, and Sarah found her own spirits rising, too.

"And we must get going on the addition," her aunt added. "I've been thinking on how best to move ahead with the work."

"Is there a problem? Surely the carpenter who started it—"

"He's a friend of Jonas's." Aunt Emma's lips pursed, and her old determination showed in her face. "When he learned Jonas didn't want me to do it, he suddenly became too busy to finish. No, I won't call on him again."

"I'm sorry." Sarah didn't know what else to say. She

didn't want to get in the middle of a family dispute, but Aunt Emma could certainly decide this for herself.

"So I think it will be best if we ask Aaron and his brothers to take the job. You can go over and talk to him after we're finished for the day."

"Me?" Her voice squeaked a bit, and she seemed to see again the negative reaction in Aaron's face at learning she was a midwife. "I'm not sure—"

"That is best," Aunt Emma said firmly. "You will be paying for it, so you must handle the plans. That is, if you're sure you want this."

Put like that, she could hardly say no, so she nodded. But she could still see the disapproval in Aaron's strong face, and she very much wondered what his answer would be.

As she walked up to the carpentry shop that afternoon, Sarah realized that despite the setbacks, her confidence had been growing throughout the day. Getting back into harness as a midwife was just what she needed. She'd been away from patients too long while she settled things back in Ohio.

In a way, this would be even better. There, she'd been one of a number of midwives. Pleasant Valley had only Aunt Emma and now her to provide for a growing Amish population.

Still, she couldn't help the faintest tinge of worry. She remembered a time when Aunt Emma saw twenty or more women on a prenatal-visits day. Did a new doctor in Pleasant Valley really account for such a change? If the practice didn't pick up . . .

She forced herself away from anxious thoughts. After all, the two women she'd met today had been welcoming. Dora Schmidt, the first, already had seven babies, and she had every confidence that number eight would arrive on time and with little fuss.

Rachel Zook was expecting her first baby with her new

husband, Gideon, although from what she said, she had three children from her first marriage. Still, she seemed as excited and happy as if this were her first.

Aunt Emma, with the indulgent smile of someone who'd delivered hundreds of babies, had let Sarah deal with Rachel. Sarah had felt an instant bond with the woman, and they'd spent several minutes talking about whether they'd met when Sarah was here before.

Rachel had bloomed with joy over the coming baby. Sarah firmly suppressed the faintest hint of envy. She would never allow her longing for a child of her own to interfere with her happiness for the mothers in her care.

She was approaching Aaron's shop. Sarah stiffened her backbone in preparation for meeting him again.

Maybe she was being unfair to him. She shouldn't let a moment's impression affect her attitude toward the man. She deliberately quickened her steps.

Sarah opened the shop door to the sounds of a generator and saw, and the scent of freshly cut wood. The shop was larger than she'd thought from the outside—as big as the whole downstairs of Aunt Emma's house, maybe. The Miller brothers probably held church here when it was their turn to host worship.

And despite the piles of lumber and the machinery, the shop was as neat as a housewife's kitchen. That didn't surprise her. Aaron struck her as a man who would be methodical and neat at anything he attempted.

But the man who turned off the saw at her entrance wasn't Aaron. He had Aaron's height and coloring, but his face was relaxed and open in contrast to the gravity that seemed to sit constantly on Aaron's expression.

"I am Nathan Miller." He dusted his hands off on a rag as he came toward her. "And you must be Emma's niece."

"I am. But how did you know that?" She found herself responding to his smile.

"Easy. I know every Amish person in Pleasant Valley, so since I don't know you, you must be newly komm." He nodded toward the window, grinning. "And since you walked, you didn't come far. So it was simple."

"I guess so." Nathan was easier to talk to than his older brother—that was certain sure. "I think I must have met you when I visited my aunt years ago, but you would have been a small boy then."

"Not so small as all that," Nathan said. "But you are not here to talk about how much I have grown. What can I do for you?"

He sounded very much the grown-up businessman when he asked the question, so she changed her mind about waiting for Aaron. Surely it did not matter which of the Miller brothers she talked with.

"My aunt and I would like to finish the addition to her house that is already started. She hoped you might want the job."

"Ach, ja." He seemed to put a curb on his eagerness. "But Solomon Gaus started that job, ain't so? It wouldn't be right if we took his work from him."

"He told my aunt that he didn't have time to finish the project, so I don't think you need to be concerned about that."

Her fingers clenched as she thought about Jonas's interference. Sooner or later she'd be talking to her cousin, and she might have trouble keeping from expressing her opinion.

"Well, if that's so, it's no problem." His expression cleared.

"You don't have too much other work to do? We're eager to have the job completed as soon as possible."

"We are finishing up a kitchen for an Englisch lady now, but after that we should have plenty of time."

A shadow bisected the patch of sunlight that lay on the floor. "Plenty of time for what?"

Nathan greeted Aaron's entrance with an open smile. Sarah took a moment to compose her features before she turned to him.

"I was just speaking with your brother about having you

finish the addition to Aunt Emma's house. She is eager to have it done as soon as possible."

She wasn't imagining the way Aaron's tall figure stiffened at her words.

"I'm sorry. But we are busy—"

"But Aaron." Nathan's astonishment couldn't be hidden. "I chust told Sarah that we don't have anything after we finish the kitchen cabinets for Mrs. Donohue. Have you taken on another job?"

Aaron probably wouldn't like it that Sarah had no trouble reading his feelings, despite that stoic expression he wore. He didn't want to do the work on the birthing rooms. She hadn't been wrong about his reaction to her presence here.

Sarah was unaccountably disappointed. She ought to be used to the fact that some people had little respect for midwives. It was unreasonable to care about the opinion of a man she barely knew.

"Nothing definite." He answered his brother in a tone that said he wanted no further discussion on the matter. "But there are a few things pending."

Nathan snorted. "If you're talking about Eli Schmidt, we could be waiting until next year for him to make up his mind about that barn roof."

"Eli is a gut customer for us. It wouldn't be right to take on another job if he's decided." Aaron had begun to sound harassed.

She was tempted to press him on it, especially since Nathan still looked unconvinced. But she'd spent too many years evading confrontation to be looking for it now.

"Perhaps you could talk to Mr. Schmidt and let us know," she offered.

"Ja. I will do that." Aaron didn't seem grateful for the olive branch she held out.

"Denke. I must be on my way. It was gut to meet you, Nathan."

Nathan murmured something in reply, his gaze still fixed, frowning, on his brother.

"I'll wait to hear from you, then." Sarah escaped as quickly as possible, only to find Aaron following her, holding the door. He closed it behind them.

She started to move away, but he stopped her, one hand closing over hers. His hand was warm and work-hardened, and it seemed to envelop hers. His expression was frowning.

"I thought that Emma had given up the idea of expanding. That she was going to retire."

"Have you been talking to my cousin Jonas?" She couldn't seem to prevent the snap in her voice.

His gaze held hers. "Jonas is her son. I'm sure he wants what is best for her."

"Perhaps Aunt Emma is the one to decide what that is."

His gaze seemed to bore into her, and his grip was firm. He let go quite suddenly and took a step back.

"Perhaps. I will check on the other job and stop by the house later to let you know."

"Fine." She headed back down the lane.

Fine. Except that her plans weren't fine with Aaron—that was certain sure. And she wished she understood why.

Aaron felt Nathan's accusing gaze on him when he reentered the shop. He had a feeling his younger brother wasn't going to let the subject rest.

"Why did you try to put Sarah off like that?" Nathan, usually easygoing, didn't let a moment pass before launching into the subject. "You know as well as I do that we'll be looking for a job once we finish this one, and one more day's work ought to be enough."

"Unless Mrs. Donohue thinks of some other change she wants made." Aaron tried to divert Nathan, but he suspected Nathan wasn't going to let go.

"There's not much else she can change, ain't so? And I'll eat my hammer if Eli actually decides he wants that job done next week. You should be happy to have a bit of work fall right into our laps."

Nathan's persistence began to annoy him. "The last time I looked, I was the one to handle the scheduling around here."

Nathan planted his hands on the workbench. "The last time I looked, you were telling me I ought to take on more responsibility for the business. How do you think it seemed, you coming in and telling Sarah we couldn't do the job when I'd just told her we could?"

The fact that Nathan was right only made matters worse. "I wasn't trying to make you look bad. I just don't want . . ." He had to let that die away, because he didn't want to go anywhere near the real reason he felt as he did.

"Maybe the truth is that you don't want to share the responsibility." Nathan looked younger than his years, suddenly—young and vulnerable, as if discovering that the big brother he admired wasn't the man he'd thought.

Aaron took a deep breath and let it out slowly. "I'm sorry," he said. "I shouldn't be interfering when you're talking to a customer. Maybe we both ought to consult each other about taking on new jobs. What do you think?"

The hurt drained from Nathan's face. "Do you mean that?"

"I do." He rested his hand on his brother's shoulder, thinking of all the times he'd done just that as Nathan grew from a little boy suddenly without a mother to a man. "Suppose I check with Eli, just to be sure. Then I'll go over to Emma's place and talk to them about the work. All right?"

"All right." Nathan's smile returned. "I'll finish up the last of these cabinet doors this afternoon already. Then we can move on."

A couple of hours later, Aaron cut across the brittle brown grass of the pasture toward Emma's house. He paused to pat Dolly, grazing in the field. The early frost had left little for the horse to eat this winter, and he could see that Emma had already started to give the animal extra hay. If the weather kept on this way, they'd be in for a hard winter.

The half-finished addition came into view as he approached Emma's, and his stomach tightened. Birthing rooms, Sarah had said it was for.

Plenty of Amish used midwives, and most of them praised Emma Stoltzfus for her skill and caring. But most of them didn't have his memories of his mother dying, leaving him responsible for the younger ones when he was only fourteen himself.

He forced his thoughts away from that. He didn't want to let his feelings interfere with business, but he also didn't want this job. So he'd look over the situation, talk about how much time it would take, and offer to help find someone else to do the work.

It wasn't the best solution, but it was one he could live with. As for what Nathan would think—well, he'd just better come up with some other job offers to distract the boy.

Not a boy any longer, his conscience reminded him. A man now, and one he'd promised to consult on jobs.

His jaw clenched. This was Sarah Mast's fault. If she hadn't come to Pleasant Valley, he wouldn't be faced with this unpalatable situation.

A horse waited patiently at the hitching rail behind Emma's house. Bishop Mose's horse and buggy. What was the bishop doing at Emma's house this afternoon?

It was too late to think of backing out. Emma had opened the back door and was beckoning him in.

"Aaron, it's gut to see you. I was chust telling Bishop Mose how you brought Sarah to me yesterday when I forgot to send someone for her."

Emma seemed to have taken on new life since the arrival of her niece. Her cheeks were rosy, and her eyes snapped with life.

Aaron followed her into the kitchen. "Bishop Mose." He inclined his head to the spiritual leader of the Pleasant Valley Amish. "Sarah."

Sarah responded to his greeting with a watchful look. Well, no wonder about that. They hadn't exactly parted on the best of terms.

"I came to say how happy we are to have Sarah with us," Bishop Mose said, gesturing with his coffee cup. "And I stayed to enjoy some of Emma's wonderful-gut cinnamon buns."

Emma was already headed for the coffeepot. "Aaron, you'll have something, won't you?"

"Not now, denke, Emma. I wanted to have a look at the addition while it's still light."

"Aaron is going to finish the birthing rooms for us." Emma beamed as she sat down opposite the bishop. "We are so fortunate to have such a fine carpenter."

"Plenty of fine carpenters around," Aaron said quickly. It was no part of his plan to be committed to this project in front of the bishop.

"People have choices, then," Bishop Mose said placidly. "In carpenters, and in how they have their babies."

Before Aaron could decide how to take Bishop Mose's words, Sarah was opening the door that led to the addition.

"This way," she said.

He followed her out into the addition, closing the door so that the heat wouldn't escape the house. He glanced around the raw, unfinished space.

"You have a start on the project, at least."

She nodded. "Aunt Emma says we can trust you to tell us whether it's been done right and what it will take to finish it."

He could already see that some shortcuts had been taken in the job. Little though he'd want to criticize a brother, he couldn't in all honesty say that it was the best of work.

"Well, we all work a little different. If it was me, I would use four-by-fours instead of the two-by-fours here. And you'll need thick insulation in these walls, I'd say."

"Ja." She smiled, as if she saw something other than the roughed-out exterior. "We want our mothers to be comfortable when they come to us for births."

"You won't be doing home births, then?" He paced the measurements of the space, pulling out his notebook to jot down figures, interested in the project in spite of himself. He couldn't see a bit of building done carelessly without wanting to fix it. A man should do his work, whatever it was, as if it were done for God. That was what the Bible taught and what he believed.

"Oh, ja, home births for those who want it. But some women would rather go to a birthing center, and it is gut for us to work in a place where everything is ready to hand. It also helps if two mothers decide to give birth at the same time."

"Is that what you did in Ohio?"

It seemed the polite thing to ask, even though he had little interest in talking about the subject. Still, he did like the way Sarah's face came to life. Her enthusiasm made her look more like the girl he remembered from that long-ago summer.

"Ja, I worked with two other midwives there. Aunt Emma and I won't need as much space here, maybe, but we want two rooms, each with windows, and two bathrooms between them. Then we'll want cabinets built in to hold our equipment and supplies."

It was time to stop watching the way Sarah's face lit up at the prospect and start working his way out of this situation.

"It's a bigger job than I thought," he said, staring at his notes to avoid looking at her. "With only Nathan and me working, it will take a while to do. And as for the cost—well, I'll have to figure that out, but it's going to be substantial."

He was trying not to look at her, but he couldn't miss the flicker of dismay on her face.

"If you think Emma isn't prepared to take on the expense—"

"It's not my aunt who's paying for it," she said, her voice firm. "I am doing that. It is my investment in the practice."

"I see. I didn't realize . . ."

"My husband's share of the farm out in Ohio provides

me with enough to cover the project, if you're concerned about being paid."

He'd offended her now, and that wasn't his intent. He just didn't want to be involved in this project. Let someone do it who believed in midwives.

"I didn't doubt that." He said the words gently. "But if you're talking about investing all that you have in this—Well, I don't want to see you get hurt if it doesn't work out."

"It will work out." The words were filled with such longing that they touched his heart. "My life is here now."

The door opened, and Bishop Mose stepped out to join them before Aaron could think of any proper response.

"Well, have you two figured everything out? Aaron, how soon will you be able to start the work here?"

With Bishop Mose's wise old eyes on him, with that vulnerable expression on Sarah's face, Aaron discovered that it was impossible to say what he'd intended.

"Next week." He heard the words come out of his mouth with a sense of disbelief. "We should be able to start next week."

CHAPTER THREE

People were looking at her. That was only natural, arriving as Sarah was for worship for the first time, but it still made her feel self-conscious.

She walked beside Aunt Emma toward the barn at Leah and Daniel Glick's place. Just being with her aunt was a lesson in humility. Every person knew Emma Stoltzfus, of course, as any Amish person knows everyone in the church district.

But people greeted Emma with a special combination of affection and respect. She'd served them faithfully for so many years—how could they help but feel that way?

Would the Amish of Pleasant Valley ever accept Sarah? If she modeled herself on Aunt Emma, perhaps.

Her aunt crossed the frosty stubble of grass to a group of older women, some widows, as people began to gather into the groups in which they'd file into the barn for worship. The Glick family would no doubt have spent the week scrubbing and clearing the barn to prepare for this day. Each family in the congregation would take a turn hosting church in home or shop or barn, and that space, no matter how humble, became a house of worship for the day.

She was about to join the group of older women when someone caught her arm. She turned to see Rachel Zook smiling at her.

"Wilkom to worship, Sarah. I want you to meet my friend Leah Glick."

The woman who stood next to Rachel was the one hosting services that day, then. Seeing them together it was clear that they were friends, just by their quick exchange of glances.

"We are so glad you have come to join us." Leah's serene smile seemed to radiate warmth. "We've been working our Emma so hard. Now she will have someone to help share the load."

"That's what I hope." Sarah smiled at the toddler pressed close to Leah's skirt. "Are you one of my aunt's babies?"

"Ach, no, my sister Leah didn't wait for the midwife to arrive," another young woman said as she joined them, smiling at the question.

"Sarah, this is my sister, Anna Fisher, just back from her wedding trip." Leah patted the newcomer's arm. "She means that Rachel here had to deliver her namesake when our little Rachel arrived ahead of schedule."

"She must have done a wonderful-gut job, then, to bring such a beautiful little girl into the world."

Leah's child stared at her with a solemn expression in her huge blue eyes and then reached out a chubby hand, patting Sarah's skirt.

The women laughed.

"See, she knows already that you are someone who loves a boppli." Anna leaned a little closer. "I'm so glad you are here as well, Sarah. I pray that I'll have reason to visit you soon."

"Ser gut," she said. "My aunt and I will be happy to see you."

This warm welcome was what she'd hoped for, but at the

same time it made Sarah a tiny bit uneasy. She wanted to help Aunt Emma, not replace her. Their relationship might be difficult if patients started asking for her instead of her aunt.

"There will be plenty to keep you both busy," Rachel said, as if she understood the concern that lurked in Sarah's heart.

"I hope so." The words came out perhaps too fervently. "We're adding two birthing rooms to Aunt Emma's house, so that anyone who wants to give birth there instead of at home can do so."

"That's gut, that is," Rachel said. "I was afraid Emma had given up on that plan. Who is doing the carpentry work for you?"

"Aaron Miller and his brother have agreed to finish it." Sarah had already spotted Aaron's tall figure among the men, looking even more severe than usual in his Sunday black.

"He is?" Rachel sounded faintly surprised. "He'll do a fine job for you, that's certain sure," she added quickly. She glanced across the group of young women assembling for worship as if looking for other possible clients for the midwife practice.

"Mary Esch is expecting," Leah said, her voice soft. "But she is going to Dr. Mitchell, I hear."

"My aunt mentioned that there is a new doctor in town. In our practice in Ohio, we had a wonderful-gut relationship with a local doctor. He referred women to us who wanted a midwife for the birth, and we sent patients to him when we felt they needed special care. Perhaps I should go and talk to Dr. Mitchell."

Leah and Rachel exchanged glances that seemed to contain a wealth of meaning. "Maybe that's not such a gut idea," Rachel said.

"Why is that?"

Anna prodded Rachel. "Go on, tell her. She ought to know."

"Whatever it is, I think you should tell me." Sarah forced a smile.

"Ach, Anna is such a blabbermaul." Rachel elbowed her friend affectionately. "I hope it's not so bad as I've heard, but I wouldn't want you to get caught in an awkward situation."

"Tell her," Anna insisted. "If I were Sarah, I'd want to know."

"It's just that I've talked to a few women who are going to Dr. Mitchell for their babies." Rachel looked unhappy at being pushed into delivering bad news. "They said that Dr. Mitchell is very outspoken on the subject of midwives. He thinks they're not qualified to deliver babies."

The women had begun to file into the barn for worship, so Rachel couldn't say more if she wanted to. And Sarah didn't think she wanted to hear any more.

Her stomach churned as she followed Rachel through the wide doors into the barn, where several kerosene heaters had been set up to take the chill from the air.

It wasn't unheard-of to meet people who felt that way about midwives. Even doctors. She had probably been fortunate in her previous practice to have Dr. O'Neill's generous support.

The doctor's opinion needn't be a problem, she assured herself as she sat between Rachel and Anna on one of the backless benches that were taken from house to house for worship. Dr. Mitchell could go his way, and they would go theirs.

If he would let them.

The thought intruded and did not want to go away. The last thing she and Aunt Emma needed when they were trying to expand their practice was the enmity of the local doctor.

Three hours later, Sarah emerged into the chilly air, blinking in the bright sunlight. She pulled her long black coat closer, feeling a little adrift, as she so often did after worship.

It was a fault to feel this way. She could remember a time when meeting with her church family to worship together was unalloyed joy.

But that was before the grief of her childlessness had grown like a chasm between her and Levi. When the love she'd been so sure was strong enough for a lifetime had grown cold with his disappointment. She had prayed, at first humbly, sure God would answer, and then with growing desperation.

Was that wrong? The church's teachings said that a believer should accept whatever happened as God's will. But women in the Bible like Sarah and Hannah had prayed endlessly for a child, and their prayers had been granted.

Her thoughts began to circle, and they always did on this subject, and she tried to push it to the back of her mind. She'd be far better off to keep herself too busy for such wonderings.

Behind her, some of the men were rapidly setting up tables, so that the congregation could eat in the relative warmth of the barn instead of outside, as they would in milder weather. Leah could use some help in the kitchen, if Sarah knew anything about serving lunch after church.

She headed for the back door of the farmhouse, spotting Rachel headed in the same direction, probably for the same reason. But when Sarah reached the porch steps, a tall figure intercepted her.

"Sarah." Aaron inclined his head politely. "Are they putting you to work already?"

She managed a smile despite the fact that she could sense the tension that always seemed to grip Aaron when he was around her. "I know how busy it is in the kitchen on a church day. I'm sure Leah could use an extra pair of hands."

"I won't keep you. We can come over tomorrow to do some preliminary work, if that is all right." His face tightened. "I know that Emma sees patients on some days, and we would not want to interfere."

"Tuesdays and Thursdays are usually patient days, but I don't think—"

She broke off as a small figure hurtled past them toward the steps, tripping over Aaron's feet. Before she could move, Aaron had set the boy on his feet, his big hands gentle.

"Ach, Joseph, there will be plenty of food for you," he teased. "You don't need to be in such a rush."

Sarah's heart gave a funny little bump at the smile Aaron gave the boy. She should have realized he'd be gut with kinder, after practically raising his own siblings. But she hadn't seen that affectionate smile before, since all he had for her, it seemed, was that expression of stolid disapproval.

The boy looked up, grinning, obviously not worried about the reproof. "I know," he said. "But I just remembered that I promised Mammi I would help carry the food out. It must be almost time, ain't so?"

"Almost," Aaron agreed solemnly. "I'm sure your mammi will call when she needs you, so you'd best stay close." Aaron tousled the boy's fine hair and set his hat back into place. "Sarah, this is Joseph, Rachel's boy."

"Wie bist du heit, Joseph. It's nice to meet you." So this was one of Rachel's kinder. He had a bit of her looks, with those big, serious eyes and gentle expression.

"You are Sarah, the new midwife, ain't so? Are you going to help in the kitchen? If my mamm is looking for me, will you tell her I'm here?"

"I will."

Aaron patted his shoulder. "Off you go and play with the other boys 'til it's time."

Sarah watched him run off, a little slower this time. "A nice boy to be so concerned about helping."

"Ja. Gid and Rachel are fortunate in their family."

Was there wistfulness in Aaron's tone, as if he wished

he were a father by now? Or was he wondering why she didn't have a family after four years of marriage? She tried to shake off the thought. That was foolishness, and self-centered as well. She'd best concentrate on business.

"We were talking about your working on patient days. I don't think it would be a problem. You will be working in the addition, after all."

"We'll see." Aaron sounded as if nothing would get them there on a patient day.

She was imagining things, surely. "We will look for you tomorrow, then."

He nodded, and she went on into the house, maybe a little more quickly than she needed to.

Several women were already at work in the kitchen, including Rachel, who was slicing cakes at the far end of the room. A girl who must be her daughter stood at her elbow to help.

Like most Amish kitchens, this one looked like any Englisch kitchen, except that the appliances were powered by gas. The long wooden table that would seat Leah's family for meals had been pressed into service as a staging area for all the food necessary to feed such a crowd.

Leah's small daughter toddled across the kitchen floor to grasp her mother's skirt. Sarah smiled at her and then transferred her attention to Leah.

"I hoped that I might be able to help with the lunch."

"Ach, Sarah, you need not do that on your first Sunday with us." Leah sliced a loaf of wheat bread with rapid strokes.

"But I'd like to. Doing something will make me feel at home."

Leah gave in with a smile. "Why don't you help my sister-in-law put sandwiches on trays, then? Some of the boys are waiting to carry them to the barn."

Sarah joined the buxom woman at the table who was quickly putting bologna sandwiches onto large metal trays. "Can I do that?"

"Ja, denke." The woman swung toward the refrigerator. "I will get more out. I am Barbara Beiler, Leah's sister-in-law." She had rosy round cheeks and a pair of snapping brown eyes. "You are Sarah Mast, of course."

Sarah nodded, taking over the sandwiches.

Barbara was back in a moment, carrying more sandwiches covered with plastic wrap. "We're glad to have you here, for sure. Emma is not getting any younger."

"None of us are," Leah said quickly, as if afraid Barbara had offended Sarah by her comment.

"Ja, but Emma has started to forget things," Barbara went on, undeterred.

Sarah took a moment to smooth out a ruffle of annoyance. Barbara was obviously one of those people who said everything that came into her mind. But was that really what people were thinking?

"I'm sure things will be better now that I'm here. My aunt has just been a little overworked."

"Ja, that must be it," Leah said, before Barbara could speak. "Barbara, did you bring this pickle relish? It looks wonderful gut."

"Ja, that is mine." Barbara's round face beamed. "I brought a chocolate cake with peanut-butter icing, too. Your kinder love that cake, I know."

"You have other children, besides little Rachel?" Sarah asked, relieved to have the conversation off her aunt.

"Three older ones. Stepchildren, but just as dear as if I carried them." Leah drew a young girl close to her. "This is Elizabeth, my older daughter. The two boys are supposed to be near the porch, ready to carry trays out, unless they've been distracted by their friends."

Elizabeth leaned her head against Leah's shoulder, her affection showing. "I will check on them, Mammi. Should I take Rachel with me?"

"Ja, gut." Leah detached the little girl's fingers from her apron and gave her a gentle shove. "Go with Elizabeth now. Go and find your bruders."

Sarah watched them go, smiling at the obvious love between them. "Little Rachel is fortunate to have such a caring big sister."

"Like I did," Anna said, glancing up from cutting a cake. "Although there were times when I didn't know how fortunate I was."

"We are all foolish when we are eighteen," Leah said, with a gentle smile for her younger sister.

"I left for a while," Anna said in explanation. "Like so many, I thought I'd find my heart's desire in the Englisch world. And all the while it was waiting here for me."

"Ach, you probably wouldn't have appreciated your Samuel near as much at eighteen," Barbara said. "He is one of the quiet ones. Like Aaron Miller." She darted a questioning look at Sarah. "You were talking with him, I see."

Sarah added curiosity to Barbara's ability to say things others wouldn't. "He was just asking about starting work tomorrow. Aaron will be finishing the carpentry on the birthing rooms for us."

That got the reaction she'd noticed from the other women—a quick look of surprise and speculation. But Barbara didn't bother to change the subject.

"That is odd, that is. I'd have said that Aaron Miller would not do such a thing in a million years."

"You're exaggerating," Leah said, a warning tone in her voice. "I'm sure we don't know anything about what jobs Aaron takes on."

"Ja," Anna chimed in, as if equally intent on heading off an indiscretion on Barbara's part. "This time of year I'd guess a carpenter is eager for any job he can get. It's a gut thing my Samuel still has plenty of horse training to do when the machine shop is quiet."

"That's all very well, but I'm still surprised at Aaron." Barbara would not be diverted. "Everyone in the church district knows how he feels about midwives, whether he talks about it or not."

"They don't—"

"He isn't—"

Leah and Anna both tried to get a word in, but they spoke together and cancelled each other out. Barbara swept on.

"Aaron's mother died in childbirth when he was no more than fourteen or so. When Benjamin was born, that was. And whether you want me to say it or not, that's true." Barbara's ruddy cheeks grew redder.

"That doesn't mean he has a prejudice against midwives," Leah said, her voice firmer than Sarah had yet heard. "I think it's a subject best left alone, Barbara. Sarah doesn't want to hear gossip."

Barbara planted her hands on her ample hips. "Ja, well, I'm not spreading lies about anyone, and it's chust as well if Sarah knows what she is dealing with. Aaron may try to hide it, but it's as plain as the nose on my face. He blames Emma Stoltzfus because his mammi died in childbirth, and you all know that's true."

The kitchen went still, seeming to echo with the sound of Barbara's words. Sarah's hands were frozen on the sandwiches while her mind spun crazily, trying to take it in. Aaron blaming Aunt Emma for his mother's death? Surely if that were true, Aunt Emma would have said something.

A board creaked in the back hall. Every woman in the kitchen turned to look.

Aaron Miller stood there, his face an impassive mask. Then he turned on his heel and walked off.

Sarah couldn't get the image of Aaron's face out of her mind. She'd tried to find him in the after-church group, hoping to explain, to apologize, but he must have left immediately.

Now, driving home after lunch, she found her mind going over the whole situation again and again. Surely Barbara had exaggerated. The other women had tried to deny or explain away what she'd said, but it was too late. Aaron had heard

Barbara's careless words, and the damage had been done. And if he thought that Sarah had been gossiping about him . . . her face burned at the idea.

Somehow, she had to set this straight. She gazed at the horse's head, bobbing along ahead of them as Aunt Emma drove down the quiet country road. Other Amish buggies could be glimpsed on a lane that ran perpendicular to this one, and probably there were others behind them. It was a typical Sunday scene in Amish country, serene if not for Sarah's troubled thoughts.

She didn't want to believe that Aaron blamed Aunt Emma for his mother's death. But if he did, it certainly explained his reluctance to be at the house on days when pregnant women were coming in and going out.

They were turning into the lane already. She'd wait until they were settled inside for the afternoon. Then she'd bring the subject up and pray Aunt Emma would not take offense.

When she returned to the house from stabling Dolly, her aunt seemed more animated than usual, as if the three hours spent in worship with her church family had lifted her spirits.

"I was so happy to see you with the other young women." Aunt Emma was already warming the coffee. "They were making you feel welcome, ja?"

"That's certain sure." Sarah hung up her black coat and bonnet in the hall and smoothed her hair back under her kapp. "Our hostess, Leah, is a lovely person."

"Everyone loves Leah. She was our schoolteacher for quite a few years, and folks thought she'd never marry. Then Daniel Glick and his children moved in next door, and soon they were a family."

Aunt Emma sat down at the kitchen table. She was carefully not looking at Sarah, maybe because she was comparing Sarah with Leah.

But it wasn't a fair comparison, was it? Leah had a child of her own.

She had to force a smile. "I understand Leah's baby arrived before you could get there."

"Ach, that was a day, that was." Aunt Emma shook her head. "Of all the mothers I've worked with, there were only five or six where I didn't get there in time."

"You remember all of them, don't you?" Sarah sat down across from her aunt. Despite Barbara's tactlessness, something positive might still come of this. If Aaron had been holding on to a false idea all these years, maybe it was best that it come out into the open.

"For sure I remember. Don't you?"

"Ja, but I don't have so many as you to keep track of." She smiled, thinking of the very first birth she'd attended. She wasn't sure who had been more nervous, the mammi or the midwife.

"Lots of healthy babies." Aunt Emma sighed. "And a few who weren't. Sometimes it's hard to accept God's will."

Sarah nodded. The Amish were more prone than most people to pass on genetic illnesses. The common background that kept them together also made them vulnerable. Still . . .

"A boppli is a blessing, no matter what." Sarah hesitated, knowing she had to bring up the subject and not sure how to do it. Maybe she should just plunge in and tell it as it had happened.

"When I went to ask Leah if I could help with the lunch, she introduced me to her sister-in-law."

"Ja? Which one?"

"Barbara."

"That's Leah's oldest brother's wife. She and her husband have the farm now, and Leah's daadi lives with them." Aunt Emma's knowledge of the families of Pleasant Valley couldn't be matched.

"Barbara said something that troubled me." Sarah paused for a silent prayer. "She said . . . She seems to think . . ." This was harder than she imagined. "She thinks that Aaron blames you for his mother dying when Benjamin was born."

Pain glazed her aunt's eyes. She shook her head. "Barbara has a gut heart, but sometimes I think her mind and her mouth are not connected. Don't let her foolish talk trouble you."

"Maybe it was tactless, but . . . is it true? Does Aaron really feel that way?"

"That's foolishness." The words were tart. "The Miller boys have always been gut neighbors to me. You know how people can talk in a small community. If there's nothing to tell, they make something up."

True enough, but . . . "So you don't think Aaron has any bad feelings about his mammi's dying that way?"

"Would he have agreed to do the work for us if he held a grudge?" Aunt Emma stood abruptly, shoving her chair in with a sharp movement.

Maybe, maybe not. Sarah couldn't forget the way Aaron had talked the day they'd discussed the addition. As if he'd been building up to saying he couldn't do it. Then Bishop Mose had come in . . .

"He might have said yes because of the bishop."

Aunt Emma's eyes crinkled suddenly. "He might have said yes because it was you doing the asking. Seems to me he was looking at you with a lot of interest."

"I . . . I'm sure it's not that," she said quickly.

"Why not?" Aunt Emma leaned on the back of her chair, as if suddenly tired. "You are as sweet and pretty outside as inside, Sarah Mast. You have to expect men to notice that."

Sarah rubbed her arms. The suggestion was a chill wind, reminding her of her childless state. "I am not looking for a new love."

"Sometimes love comes when a woman is not looking for it."

"Not for me." And especially not with Aaron Miller. "About Aaron's mother—"

"Are you thinking I made a mistake, Sarah?" Her aunt's face tightened. "Is that it?"

"No, of course not. Aunt Emma, I didn't mean that."

Her aunt wasn't mollified. "Look at my notebooks if you want to find out about Aaron's mother. I keep records of every birth. You will see." She turned away, stalking toward the stairs.

"I didn't mean . . ." she began, but Aunt Emma was already gone.

So quickly. Sarah clasped her hands together, searching for calm. So quickly, and a chasm had opened up between them.

Chapter Four

After what he'd heard on Sunday, Aaron found it hard to believe he was letting himself get anywhere near Sarah Mast again, let alone continuing the project. But here he was in the unfinished addition, laying out the work to be done with Nathan, while Benjamin lingered, listening. At least he hoped the boy was listening.

He'd decided it was more difficult to explain his feelings to Nathan than to simply get on with the job at hand. The sooner the work was finished, the sooner he could begin ignoring his new neighbor.

"So we'll replace these two-by-fours with four-by-fours." He knocked on the offending posts, annoyed as always by carpentry that wasn't up to par. He wasn't prideful about his own work, but he liked the idea that what he built would be here when he was long gone.

"Ja, gut." Nathan shook his head. "I would not like to accuse a brother of doing shoddy work, but . . ."

"But we'll do better." Benjamin rubbed his arms. "Let's get on with it. It's cold to be working here."

Nathan snorted. "You think this cold is something? You should have seen us repairing the roof on Jacob Yost's barn in the midst of the big January snowstorm two years ago. Ain't so, Aaron?"

Benjamin got his mulish expression at the words. Keeping peace between the two youngest had always been Molly's role, and she did it much better than Aaron did. Still, he had to try.

"Ja, but this is the coldest November I can remember. The pond is skimming over with ice already."

Benjamin nodded, mollified. "Wish it would freeze. I'd try out my new skates."

"Well, the more we get done, the warmer it will be to work. You can tack plastic over the window openings for starters."

For some reason Aaron found he was picturing the hope in Sarah's face when she talked about the use to which these rooms would be placed. He didn't want to think about Sarah at all, and certainly not with any sympathy.

Better to remind himself of how he'd felt when he'd walked into the back hall of the Glick house and heard the women talking in the kitchen. Gossiping about him . . . about feelings he'd spent years hiding.

His hands clenched into fists. He swung around, nearly knocking Benjamin over.

"Sorry." He grabbed his younger brother by the elbow, steadying him. "I'm going to bring a couple of four-by-fours from the wagon." Maybe a dose of cold air would clear his head.

It didn't help. He pulled the posts from the wagon, arguing with himself. He ought to be fair to Sarah. After all, he hadn't heard her say anything about him. But surely it was her presence that had precipitated that conversation. And she'd stood there listening to the gossip.

He stalked back to the site, balancing the posts on his shoulder. He stepped inside and halted, the posts swinging. Sarah was there.

She caught his eye and looked quickly away, and he seemed to feel her tension across the width of the space.

"Aaron. I was just telling your brothers that chicken pot-pie is hot on the stove whenever you're ready to take a break for a meal."

"Denke." He turned to put the posts down.

"I could smell it when you opened the door," Benjamin said. "Sure smells wonderful gut." He looked ready to break for middaagesse already. "Isn't it time to eat yet?"

"You're always hungry," Nathan said. "Sarah will think you're greedy."

"I think he's a growing boy, that's all," Sarah said. "And growing takes a lot of fuel."

"That's what Molly always said." Benjamin grinned, turning from a sulky adolescent into an excited kid all in a moment. "Molly is our sister. She is coming back from Indiana to stay with us for a while."

"She's not coming to cook for you," Nathan said.

"Anything she cooks will be better than what you do," Benjamin retorted. "And once her boppli comes, I won't be the youngest one in the family anymore."

"That is wonderful," Sarah said. "I'm sure you'll be a gut onkel."

The warmth in her eyes touched Aaron in spite of his feelings. Strange, that a woman who took such pleasure in babies had none of her own. She had been married for several years before her husband died.

Maybe she couldn't have children. His heart twisted in a surge of sympathy that he couldn't prevent.

"If Molly comes to you for the baby—" Benjamin began.

"We might as well break for lunch, since you're so hungry. Go on and wash up." Aaron rushed the words, intent on keeping Benjamin from saying anything else about Molly and the baby.

The eagerness in his brother's face vanished, and he shot Aaron a look full of resentment.

He shouldn't have spoken sharply to the boy. But he

couldn't have Benjamin talking as if their Molly would be coming to Sarah for this baby.

"Komm, komm." Sarah ushered his brothers through the door. "The meal is waiting."

"Denke, Sarah." Nathan led the way, with Benjamin close behind him.

But when Aaron approached, she pulled the door to, looking up at him. "Do you mind waiting for a moment, Aaron?"

His jaw set. This was about yesterday. If Sarah asked for his forgiveness, he'd have to forgive, no matter how little he wanted to.

He looked at her, frowning, not speaking. Let her begin, since she was the one with something to say.

"I wanted to talk with you about what happened yesterday after worship." She took a breath, seeming to find it difficult to go on. "Please believe that I wasn't prying about you. Barbara Beiler burst out with that even though the others tried to stop her. I would not gossip about you behind your back."

It might well be true. He hadn't heard Sarah speak, and everyone knew what a blabbermaul Barbara Beiler was. Still, the subject had only come up because Sarah was there.

He battled the thoughts, knowing she was waiting for his response. "Ja. All right. It's best forgotten."

But Sarah didn't move, and she stood between him and the door, looking up at him with a question in those clear eyes. "I wouldn't have asked. But what Barbara said—is it true? Aaron, are you blaming Aunt Emma for your mammi's dying?"

"No." He forced out the word. He had no choice but to deny it. "It's a long time ago. The others will be wondering what we are doing. We must go in."

Sarah shook her head, something that might have been pain crossing her face. "If people believe you feel that way—"

"Barbara loves to gossip." He couldn't let her finish the thought. "Even if she's imagining things."

Her look rebuked him for the harsh words. "Other people besides Barbara showed surprise that you were working on the birthing rooms. Aaron, if you feel that way, we must talk about it."

"There is nothing to talk about." He reached past her for the door. She put her hand on his arm to stop him.

Aaron seemed to feel the warmth of her touch through the layers of shirt and coat. He stared at her, frowning. Angry.

And something more. Attracted. He saw in her eyes the same startled awareness.

No. This could not be. He brushed past Sarah abruptly and went into the house.

Sarah found herself increasingly keyed up as the time came for patients to start arriving the next afternoon. Aaron and his brothers had worked steadily all morning. Would they stay or would Aaron insist on leaving? If he left, that would seem to confirm the belief that he had unresolved feelings about his mother's death.

Sarah glanced out the window toward the addition. Aaron was packing up his tools. Even as she watched, he walked away toward the wagon.

She pressed her hand against her heart. No matter how he denied it, Aaron was hurting. She longed to ease that hurt, but she was probably the last person in the world who could do that.

Bless him, dear Father. Please, grant me your guidance, for I don't know what to do.

"Sarah."

She turned to find Aunt Emma standing in the doorway. "Ja, I'm here."

"Alice Straus is our first patient this afternoon." Aunt Emma's weathered face crinkled in a smile. "She has done this five times already, so there should be no surprises. You handle the visit, so she gets comfortable with you, ja?"

"I will. Denke." It was a sign of acceptance, and she valued that.

Alice Straus, however, didn't seem so sure of that when she found herself alone with Sarah in the small room Emma used for meeting patients. "Is Emma not well, then?" She frowned suspiciously as Sarah approached with the blood pressure cuff.

"My aunt is fine. She just wants all her patients to meet me, since I'll be working with her."

"I guess that's all right, then." Alice extended her arm, allowing Sarah to wrap the cuff around it. "So long as it's Emma who is there when the boppli comes." She smiled suddenly. "Not that I don't think William and I could do it on our own after all this time."

"I'm sure you could." Sarah watched the pressure—in the slightly higher range of normal, but probably not at a worrisome rate. "How have you been feeling? Any tiredness?"

Alice patted her belly. "Who wouldn't be tired, lugging all of this around? I keep telling William this one is going to come out big enough to shovel snow."

"How big were your other babies?" She helped Alice lie back on the narrow bed.

"Eight pounds. Little Jacob was almost nine." Alice frowned again as Sarah approached with the tape measure. "Emma doesn't do that every time."

"I just like to see how the measurements are increasing. That helps us know how your boppli is growing." She'd told herself she wouldn't second-guess Emma's methods, but taking the abdominal measurement at each visit was standard at her previous practice. "Ser gut." She jotted down notes.

Unfortunately the notebook reminded her of Aunt Emma's angry suggestion that she look at the older woman's notes on Aaron's mother.

She hadn't done it. She wasn't sure that her relationship with Aunt Emma would survive that.

You could look at the book when Aunt Emma is out, a little voice whispered in the back of her mind. *She wouldn't ever have to know.*

No. She couldn't. Sarah kept a smile on her face as she completed Alice's examination, but her thoughts were in turmoil. She had to know the truth, but not that way.

Somehow, she had to get either Aunt Emma or Aaron to talk about his mother's death. Right now, that seemed impossible on both sides.

"Everything looks wonderful gut," she said, helping the woman sit up. "It won't be long now until that boppli is in your arms."

"Gut, gut." Alice patted her kapp to be sure it was in place. "You have a nice way about you," she said, perhaps a little reluctantly. "I'm glad Emma has someone to help her."

"I am happy to be here." Sarah's fresh start might not be turning out exactly as anticipated, but the words were true. "Now, about the tests on the newborn—"

She didn't have a chance to finish. Alice drew back, face setting. "No need for that. There's none of the diseases in my family, nor William's."

Given the prevalence of genetic diseases among the Amish, Sarah was relieved to hear that, but it didn't mean Alice's baby shouldn't be tested. The possibility was still there.

"I think . . ."

"Ach, Alice, how are you doing?" Aunt Emma bustled in. "Is my niece taking gut care of you?"

"All right." Alice sounded a bit grudging. "She wants me to have the boppli tested, but I was telling her there's no need, ain't so?"

"Probably not . . ." Emma began, and then checked herself. *Don't disagree in front of the patient,* her expression said. "Time enough to talk about that later. Now, you let William and the girls help you a bit, ja? You'll be busy enough once this little one arrives. Get a bit of rest before that."

They both escorted Alice to the door, but under the casual conversation ran a thread of worry on Sarah's part. Genetic testing might seem newfangled and unnecessary to women who'd had several healthy babies, but genetic diseases were a constant concern in Amish communities, with their common pool of ancestors.

Sarah didn't want to wrangle with Aunt Emma on the topic, but testing was too important to compromise. This point she'd have to press.

Aunt Emma stood at the door for a moment, watching as Alice got into the waiting buggy. Then she turned to Sarah.

"I know my patients," she said, as if Sarah had challenged that.

"I'm sure you do, better than I ever could." That cost a pang of regret. "It's encouraging that there's no history of genetic illnesses in Alice's family."

"So why bother with the testing? I know William, and he'll say he can't afford needless expenses."

"Would he say that about buying a new cow for his dairy herd?" Somehow she doubted that. Seeing the stubborn look on her aunt's face, she touched Emma's arm lightly. "I understand your feelings, and of course you know the families best."

Aunt Emma nodded, looking mollified.

"Still, there's always a chance," Sarah went on. "We both know that. When the parents know immediately, they can start the proper care right away. If every newborn is tested as a matter of course, then no one will argue about it, ain't so?"

The stubbornness eased out of Emma's face. "It's true enough that it can be hard to talk about testing to those who need it."

"Ja." Sarah had to blink back tears at the memory of the first client she'd had whose baby had been born with the maple syrup urine disease. The happiest time in a young couple's life together had turned so quickly to sorrow.

Aunt Emma put her arm around Sarah, surprising her with a hug. "Ach, this is why I need you, my Sarah. You will keep me up-to-date, ain't so?"

The tension drained out of Sarah as she returned her aunt's hug. "And you'll teach me what you've learned in a lifetime of being a midwife. It's a fine trade, ja?"

"Ja." Aunt Emma released her, blinking away what might be tears. "This will work out. For both of us. You'll see."

Sarah's heart clutched. It would work out. It had to, because she had no other choices.

Sarah watched the last patient of the day leave with a sense of satisfaction. Certainly some of the women had shown their preference for Aunt Emma, whom they knew and trusted, but that was only to be expected. And Aunt Emma had shown herself willing to compromise, which was a feat in itself. All in all, they were off to a fine start.

At some point during the afternoon Sarah had realized that she was listening for the sound of Aaron's wagon. It hadn't come. Apparently he was determined not to be here when their clients were.

She frowned, staring out at the brown winter grass. Aaron's attitude was worrisome, and worse still was that moment when she'd looked into his face and felt . . . what? Attraction?

Her cheeks grew warm. She hadn't felt so much as a flicker of interest in a man since Levi's death over a year ago. She hadn't expected to, ever. And if that interest was only sleeping, and not dead, why would it rouse for Aaron, of all people?

She brushed her apron straight with an impatient hand. These thoughts brought nothing constructive with them. Far better to make herself useful in the kitchen. Staying busy was always a remedy for worrying.

"I had thought we'd have the rest of the chicken potpie for supper tonight." Aunt Emma was busy at the stove. "But those Miller boys cleaned it all up. Goodness, but young Benjamin can eat."

"He's still growing, that's certain sure." Sarah crossed the kitchen. "What can I do?"

"I'm heating some beef stew I put up in September." Aunt Emma emptied the contents of a mason jar into a kettle. "You might start some biscuits to go with the stew."

"I'll do that." Sarah reached into the cabinet for the earthenware bowl she always remembered Aunt Emma using for biscuits and dumplings. "It was nice, working together today, ain't so?"

"Ja. Reminded me of when you were here before, so serious and eager to learn." Her aunt stirred the stew to keep it from sticking.

"I wanted to be just like you, that's why. You're the reason I became a midwife. You know that." She measured flour into the bowl.

"I know." Aunt Emma glanced at her, face serious. "Sometimes I thought . . . well, I worried that maybe the midwifery came between you and Levi."

Sarah's fingers tightened on the handle of the wooden spoon, and she forced them to relax. "There was a time when I thought he was proud of my work. But when our own babies didn't come . . ." It still hurt, thinking of the distance that had grown between them.

"I know." Her aunt's voice was soft. "That's hard on a marriage, for sure."

"My being a midwife didn't help, I guess, but it didn't cause the problem. And now . . . well, I'm just so glad I have a job to do that helps other women have babies."

Aunt Emma nodded, her eyes suspiciously bright. "It is gut work, that's certain sure. Important work."

"Ja." Maybe this was the right moment to bring up the testing again, to be sure they were in agreement. "I didn't think to ask you earlier, but where do your mothers go for testing? In Ohio, we had a clinic we worked with. Is there anything in town?"

"Not in Pleasant Valley, no. Only Dr. Mitchell, and I hear tell that he would talk every woman out of using a midwife if he could."

"That's a shame." It was what she'd heard from the other women, and apparently Aunt Emma believed the same. "Still, maybe he'd be willing to cooperate on the newborn testing."

Aunt Emma shook her head decidedly. "Better to use the clinic over near Fostertown. It's farther, but Dr. Brandenmyer does gut work, and they're doing research on the genetic diseases besides. Leah Glick does volunteer work for them. She can tell you all about it. In fact, you ought to go along the next time she's going to the clinic. Just to let Dr. Brandenmyer know who you are."

Before she could respond, Aunt Emma had moved to the window. "A buggy. Who would be coming now . . . ach, it's Jonas." Her voice lifted. "What a nice surprise."

Aunt Emma hurried to the door, and Sarah followed more slowly. Not that she wasn't happy to see her cousin, but what Aunt Emma had said about Jonas urging her to sell the house and move in with him . . . Well, Jonas might not be best pleased with Sarah right now.

But Jonas, turning to her after hugging his mother, enveloped her in a hug, too. "My little cousin, all grown up. It is gut to see you, Sarah."

"And you." She pressed her cheek against his, ruddy from the cold. "It's been too long. How is Mary? And the kinder?"

"All well. The little ones are growing like weeds, for sure." He hung his coat on a peg in the back hall.

"Having a family agrees with you." She hadn't seen Jonas since his wedding. He'd broadened out since then, and his chestnut brown beard was down to his chest.

Jonas patted his stomach. "My Mary is a gut cook, for sure. But not so gut as my mamm."

Aunt Emma shook her head, smiling. "Don't you let

Mary hear you say that. A man should always like his wife's cooking best. Ach, it's so gut to see you."

"I'm sorry I didn't let you know I was coming." Jonas followed them into the kitchen. "I had a chance at a ride from Fostertown all of a sudden. I needed to see Bishop Mose about some new harness. My driver isn't going back until later, so I borrowed a buggy from Bishop Mose and came to see if there might be enough supper for one more."

"There's always enough." Aunt Emma was beaming. "I'll just get another jar of stew from the pantry."

"I'll do that," Sarah said quickly. "You sit down and visit."

She was just as glad to have a moment to think, so she took her time about locating the stew in the rows of jars that lined the shelves of the pantry. Jonas might be feeling that her coming had interfered with his plans for his mother. And he'd be right about that. Still, Emma seemed well able to decide for herself what she wanted.

Sarah walked back into the kitchen ready to tell Jonas exactly that, should he bring the subject up.

However, it seemed Jonas had no such thing in mind. The talk over supper was mostly about his growing family, the downturn in the economy that had left some Amish without the factory jobs they'd had, and the problems of keeping a good teacher at their school.

It was only after the meal was over that Jonas seemed ready to tackle something else. "You sit down and put your feet up," he urged his mother, leading her toward the living room. "I'll help Sarah with the dishes."

"You don't need to help me," she said, when he returned and picked up a dish towel. "I can take care of these while you visit with your mother."

"When you don't have sisters, you have to learn to help in the kitchen from time to time." Jonas dried a plate vigorously. "Mary always says she's glad my mamm taught me so well."

"Your mamm thinks the world of Mary, from everything she's said." She suspected that Jonas wouldn't take long to reach the subject of his desire for a private chat.

"Ja, that's so. It's a lucky man whose wife and mother get on so well as they do." He slanted a glance toward Sarah. "That's why we thought it best for Mammi to move in with us."

And there it was. "I'm sure Aunt Emma would like that when she's ready."

"We thought she was ready now. Neither of us wanted to see her go through another winter here alone. But then you came."

It was not said angrily, but Sarah still felt the words were an accusation.

"I came because your mother asked me to."

"Ach, ja, I know that." Jonas frowned at the bowl he was drying. "If you'd talked to us before you agreed, things might have been different."

She couldn't argue with that. "They might have been, I guess. But why would I think of talking to you? Your mamm has always been an independent woman, able to make decisions for herself."

Jonas drew himself up, as if about to say something important. "Now that my father is gone, the responsibility for my mother is mine. It's time she gave up working so hard and took it a little easy for the rest of her days."

Sarah raised her eyebrows. "Is that what your mamm thinks?"

For a moment she thought Jonas would flare out at her. He looked very like the boy cousin who'd ordered her not to climb the apple tree when she was six. Of course she had, and had gotten stuck, to boot.

Then a smile tugged at Jonas's mouth, and the pompous air vanished.

"No, I guess it's not." The smile widened into a grin. "My mother is not the only independent woman in the family."

Sarah smiled back, her defensiveness evaporating. "Jonas, you know I wouldn't do anything to harm your mamm.

She's not ready to give up yet, and now that I'm here, she needn't work so hard. Or be alone in the house."

"Ja, that's so."

She heard a reservation in his voice, and it troubled her. "If something else is wrong, just tell me."

Jonas rubbed the back of his neck, hesitating. Finally he seemed to make up his mind. "It seems to us that Mammi is getting a little forgetful these days. Mary tried to get her to go to the doctor about it, but Mammi wouldn't hear of it."

If anything would strain the relationship between mother-in-law and daughter-in-law, unwelcome advice would be it.

"I'm sorry, but—"

"Have you seen any sign of her forgetting things?" Jonas leaned on the sink, looking into her face. "Sarah, it has me worried."

She tried to smile. Jonas had become a boy who was worried about his mother, not a man who was trying to make decisions for her.

"Only once or twice since I've been here," she said. "Just little things, like mistaking the day. And when someone lives alone, that's not unusual."

"You think she's all right, then?"

She put her hand over his. "Will it make you feel better if I promise to keep my eyes open for any problems? If there are any, maybe I can find a way of getting her to the doctor."

He blew out a breath. "Ja, that would be a relief. Maybe it's gut that you've komm after all."

He didn't sound totally convinced, but that might be too much to hope for. She smiled and patted his hand. "I'll look after her. I promise."

Chapter Five

Sarah heard the sounds of hammering early the next morning. Obviously the Miller brothers were hard at work after their disappearance the previous day.

She hesitated for a moment. There was something she wanted to discuss with Aaron about the storage areas. Legitimate as that concern was, she was reluctant to press him into a discussion that involved the purpose to which the rooms would be put.

That was foolish, wasn't it? She'd prayed for the wisdom to deal with Aaron. Staying away from him wasn't dealing with him—it was hiding. Pulling her shawl around her shoulders, she opened the door to the addition.

All three brothers worked today—maybe with the idea of making up for missing yesterday. Aaron looked up at the sound of the door opening, his face unreadable.

"Sarah." He nodded in greeting.

"You are making progress." The uprights had been replaced and the framing was finished. "Already it is warmer to work out here, with the wind cut off."

"It will be even better when we have the insulation installed." Nathan's relaxed smile accompanied the words. In the face of Aaron's apparent disapproval of her and Benjamin's teenage sulkiness, Nathan seemed most ready to be friends.

"You won't freeze your fingers when you work, then." She'd noticed that while the two younger boys wore work gloves, Aaron seemed to prefer touching the wood with his hands as he cut and hammered. Even now his hand caressed the board he handled as if it were a living creature.

"Ja, that's for sure," Nathan said. At a look from Aaron, he turned back to his cutting.

She'd like to believe that Aaron was only concerned with his brother giving his attention to the job, but she suspected his reaction was more personal than that. She rejected the temptation to escape back into the house and forced herself to approach him.

When she stood next to him, he kept his gaze on his hand for a long moment. Then he turned to her.

"Is there something you need, Sarah?"

"I'd like to discuss the storage areas with you. If you can come into the examining room with me for just a moment—"

"Not now." The words were curt enough to be insulting. He seemed to realize that, and he gave a twitch of his firm lips that might have been meant for a smile. "It's best we finish what we're doing at the moment, so we can get on with the insulation this afternoon." He turned to Benjamin, seeming to dismiss her. "You can start cutting the insulation now, so it will be ready."

Benjamin seemed to freeze, and even she could read the guilt in his face.

"Well?" Aaron's voice was sharp. "Was ist letz? What's wrong?"

"I . . . I forgot to put the cutter in." Benjamin's embarrassment was probably doubled because she was here.

"Forgot it?" Aaron's face tightened even more, if that was possible. "How are we to cut the insulation without it?"

Benjamin's guilt turned to a pout, and he looked so like her own little brother when he'd done something wrong that Sarah wanted to reach out to him. But Aaron would hardly welcome that.

"It's no big deal," Benjamin muttered.

"Don't talk to me as if I were one of your Englisch friends." Aaron glanced at her and then caught the boy by the arm. "Komm. I'll tell you some other things to bring when you go back for the cutter." He marched Benjamin outside.

Sarah had to press her lips together to keep from voicing her opinion. Didn't Aaron see that being sharp with the boy would only make him more rebellious?

"Do you have bruders, Sarah?" Nathan's question pulled her attention away from the two of them who stood out by the wagon.

"Ja, five of them and no sisters, so I know a little about getting along with boys." She thought of her own youngest brother. "James, the youngest, is fourteen. He's going to be a dairy farmer, just like Daad, if he has his way."

"That's nice, that is." Nathan paused for a moment, straightening so that he could see out the door opening to where his brothers stood. "Often boys that age don't know what they want."

"True enough. Did you?"

Nathan grinned. "For sure. Aaron put tools in my hands as soon as I could hold them. I never wanted anything else."

Obviously Aaron had taken time and patience with his siblings. "It seems as if Aaron is more like a father to you two than a brother sometimes." She remembered what Aunt Emma had said about the father's drinking problem and wished the words back.

But Nathan didn't seem to take offense. "Ja, he always has been. He was fourteen when Mammi died, so he just took charge." His smile flickered again. "Molly reminds him that we're most all grown up now and he can relax, but I don't suppose he ever will."

"Parents don't, do they? My daad still worries over me." She felt a rush of longing to have Daadi's arms around her shoulders. "Now I know how much that concern means, but there were times when I was impatient with what seemed like endless fussing."

"Like Benjamin." Nathan didn't seem too concerned. "It will all komm straight."

She hesitated, wondering if she could say the thought in her mind. But if she didn't speak, how could she know what Nathan might say?

"I'm afraid that this project is difficult for Aaron. Because of your mamm."

He was silent for so long that Sarah feared she'd gone too far. Then he nodded.

"Maybe. But maybe that's gut. Bishop Mose would say that all of this—you being here, our doing the work—is God's will, meant for our well-being."

She smiled despite the tears that filled her eyes. "Nathan, I think that you are very wise for someone so young."

"Not me. But Sarah . . ." He hesitated a moment. "If Aaron gives you trouble, just remember that you're the boss on this job, ain't so?"

She couldn't respond because she heard Aaron returning, but she gave Nathan a grateful smile before she turned toward Aaron.

He glanced from Nathan to her as if wondering what was going on between them. "Benjamin will be back soon. That boy would forget his head if it weren't attached."

"Most nearly-sixteen-year-olds are like that," she said easily. "Now, about the storage areas." She didn't give Aaron time to protest. "When you break for lunch, I will show you what we have now in the exam room and what things I want changed."

She was pleased to hear that her words didn't leave any room for excuses. Aaron must have felt that way, too, because he simply gave a sharp nod of agreement before turning back to his work.

. . .

Aaron followed Sarah into what she called the exam room, and the beef-and-onion pie Emma had served for lunch seemed to form a clump in his stomach. He didn't want to talk about what Sarah and Emma needed for delivering babies. But Sarah hadn't left him much choice in the matter, now had she?

Her firmness had taken him by surprise. He didn't remember such spirit in the girl she'd been. Maturity had changed her in a number of ways, it seemed.

His gaze lingered on the long curve of Sarah's slim back as she moved to the closet and opened it. He blinked and stared at a hairline crack in the plaster instead. He didn't need to be noticing anything about Sarah Mast—that was certain sure.

"You can see that we're a little cramped for space." She gestured at two large black bags on the bottom shelf. "We manage to fit what we need in our bags when we do home births, but we'd like to have about half again the storage in the birthing rooms." She darted a glance at him. "Is this making you nervous, Aaron?"

He shrugged, pulling his measuring tape from his pocket. "Don't most men feel that way when it comes to talking about babies?"

She considered, head tipped slightly to one side. "I would say that Amish men usually take birthing fairly calmly, even though they don't talk about it much. Englischers are another matter." Her face relaxed in a smile. "I remember one husband—a great big fellow he was, and so sure he'd be able to help his wife through delivery. Instead he passed out flat on the floor, and we had to tend him."

Aaron managed an answering smile, though he didn't feel anything resembling humor. His father hadn't done so well when Mamm was in labor, as he recalled. He'd slipped away, leaving everything to the midwife.

Sliding out the metal tape, Aaron knelt to measure the

length of the closet. The tape snapped back when he pulled out his pad and pencil.

"Let me." Sarah took the pencil and paper from his hand, her fingers brushing his. "You tell me the measurements, and I'll write them down."

"Ja, fine." He needed to concentrate on the job, not let his mind wander off into the past. Or onto his own personal feelings about midwives.

Bishop Mose had pushed him into this job, and he would do it. But he didn't have to like it.

"Forty-eight inches long." Still, he couldn't help being aware of Sarah standing just behind him, the hem of her skirt brushing his arm. He swung the tape vertically. "Looks like the spacing between the shelves is fourteen inches, and the shelves are ten inches wide."

Sarah jotted down the numbers before she spoke again. "Deeper shelves would be more useful. Can you do that?"

"Sure." He glanced up at her, sidetracked for a moment by the view of her face from this unexpected angle. He stood, taking a careful step away. "Anything else?"

"Aunt Emma loves her corner cupboard in the kitchen. I was thinking to put one in each room, if you and your brothers could do that."

He nodded, making a note of it. "We can. Nathan has a gut hand with designing shelf units."

"Nathan loves working with you. He says you started teaching him when he was barely old enough to hold the tools."

When had she gotten on such friendly terms with Nathan? "Ja, I guess that's so."

"And I suppose you did the same with Benjamin, as well."

Her tone was casual, but he didn't doubt that her thoughts were on how he'd handled the boy this morning. Already he regretted that, but he wasn't going to say so to Sarah.

"Benjamin does well, when he puts his mind to it. Unfortunately, that's not often enough." He snapped the tape closed and slid it back into his pocket.

"Ach, he reminds me of my youngest brother, James. I think they're all a little befuddled at that age, don't you?"

"Benjamin must learn to be responsible." His voice snapped like the tape had, snicking back into its case.

"Like you?" Her gaze met his, and there was a spark in her green eyes.

"I have to be responsible. As you do."

"We're adults. Benjamin is a boy still."

"And he is my brother. I will handle him as I see fit."

For an instant they glared at each other. Were they arguing about Benjamin? Or about the other thing that lay between them?

The door swung open, and Emma hurried in. "Ach, Sarah, we must hurry. It's almost time for the patients to start arriving."

Tension tightened his hands into fists. "I thought you didn't see patients today," he said.

"We don't." Sarah had paled. She moved quickly to Emma and took her arm. "We don't have any patients coming today, Aunt Emma. Remember? This is Wednesday."

For a moment Emma just stared at her. Then she shook her head, her concerned expression dissolving in ruefulness. "Ach, I'm ferhoodled today. I don't know what's wrong with me."

"You're tired, that's all." Sarah took the older woman's arm and turned her toward the door. "Why don't you have a rest? I'll clean up from lunch as soon as Aaron and I are finished."

Sarah's caring, her gentleness, seemed to touch something inside him. But the incident just confirmed what he already felt. Emma should retire. Surely Sarah could see that as well as he did.

Emma went out, still shaking her head at herself. Sarah swung toward him, face defensive.

"I suppose you think that means something."

"I think it means what any sensible person would think.

Emma is growing forgetful. She shouldn't be delivering babies."

Sarah folded her arms across her chest. "Just because she loses track of the days doesn't mean she has to be put out to pasture."

"What if she forgets when she's supposed to be delivering a baby?"

"That won't happen. I'm here. I won't let it."

"You can't do everything, Sarah." His voice softened despite himself. She seemed so alone. He didn't want her to be hurt. "It's not too late to pull back from the project. You don't have to sink your savings into something that may not work out."

"You'd like to get out of this, wouldn't you?" The flare of defiance that accompanied the words startled him. "You may as well forget that idea, Aaron. I'm not changing my plans for you or anyone else."

Aunt Emma might have grown a little forgetful, but not when it came to the activities of her church. So Sarah found herself in the kitchen at the township fire hall at five in the morning. The cement-block building was filled with a group of women putting on a hunters' breakfast to raise money for charity.

She'd already been awake when Aunt Emma came to call her at four. Her sleep had been troubled by the guilt that hung over her. She had lost her temper with Aaron and spoken hasty, angry words. She almost never did such a thing, and she couldn't understand what had gotten into her.

She'd already asked God for forgiveness. She'd have to ask Aaron, as well, before things would be right.

"Do you do this every year?" She stood next to Leah at the huge commercial gas range, watching over griddle after griddle filled with pancakes.

"Just about." Leah flipped blueberry pancakes with an

expert hand. "Everyone comes, Amish, Mennonite, and Englisch alike, and not only hunters. This year the money will go to Mennonite Disaster Relief for hurricane victims."

"My church in Ohio raised money for that, too." Sarah scooped buckwheat batter onto a griddle. "This was a bad year for hurricanes, for sure."

She glanced through the pass-through at the large open room filled with long tables. They were already lined with people in hunter orange, eating their way through mountains of pancakes, sausage, bacon, and eggs prepared all ways, to say nothing of all the coffeecakes and breads the women had brought.

"Looks like you'll raise plenty of money today," she said.

"*We'll* raise plenty," Leah said, correcting her with a smile. "You are one of us now, remember?"

"Ja, I remember." It felt good, being accepted here. The warmth, chatter, and laughter of the kitchen seemed to envelop Sarah with a sense of familiarity. This day was such an example of what it meant to be Amish.

"It's gut, working together this way." Leah seemed to echo her thoughts. "Some folks would just write a check to help, but I like actually working. I like teaching the children that this is the right thing to do."

Sarah nodded. She'd already seen Leah's stepchildren hard at work, carrying trays and coffeepots around the large room.

"You are setting them a gut example. And they are finding out that it is fun to work together."

"It is, isn't it?" Leah gave her a quick smile. "This is how we get to know each other so well, ain't so?"

Sarah nodded. What Leah said went to the heart of what it meant to be Amish. This time together, working with sisters, was part of what wove the tough, durable fabric of the Amish community.

Leah was quiet for a few minutes, concentrating on the

next batch of pancakes. Once they were all going, she turned back to Sarah.

"I hear that you might want to go to the clinic with me one day."

Sarah couldn't help smiling. The Amish might not have telephones, but news traveled fast—the Amish telegraph, some folks called it.

"Ja, I would like to. Aunt Emma says that is the best place to arrange for newborn testing."

Leah nodded. "You must meet Dr. Brandenmyer. He is so dedicated to helping babies. The research his clinic does will lead to solving the genetic diseases, I pray."

"I pray that, as well." Sarah's throat tightened at the thought of no more babies doomed to a short, difficult life. "What is the work that you do for the clinic?"

"Collecting family tree information, mostly," Leah said. "They can trace the incidence of genetic problems through the families."

Sarah nodded, impressed. "Our people trust you. They wouldn't give up that information easily to a stranger coming to the door."

"That is my part," Leah said. "And I understand that you believe in testing every newborn, even when the families have no history of disease."

That news had spread fast, as well. People would have varying reactions to it, Sarah feared.

"I think testing everyone is for the best. If everyone's child is tested automatically, then no one can object. Early detection can save babies. That's what is important. And it's gut for the parents, also, to know from the start what they are facing."

"I'm so glad to hear you say that." Her gaze warm, Leah clasped Sarah's hand, and Sarah had the sense that she'd gained a valuable ally. "That has not always been the case in the past."

Sarah closed her lips. There was nothing she could say.

She wasn't going to criticize Aunt Emma to anyone, even if she agreed.

"I would like to go to the clinic with you," she said. "But are you sure Dr. Brandenmyer will welcome a midwife to the area?"

"I'm sure," Leah said. "He's a believer in midwives. Especially one like you, who is so dedicated. Will this coming Wednesday be all right for you? I can arrange for a driver."

"Ja, that will be wonderful gut." The trip was settled so easily, and she would walk into the clinic with a friend. That meant a great deal.

"Ach, here is someone who also loves Dr. Brandenmyer." Leah turned from the stove to embrace a woman who had just come in. "Sarah, this is my sister-in-law, Myra. And her little girl, Anna Grace."

Myra was a sweet-faced young woman with shy dark eyes. The child on her hip reached for Leah, smiling, sure of her welcome. She was adorable, with chubby pink cheeks and wispy blond hair. She was also a Down syndrome child.

The thought went through Sarah's mind in an instant. She smiled at Myra. "I am glad to meet you. And this little one, also." She touched one chubby hand and was rewarded with a chuckle.

"We are so fortunate to have another midwife in Pleasant Valley." Myra's greeting was warm. "I hope to have a midwife the next time I have a baby." She bounced little Anna on her hip. "I went to the clinic for my first two babies."

Sarah nodded. It wasn't unusual for an Amish mother to choose a doctor for her first birth and then, if all went well, to switch to a midwife for other births.

And if that next baby was Down syndrome, as well, he or she would be loved and cherished just as Anna Grace obviously was. It would be God's will.

"You two have been cooking over the stove long enough." Barbara, Leah's other sister-in-law, bustled up to them, her cheeks bright red from the heat of the kitchen. "You go and take over the serving table, and I'll set someone else to turning pancakes for a while."

"I don't mind staying at the stove," Sarah said.

Leah took her arm. "Komm, now. Barbara is in charge today, so we will follow orders. We'll get a chance at every job before the day is over."

Filling plates for people as they came to the table was definitely cooler than working over the hot stove. Almost too cool, in fact, as a blast of cold air filtered through the room each time the door opened.

Leah shivered a little. "That inch of snow on the ground will make the hunters happy. If the old-timers are right, we're in for a snowy winter."

"Midwives aren't so happy with snowy winters, no matter how much hunters like them," Sarah said. "I've never missed catching a baby, but it has been nip and tuck sometimes."

A fresh group came to the table, cutting off their conversation. Sarah filled plates quickly with generous helpings. The breakfast was all-you-can-eat, and most people took that seriously.

"Can I have some extra scrambled eggs?"

Sarah looked up to find Benjamin Miller standing in front of her. "Of course." She piled an extra scoop on his plate. "You can komm back for more, you know."

"He will." Nathan clapped him on the shoulder. "You can be sure of that."

"Gut. We don't want to have any leftovers." She managed to keep a smile on her face as she realized that Aaron was standing behind his brothers. She'd just been thinking that she owed him an apology. God was giving her the opportunity.

In a moment Aaron was in front of her. Her tongue seemed stuck to the roof of her mouth. She filled the plate for him silently, trying to find a way to say the words she needed to speak.

As she held out the plate, she met his eyes and saw the same struggle in his face that she felt.

"I'm sorry—"

"I should—"

They both spoke at once; both stopped at once.

Aaron gestured toward her. She swallowed.

"Aaron, I am sorry. I had no right to be angry with you for what you said."

He took the plate, his fingers touching hers. "And I had no right to say it. I am sorry. I was wrong."

"Can we forget it?" She tried to smile, knowing others were watching. She should take her hand away, but his fingers had become wrapped around hers.

"Ja, that is best." Aaron seemed to become aware that people were watching them. He took the plate, gave her a meaningless smile, and went quickly to join his brothers.

Chapter Six

On the off Sunday when worship wasn't held, the Amish of Pleasant Valley went visiting. Aunt Emma's sons didn't live close enough to come often, but since most Amish were related if you went back far enough, she didn't lack for invitations.

Today, joining the other women in Anna Fisher's kitchen as they prepared the meal, Sarah thought how familiar this all was. Sunday visits were an integral part of their lives. In the outside world folks might use Sunday for football games or shopping, but not here. On Sunday you were either in church or visiting family or having family come to visit.

Myra and Joseph Beiler were here, as well. Apparently they lived next door. Samuel helped Joseph in his machinery shop when he wasn't training horses, and Joseph and Anna were brother and sister, as were Samuel and Myra—another example of the connections that marked Amish life.

In this case, that had perils as well as strengths. Sarah

glanced toward the living room, where Myra's daughters played with their cousin. Since there'd been a case of Down syndrome in the family, there was all the more reason for Anna to be tested when she became pregnant.

Sarah sliced a loaf of oatmeal bread, stacking it in a napkin-lined basket. She glanced at Anna, bending over the stove to check her pot roast. With some women, testing might be a difficult subject to bring up, but Anna struck Sarah as being mature and clear-minded. She'd probably already thought of it.

With two mothers and two midwives in the room, the talk naturally centered on babies. This pattern, too, was familiar. The men in the living room talking about work or weather, the women in the kitchen talking about pregnancy and babies, something they wouldn't discuss in front of the men.

Myra added hot biscuits to the bread basket, giving Sarah a shy smile.

"I'm glad we met at the hunters' breakfast. I've been wanting to meet you. You are getting acquainted with everyone, ain't so?"

Sarah smiled. "It will take a while, I guess. I'm still figuring out how everyone is related."

"You must ask your aunt about that. She knows everyone's family tree, from delivering all those babies. I saw that you were chatting with Aaron Miller at the breakfast. You must be getting to know him."

"Not really." The words came out too sharply, and she regretted that instantly. What was it about Aaron that brought out her most disagreeable qualities?

Myra's cheeks flushed. "I didn't mean—"

"No, no, I am the one who's sorry. Aaron and his brothers are building the new birthing rooms for us, that's all. That's what we were talking about." Well, in a way it was.

"And you don't want folks pairing you up already," Myra said, smiling. "You have to forgive us. I'm so happy with Joseph that I'd like to have everyone feel this way. And you must be lonely since your husband died."

Maybe it was as well to get this out in the open. Then word would get around, and folks would stop wondering.

"A little lonely, I guess, but my work keeps me busy. I don't really think I'll marry again. What man would put up with the crazy schedule a midwife keeps?"

Myra glanced toward Emma. "Your uncle didn't seem to mind."

"Onkel Ezra was one of a kind." Her voice softened as she remembered Aunt Emma's husband. "He didn't seem to mind any inconvenience, but I don't think there are many men like that around. Anyway, I guess I am promised to my work."

"We are the winners, in that case," Anna said, coming up behind them in time to hear the words. "Myra, would you mind mashing the potatoes? They always come out so light when you do them."

Myra smiled, shaking her head at the compliment, and crossed the kitchen.

"I thought maybe Myra was asking too many questions," Anna said under the clatter of dishes as Aunt Emma got serving bowls out.

"Not at all. Well, I know everyone is curious when someone new comes to the community."

"Or someone old comes back." Anna shrugged her shoulders. "I was three years in the Englisch world before I came home. I remember how it was, feeling as if everyone was watching and wondering. You're going through that now, ain't so?"

"It does make me wonder if I've put my kapp on upside down sometimes," she admitted. That explained the maturity and assertiveness she'd sensed in Anna. She'd earned them, perhaps the hard way, being out among the Englisch.

"One thing I learned out there." Anna seemed to be sensing her thoughts. "To ask when I want something." She lowered her voice with a glance at Emma. "I'm almost certain sure now that I am expecting, and if so, I want you to be the one to deliver my baby."

Sarah didn't know what to say, and she should have come up with an answer for that by now. "I hope it works out that way," she said carefully. "Aunt Emma and I haven't yet decided exactly how we'll divide up the cases."

Anna nodded. "So long as you know. When it was thought Emma was going to retire . . . well, I wasn't sure what I would do." She hesitated. "I don't know if Emma has told this to you, or even if she knew it, but rumor was that Dr. Mitchell wanted the law to shut down Emma's midwife practice."

"I don't— No, I didn't realize that." Her mind spun crazily. Had Aunt Emma known? Was that maybe behind the fact that she hadn't had the birthing rooms finished? "What on earth did the man have against Aunt Emma?"

"Maybe not Emma in particular," Anna said. "Seems from the time he came to Pleasant Valley he's been intent on having things his way, and he just plain doesn't believe in midwives. Well, anyway, I thought you should know." Her smile flashed. "Hope that doesn't make me a blabbermaul."

She turned before Sarah could respond, going to the doorway and getting the attention of the men in the living room. "We are dishing up now. Will you two get the little ones in their seats?"

After a few moments of confusion as the women carried food to the table, the little girls knocked over their block towers, and the men gathered the kinder up, they were all seated around the long kitchen table. The room was warm with the heat from the stove, and the bowls and platters steamed, perfuming the air. Samuel, at the head of the table, bowed his head for the silent blessing, and the others followed his example.

Please, Father. Sarah found her prayer straying from blessing the food to her other concern. *Help me see if I should do something about this doctor. And show me how to manage my relationship with Aunt Emma. I don't want her to feel that I am taking her patients.*

As if they could see with their eyes closed, everyone at the table murmured a silent "Amen" at the same time that Samuel opened his eyes. Platters heavy with food began to flow around the table.

"So, Emma," Joseph said, "when are you going to let us set up a telephone shanty for you? Seems to me that if a machinery shop can have one, a midwife should. It would make Samuel feel easier when he and Anna start having babies, that's certain sure."

Samuel grinned. "You might be right at that. Especially if a little one decides to come in the middle of a stormy night."

Aunt Emma looked up from buttering a roll for Anna's little girl. "I've never seen much need for that. Folks always seem to get me, one way or another."

"Did your practice in Ohio have a telephone nearby, Sarah?" Myra handed her the bowl of mashed potatoes as she asked.

Sarah disliked being in a position where she seemed to disagree with Aunt Emma, but she couldn't say anything but the truth. "Ja, we had a telephone shanty with an answering machine so people could leave a message. And one of our neighbors fixed up a buzzer that would go off in the bedroom if a call came in the night."

"We could fix that up, easy as can be." Joseph glanced at his brother-in-law. "Right, Samuel?"

"I'd say so. It wouldn't take much." Samuel looked as if he were seeing it in his mind. "It wouldn't take more'n an hour or two of work to do that once the phone was in place."

"Easiest if we put the shanty as close to the bedroom as possible," Joseph added, obviously eager to do the project and sounding as if it had already been decided.

Sarah looked at her aunt, and her heart seemed to clench. Emma didn't look angry or upset. That would have been a natural reaction from her when she opposed something. Instead Emma looked . . . withdrawn. Distant. As if she were sitting back and watching things go on without her.

That wasn't what Sarah wanted. She was here to help Aunt Emma, not replace her. Certainly not make her feel unnecessary.

"That is most kind of you both," she said. "But I think it will be something for Aunt Emma and the bishop to discuss."

Looking a little abashed, Joseph nodded. Anna began talking about the Christmas program the children at the school were preparing. The others joined in.

But maybe it was too late. Maybe the damage had been done. Because Aunt Emma still stared down at her plate as if she weren't really there at all.

The cold air nipped at Sarah's cheeks as she and Aunt Emma drove home from Anna and Samuel's. It was not even four o'clock yet, but the dark line of clouds, straight as a line drawn by a ruler on the horizon, made it seem later.

Aunt Emma shivered and pulled the lap robe closer. "Just the first of December, and it feels like the middle of winter."

"It does." Sarah smiled, nodding toward the two figures walking down the lane, heads close together as they talked. "Those two don't look cold, though."

Aunt Emma peered through her glasses. "Benjamin Miller, that is. Walking out with Louise Buckholtz, I see. Ach, it seems only yesterday that I delivered the two of them—not a month apart, they were, and their mamms such gut friends."

Sarah didn't dare breathe. Aunt Emma had brought up the subject of Benjamin's birth herself. Would she go on to talk about his mamm's dying?

Her aunt shook her head, shivering again despite the warm blanket. "I never could forget that, no matter how much time went by. The only mother who died in all the years I've been a midwife."

"I am sure you did everything you could do." It was the only response Sarah could think to make.

"If only he had done as I said . . ." Emma let that trail off, lapsing in abstracted silence.

"Who?" Sarah kept her voice soft, nearly a whisper, but her heart was thudding. She held her breath. "If who had done what you said?"

As if roused by the question, Aunt Emma jerked upright. "Nothing. Never mind." Her lips clamped into a straight, stubborn line.

Sarah knew the signs. Her aunt would say no more, and she was left wondering.

Their buggy passed the young couple, and she raised her hand in greeting. Benjamin nodded, his cheeks red either with the cold or maybe with embarrassment that she'd seen him with a girl.

She turned the horse in when they reached the lane, and they rolled up to the house. She shot a glance at Aunt Emma. She'd hoped to have a quiet talk about this business of the telephone once they got home, but the tired lines in her aunt's face changed her mind.

"You go on in and warm up," she said. "I'll take care of Dolly."

Her aunt didn't argue, which was in itself cause for concern. "Ja." She slid down slowly. "I think I will take a little nap."

That startled Sarah. She couldn't remember a time when Aunt Emma had lain down willingly in the middle of the day, even after being up most of the night delivering a baby.

"Are you feeling all right?" Sarah leaned down from the high seat, keeping a firm hold on the lines. Restive, Dolly tossed her head, obviously wanting to move on toward her warm barn.

"Fine, fine." Aunt Emma gave an irritated shake to her head. "I chust want a little rest, that's all." She walked off toward the porch, and Sarah stayed where she was until she'd seen her aunt get safely inside.

Dolly moved toward the barn at a quick clip the instant she loosened the lines. Once there, Sarah moved automatically through the routine of removing the harness, rubbing the horse down, turning her into her stall, seeing to the feed and water. All the while her mind revolved around Aunt Emma's out of character behavior.

Was this all to do with that business about the telephone? She'd had every intention of bringing the subject up with Aunt Emma, but she wouldn't have done it that way, in front of other people. Did her aunt feel as if they'd joined together against her? She wouldn't have Emma feel that for the world.

And what about Dr. Mitchell? Had Aunt Emma been aware of his antagonism or not?

The house was still when she went back inside. Aunt Emma must have done as she'd said. Sarah stood at the foot of the stairs, listening, hearing nothing more than a soft snore.

Well, Aunt Emma knew best about her own needs. Maybe some soup for supper would be gut. Sarah stepped into the pantry, looking along the well-stocked shelves for soup. She took down a quart of chicken noodle soup and carried it to the kitchen. As she set it on the counter, she glanced through the window. And smiled, distracted from her thoughts.

Hand in hand, Benjamin and Louise walked across the frosty grass toward the pond. Louise swung away from him, tilting her head, and then skipped back. The sight of their laughing faces warmed Sarah's heart.

She could remember when she and Levi were like that—skipping through their time together, laughing, teasing. Carefree. So sure of their love, so convinced they knew what the future held.

For once, such thoughts didn't seem to be leading her into a spiral of doubt and blame. Today, for a reason she didn't quite understand, she could look at Benjamin and Louise's puppy love and simply smile at that innocent happiness.

Well, why not? It would be a pity to let what happened later cloud the memories of her own happy days. Like Benjamin and his girl, she and Levi hadn't had a thought then for anything other than the delightful new feelings they had for each other.

She glanced out the window again, still smiling, and froze, her hand tightening on the edge of the sink. The girl had slid out onto the glossy surface of the frozen pond. She stood there, laughing, beckoning at Benjamin to join her.

The ice surely wasn't thick enough to hold one, let alone two. Sarah's body stiffened, and she leaned forward as if she could reach them through the glass.

Thank the dear Lord, Benjamin seemed more sensible than the girl. He stood on the bank, reaching out to her. Sarah couldn't hear his voice, but she could imagine the words. He'd be telling Louise not to be so foolish, to come off the ice.

Louise reacted predictably for a girl her age, with a toss of her head that seemed to say he needn't think he could tell her what to do. She took another step toward the middle of the pond.

Sarah whirled, grabbing her coat and hurrying out the back door and down the three steps. They wouldn't thank her for interfering, but maybe just the realization that an adult was watching would be enough to make the girl act sensibly.

Sarah hurried around the house, her eyes fixed on them. Should she call out? If she did—

All in a moment it was too late. The ice cracked—the sound was a shot in the cold air. The girl's arms flew out, reaching for a support that wasn't there. She plunged through the ice.

Sarah broke into a run, her jumbled prayers keeping pace with her racing feet.

Hold her up, Father. Please. Please.

Benjamin, frantic, ventured a foot onto the ice.

"Benjamin, stop! Stop!" The cry was torn from her throat. "You muscht stoppe."

He turned toward her, his young face distorted by fear and panic. But he was heeding her.

"Lie down." It took all she had to shout and run. "Lie down on the ice."

She could see the sense come back into his face at her words. He threw himself onto his belly, inching forward onto the ice.

An eternity of running, and she was there. A broken branch lay near the tree, and she grabbed it, plunging down on the ground behind Benjamin.

Louise bobbed up, arms thrashing, breaking the ice still more as she grasped for it. Her lips were blue—she'd exhaust herself, disappear under the surface . . .

"Louise!" Sarah shouted the name, putting every force of her will into it. "We are coming for you. You must stop moving. Listen to me! Stop moving. Just keep your head above the water."

Benjamin slithered out onto the ice, which was still firm near the edge of the pond. "Hold my feet."

"Ja, I will." Sarah shoved the branch into his hand. "Hold this out so she can reach it. Don't try to take her hand, or you'll go through as well."

Harsh words, but she'd seen a cousin break through the ice when she was a child. Her father's orders as he organized the rescue filled her mind as if in answer to her prayer. *Move slowly, stay flat, use whatever you can find to reach out to her.*

Benjamin took the branch, sliding it out in front of him. Not quite long enough. He inched forward.

Sarah grabbed his ankles, holding tight. The cold already penetrated her coat and dress to her skin, making her shake. Soaked with icy water, how much longer could the girl stay up?

"Grab it," Benjamin ordered, shoving the branch farther across the ice. "Louise, grab the branch. You can do it. Now."

The girl's terrified face seemed to calm for an instant. She reached, ice breaking, the effort nearly submerging her, but then she had the branch and was holding on tight.

"Gut, gut. Now the other hand." Sarah was half on the ice herself now, clinging tight to Benjamin. She would not lose him.

For a moment she thought the girl couldn't do it. Then Louise swung her arm, grabbing the branch and holding on with both hands.

"Back now, Benjamin." Sarah tugged on his ankles. "Back, drawing her with you."

Benjamin slid back. The ice breaking around her body, Louise moved closer. They were going to make it—

The ice began to crack around Benjamin. Sarah clasped his ankles, pulling with all her strength. She had to get them out, she couldn't feel her hands anymore—

Another hand reached out, closing over hers, and then Aaron was pushing her away, taking her place, pulling his brother toward safety.

"Not so fast—" Benjamin began, but Aaron already had him, pulling him and the girl toward the bank.

With a final crack, the ice gave way entirely, but it was all right. Aaron had them both.

Denke, Father. Sarah forced herself up, ripping her coat off to wrap it around Louise. *Denke.*

The girl caught up in his arms, Aaron set off for the house. Get her warm and dry—that was the important thing now.

His relief that all three of them were safe turned quickly to anger. How could Benjamin have been so foolish, so heedless, as to put Louise in danger like that? What had he been thinking?

The words burned in his throat. He choked them back.

He would not say anything in front of Louise. He certainly wouldn't do so with Sarah there.

He glanced over his shoulder to find that Sarah had her arm around Benjamin's waist as they stumbled along behind him. It was hard to tell which of them was holding the other up.

"Sarah, you need not come with us. Go back to your house and get warm and dry."

Go home. He didn't need Sarah around while he dealt with this situation.

"Unless there is another woman at your house, you need me." The chill in her voice said that she knew he'd like to be rid of her.

But she was right. He did need her.

"I hadn't thought about that. Denke."

She didn't spare breath for an answer. Sarah would be chilled to the bone as well, but she kept trudging on. Across the yard, up the porch steps, and into the welcoming warmth of the house.

Sarah hurried to his side. "Take her to the warmest bedroom. I must get those wet clothes off her."

"This way." He climbed the stairs two at a time, ignoring the sodden weight that dragged at his arms. "Molly's room is ready for her, and it has the best heat in the house."

He carried the girl through the door and set her carefully on the bed, stepping back so that Sarah could get at her.

The poor girl shivered, teeth chattering together, her face dead white. His concern deepened. "Should I send for the paramedics?" he asked.

"Let's see how she is once we get her warmed up." Sarah spared him a reassuring glance as she pulled off first her coat and then Louise's own sodden one. "More blankets, if you have them. If you have any hot water bottles, fill them. But you'd better leave now."

"Ja." Louise seemed to find her voice.

She was embarrassed by the situation. If Sarah hadn't

been here . . . well, he'd have done what he had to, but he didn't want to think about that.

He removed an armful of blankets and quilts from the blanket chest at the foot of the bed and piled them next to Louise on the bed. "I'll look for a hot water bottle. Call me if you need anything else."

Sarah nodded, her focus on the girl. Obviously the best thing he could do was leave them alone. Sarah knew what to do.

Benjamin waited at the foot of the stairs, one hand on the railing as if unable to decide whether he should go up. His wide, frightened gaze met Aaron's. "Is she . . . How is she?"

"Sarah is taking care of her." He led the boy away from the stairs. "We'd best leave it to her."

"Ja. Sarah will know what's best." Benjamin blew out a long breath, as if he'd forgotten to breathe for a while. "Thank the gut Lord Sarah saw what was happening." A shiver went through him. "I don't know if I could have gotten Louise out alone."

Aaron bit back the words that wanted to explode from his mouth. "Go and change into something dry. You can't do anything for Louise. You've done enough—"

He cut that off. Hadn't he just told himself not to speak, not now, while he still shook inside at the thought of what might have happened?

But Benjamin probably knew where that thought had been going. He stiffened, fists clenched tight against his legs, staring at Aaron.

"What do you mean? Are you saying Louise's accident was my fault?"

Aaron's control slipped. "Wasn't it? You took the girl out there. You were responsible. What were you thinking to let her go on that pond? You should have known the ice wasn't thick enough."

Benjamin was as pale as the girl upstairs. "I knew. I told her so. What was I supposed to do?"

"You were supposed to be responsible. To stop her."

"How could I do that? She ran out onto the ice before I knew she was going to do it."

"It was your responsi—"

"My responsibility. Ja, I know. You're always telling me, aren't you?" Benjamin flared up like dry tinder. "Whatever happens, it's always my fault. You never believe me."

"That's not true." It wasn't, was it? For just a second Aaron doubted.

"You never believe me," Benjamin repeated. "You always blame me. And I know why. You've never forgiven me for living when Mammi died."

Aaron could only stare at his brother as the words penetrated. He couldn't speak—it seemed he couldn't even think.

Benjamin was silent, too, as if shocked by his own words.

The sound of a step broke the stillness. Sarah walked into the living room. She'd heard them. She must have.

But when she spoke, her voice was calm. "Louise is doing much better now. She's come to no harm, I think. If I might use the kitchen, I'll make her a hot drink. That will help. Did you find a hot water bottle?"

"It is in the bottom kitchen cabinet, I think. I'll look for it." Aaron had a battle to keep his voice even after what Benjamin had just said.

She led the way into the kitchen, and the two of them could do nothing but follow. Aaron should resent the way she was taking over, but he couldn't. It was a relief to have someone else decide. He began rummaging in the lower cabinets for the hot water bottle.

Sarah put an armload of wet clothes on the counter. "These should be hung in a warm place to dry, but Louise will need some other clothes to wear when she feels like getting up."

"Ja." He tried to think, but his mind seemed as frozen as the pond.

Sarah filled a kettle and set it on the stove. "I could go and get her something of mine, but her parents will have to be told anyway. Maybe they should just bring her clothes when they come to take her home."

"I will go and tell them." Benjamin spoke before Aaron could. "It is my responsibility."

"Gut," Sarah said. "But go and put dry clothes on first."

To Aaron's surprise, Benjamin didn't dispute that. He turned and went quickly upstairs.

"He didn't argue with you. That's how he always was with Molly, too." He started hanging the wet clothes on the rack next to the stove. "Molly was always better with Benjamin than I was." Aaron's thoughts edged around the impossible, hurtful thing his brother had said.

"Do you have tea bags or hot chocolate mix?" Sarah's tone didn't give anything away.

"Ja, both." He opened the cabinet and got out tea bags, sugar, and hot chocolate mix so that she could choose.

"I happened to be looking out the kitchen window when I saw Benjamin and Louise walking across the field." She busied herself measuring the chocolate mix into a mug, not looking at him. "They were talking and laughing—flirting a bit, the way kids do."

He picked up the hot water bottle and found a towel to wrap around it. "They've always been sweet on each other, I think."

Sarah nodded. "When they reached the pond, Louise seemed to be teasing him. Then all in a moment she ran out onto the ice. I could tell that he was trying to get her to come back." She shook her head slightly. "Girls that age can be heedless. I expect she wanted to show him that she didn't have to do what he said."

The kettle started to steam. She poured hot water into the bottle, then into the cocoa mix, stirring as carefully as if everything depended on getting the chocolate just right.

She picked up the mug and the hot water bottle. "I'll take this up now. It will help to warm her."

Benjamin passed her as he came back in, shrugging into an old coat of Nathan's. Too big, but at least it was dry.

"I'll go get Louise's parents now." He didn't look at Aaron.

"Benjamin." Aaron didn't know what to say, but he had to say something. "I'm sorry. I shouldn't have spoken to you as I did. What happened wasn't your fault."

Benjamin stared at him for a moment. Then he nodded, and the very air in the room seemed to ease. "Denke." He went out quickly.

Aaron stared after him, running his hand through his hair. He should have said more. They had to talk about Benjamin's accusation. If he really believed that Aaron blamed him for Mammi's dying . . .

He shook his head. He couldn't start on that now. But soon they had to talk.

He put the kettle on the stove again and got down another mug. Sarah was chilled, too. She should have something hot.

By the time Sarah came back into the kitchen, he had a mug of chocolate waiting for her. "This is for you." He gestured to a seat at the table and pushed the mug over to her. "I wasn't thinking. You probably need some dry things, too. If you want to go home . . ."

She shook her head and picked up the mug, pressing her hands against the warm sides. "It is best if you have a woman here when Louise's parents arrive, I think."

"Ja, I'm sure you're right about that. They will be upset enough." He stared down at the table for a moment, knowing he had to say something about what had happened. "Denke, Sarah. For everything. If you hadn't seen what was happening . . ." A shudder went through him. "It was your cry I heard."

"A gut thing, too. I couldn't have held on much longer."

He looked at her then. "I think you would have held on as long as you had to. You are a strong woman in every way."

Color flooded her cheeks. "Ach, I'm just glad you

reached us when you did. Benjamin wouldn't let go, even when the ice was cracking around him."

"I have told him how sorry I am for my hasty words. I shouldn't have blamed him."

"We often say things we don't mean in the heat of the moment." She paused. "I'm sure Benjamin can understand that."

"I hope so. It's just . . . sometimes Benjamin reminds me too much of our father. I worry that he might turn out to be a man like him."

It was a relief to say the words out loud. And incredible, that he was saying them to Sarah.

She touched his hand, just for an instant, and then drew away. "I think you are worrying needlessly, Aaron. You are the one who has been a father to Benjamin. If he turns out to be like anyone, he will be like you."

Chapter Seven

Sarah stayed in the background while Aunt Emma gave Dora Schmidt her checkup on Tuesday. Sarah smiled, nodded, and listened to the lively chatter that went on between the two women who had gone through one of life's most intimate experiences together seven times already. Naturally Dora wanted Emma to deliver this baby, too.

With five women now in their final month and coming every week, this was shaping up to be a busy day. It was not, however, busy in the addition. Aaron and his brothers had put in a full day yesterday but once again had failed to come on a patient day.

After what had happened on Sunday, Sarah felt that her relationship with Aaron had passed a hurdle and moved into friendship. She'd thought perhaps that would reduce his reluctance to come today, but she'd been wrong.

Certainly she understood him better now that she knew a bit more about what drove him. Her heart had been wrung by his fears for his little brother.

Groundless fears, she hoped. She'd meant what she told

Aaron—that if Benjamin would be like anyone, he would be like Aaron. Benjamin could become just such a solid, steady, dependable person.

Maybe those thoughts said more about her opinion of Aaron than her opinion of Benjamin. If so, she'd be better off not to be thinking about him at all.

Aunt Emma reached for the tape measure, and Sarah handed it to her.

"Ach, you don't need to measure me to let me know that I'm as big as a house," Dora said. "I think it's time this little one joined the rest of us."

"There's a full moon the end of the week," Aunt Emma said, stretching the tape measure. "You know how that brings on labor. He might be in your arms soon enough, ain't so, Sarah?"

"Could be. Some might say that is nothing but an old wives' tale, but we midwives know better."

"Maybe because we are old wives," Aunt Emma quipped, making Dora laugh.

Thank goodness Aunt Emma had regained her usual good spirits. That episode on Sunday, when she'd withdrawn while they'd been talking about the telephone—that had been so out of character. At the time, the crisis with Benjamin and Louise had wiped the incident from Sarah's mind, but later the worry had come back.

She'd promised Jonas that she'd try to get Aunt Emma to see a doctor if she thought there was any need. Maybe that time had come. But how she'd bring that up, she didn't know.

Dora Schmidt's visit was nearly over. Sarah ran her gaze down the records in Dora's folder, noting that her blood pressure had sometimes been rather high. She glanced at Aunt Emma, chatting with Dora about the likelihood that the full moon would bring on her labor as she helped her up. Wasn't she going to check Dora's blood pressure?

It seemed not. For a moment Sarah hesitated, unwilling to interfere. But the patient came first. They both knew that. She picked up the blood pressure cuff.

"Let's just check your pressure before you leave," she said.

Aunt Emma's face tightened. Then she nodded. "Ja. Just to be on the safe side." She took the cuff from Sarah's hands and wrapped it around Dora's arm herself.

Then she surveyed Dora with a frown. "You've been eating salty food again, ain't so?"

Dora's ruddy cheeks deepened in color. "I've had a craving for fried potatoes lately, it seems. You know how much I love them."

"I know, but I know also they're not so gut for you, especially with the baby this near term. Now you promise me you'll stay away from the salt shaker, ja?"

Dora nodded. "Ja. I will. But sometimes I get heartburn, and I think something salty makes me feel better."

"You try having a nice cup of ginger root tea for the heartburn," Emma said. "Now you do as we tell you."

Sarah let out a slow breath. Aunt Emma had said *we*. Maybe that meant she wasn't taking offense at Sarah's interference.

But once the door had closed behind Dora, she turned on Sarah, her face tight.

"I have been catching babies since before you were born, Sarah. Do not correct me in front of a patient."

"Not correcting," Sarah said quickly. "I'm sure Dora didn't think that. Just reminding you."

Emma didn't look mollified. "I don't want Dora going around telling folks I'm getting too old for my job. If I didn't take Dora's blood pressure, there'd be no harm done. I would tell her anyway to watch her diet. I know better than you what her problems are."

"I'm sure you do." Sarah was cringing inside at pressing this issue with Aunt Emma, but it had to be done. "But we both know that checking her blood pressure was the right thing to do." She reached out to her aunt, silent pleading in the gesture. "You are the one who taught me that the patient always comes first. Remember?"

Her aunt's expression didn't soften. "That's as may be, but—"

A tapping on the door interrupted her. Maybe that was for the best.

Sarah went to answer. It was Benjamin, his cheeks ruddy from the cold, snowflakes sticking to his blond hair. He stepped inside at her gesture, grinning.

"Sarah, there are snow flurries in the air." It seemed Benjamin wasn't so far from being a small boy, excited at the idea of snow.

"Ja, I see. But I think you didn't come over just to tell me that."

"Ach, no, I am here with a message from Aaron." His grin widened, if that was possible. "Our Molly is arriving this afternoon. Aaron says we might be a little late in the morning, because she's sure to want to make a big breakfast for us, but we will be here."

"That's gut news. You must be excited to have her here at last."

He nodded. "You must come to see her sometime soon. She'll want to get to know you again."

"And I feel the same. How is Louise? None the worse for her dunking?"

He sobered a little. "She is fine. Her daad gave her such a scolding—she won't soon forget what he said."

"She scared him, just as she scared us." She could imagine how Louise's father felt. At least he didn't seem to blame Benjamin.

"Ja." He ducked his head, looking both embarrassed and determined. "Sarah, I chust wanted to say . . ." The words seemed to peter out.

"You don't need to say anything." Sarah touched his arm lightly. "I am thankful I was there to help."

"Not only that." His blue eyes were suspiciously bright. "I know you must have talked to my brother. Denke, Sarah. Denke."

"It's all right." Did she dare say anything more? "Your

brother loves you very much, I know. Maybe sometimes he speaks before he thinks."

He squeezed her hand. "You are a gut friend, Sarah. Denke." He turned and hurried away.

Sarah closed the door slowly, her heart insensibly lifted by Benjamin's words. Maybe she needed to know that someone thought well of her.

Aaron had nearly forgotten what a joy it was to have all four of them sitting around the kitchen table. Their family felt complete again—their faces relaxed and happy in the glow of the gaslight.

Benjamin had been telling Molly the story of Louise's fall through the ice. He told it lightly enough, but he knew Molly saw through that to the fear beneath. She clasped his hand warmly on the tabletop.

Odd, how he and Nathan and Benjamin got on so much better together when Molly was there with them. She seemed to smooth off the rough places where they bumped against each other.

He'd noticed that Sarah did the same, easing tension by her very presence. He frowned down at his coffee cup, trying to sort out the complications Sarah had brought to his life. It would be simpler if he could just decide to distrust her, but he couldn't.

He hadn't been able to get his mind off what she'd said to him on Sunday. Her comment that Benjamin would grow up to be like him kept echoing in his mind, as if Sarah's soft voice spoke in his ear. If Sarah's words were true, he wouldn't have to worry so much about Benjamin's future, would he?

Or did that mean that Benjamin would become a man who would expect the worst of someone he loved? The thought shocked him so that his hand clenched the cup.

He didn't think that about Benj. It was ridiculous. Just

because he'd jumped to the conclusion that his little brother was at fault in Louise's accident—

He backed away from that memory, confused, unsure of himself for the first time in a long while. That was Sarah's doing, making him question himself this way.

He wouldn't think about her. He'd just enjoy Molly's first night at home.

"I didn't know you could cook so well, Nathan." Molly pushed her empty plate back. "Seems like you won't need me to do any cooking while I'm here, ain't so?"

Nathan grinned, knowing she was teasing. "If you want to have steak-and-onion pie every night."

"That's the only thing he cooks," Benjamin said. "You should have seen what happened when he tried to make chicken potpie like you do." He rolled his eyes. "Even the dog wouldn't eat it."

"It wasn't that bad," Nathan protested. "Was it, Aaron?"

"Not if you like noodles the consistency of rubber bands." Some of Nathan's ventures into cooking were downright terrible, but if Aaron and Benjamin complained too much, he might stop entirely. Aaron had learned his way around the kitchen at an early age, but he'd far rather be washing up the dishes than cooking.

"Ach, you're kidding," Molly said, dimples appearing in her round cheeks. "I taught Nathan better than that, didn't I?"

Benjamin shook his head. "If not for the neighbors taking pity on us now and then, you'd find us looking like scarecrows."

"You'd best be careful, or Nathan will make you take over," Aaron warned.

"Speaking of neighbors, I hear you have a new neighbor that you've been getting friendly with." Molly looked at him as she spoke, laughter in her blue eyes.

"Who told you that?" The words came out sharper than they should have.

"Anna Fisher writes to me now and then," Molly said.

"She told me all about Emma's niece coming to live with her. I remember Sarah fine from when she was here a few years ago. It is nice for you to have a pretty new neighbor, ain't so?"

"Sarah is pretty," Benjamin said, with the air of one making a new discovery. "She's kind of quiet, so you don't notice it at first."

"Not like you, jabbering away to everyone you meet." Nathan jogged Molly's elbow.

Molly ignored him. "So Anna says she's a midwife, like her aunt, come to help out Emma."

Nathan nodded. "I guess Emma is glad of some help. We've seen quite a bit of Sarah, since we've been doing some work over there."

"Really?" Molly acted surprised, but Aaron had a feeling she'd already known that perfectly well from Anna or one of her other friends. "What are you doing?"

"Adding on two rooms," Aaron said shortly, having no wish to discuss what the rooms were for.

"That's so women who want to have their babies at Emma's can," Benjamin said. "Sarah calls them birthing rooms."

Molly nudged her little brother. "Next you'll be telling me that you know all about such things."

Benjamin flushed. "Well, that's what Sarah says, anyway."

"That sounds like a fine job for the three of you to catch this time of the year." Molly patted Benjamin's arm, but her gaze was on Aaron, and there was a question in it.

She knew him better than anyone, and right now she was wondering why he'd go anywhere near a job like this one. He didn't respond. He couldn't, not without telling her too much.

"So you think well of our new neighbor, then," Molly prompted, looking at him.

"She seems like a nice enough woman." But behind the neutral words he was seeing the caring in Sarah's eyes and remembering the healing in her touch.

"Such a careful answer." Molly grinned. "Ach, well, I'll see for myself, won't I?"

"What do you mean?" He couldn't help the sharpness of his tone.

Molly patted her belly. "This little one will be coming along in six weeks or so, and I am in need of a midwife."

"No." Aaron's chair scraped as he shoved it back, hardly aware of having risen. "No, you won't go to any midwife."

Three faces stared at him, showing varying degrees of shock.

"But, Aaron . . ." Nathan began, and stopped when Molly put her hand on his arm. They seemed to speak to each other without words.

Then Nathan was rising. "Komm, Benjamin. Let's go see that the horses are settled for the night."

"But we don't need—"

Nathan didn't let him finish. He took him by the elbow and propelled him out of the kitchen. In a moment the back door had slammed behind them.

"Aaron?" There was a question in Molly's voice, and she made her way around the table to him. "What is going on with you?"

"Nothing. I just think you should go to a doctor, that's all. I'll get a driver to take you . . ."

He let the words fade away, because she was shaking her head.

"I hoped . . . I prayed you were over all those feelings. When I heard about you doing the job for Sarah, I thought maybe you'd found peace about Mammi."

He pressed his hands hard against the top of the table. Pain had a stranglehold on his throat, but he had to speak.

"Mammi died because of the midwife. If she'd gone to the hospital, she'd be alive today."

"You don't know that." Molly touched his hand gently. "What is the sense of thinking that way? What happened is God's will. We must accept and move on."

He had to unclench his jaw before he could answer. "I

have accepted God's will. But that doesn't mean I want my only sister to put her life in the hands of a midwife." He closed his eyes for a second at the memory. Distant as it was, right now it seemed very close. "Please, Molly. Don't make me worry about you. See a doctor."

She looked at him for a long moment. Then she rose on tiptoe to kiss his cheek.

"I'll think about it, all right? But you need to remember something, Aaron. This is my baby. Mine and Jacob's." She moved her palm in a gentle circle on her apron, and for an instant her face seemed transfigured with love. "It's hard with Jacob so far away now, but we have to decide what's best for the boppli. Not you."

Sarah and Leah arrived at the clinic on Wednesday in a car driven by Ben Morgan, an elderly Englischer who seemed to enjoy earning a bit of money ferrying the Amish to places they couldn't easily reach by horse and buggy.

"You ladies take your time," he said as he pulled up at the front entrance of a long building—new, but built in a style that imitated a large farmhouse. "I'm heading down the road to the coffee shop, but I'll come back in about an hour or so."

"Denke, Ben." Leah was obviously used to the process. She handed money to Ben as she slid out of the car. "We will see you later, then."

Sarah walked up the steps with Leah, trying to ignore the way her stomach crunched in anticipation. She needed to develop a working relationship with the people she'd meet in the clinic. Unfortunately, she was well aware of how some medical personnel regarded lay midwives.

"Don't be nervous." Leah squeezed her arm, apparently well aware of her feelings. "Honestly, I was that frightened the first time I came here—well, I can hardly believe it now."

"You're a valuable volunteer to them." Sarah had learned enough about the work Leah did, gathering Amish family tree information to track genetic diseases, to know that the clinic was very fortunate to have her. "Some of these people may see me as a competitor, and an unqualified one at that."

Her mind flickered to Dr. Mitchell and his apparent opposition to midwives. If it was true that he'd hoped Aunt Emma was going out of business, what must he think now that Sarah had joined her?

"Then we'll have to change their minds about the value of midwives, won't we?"

Leah opened the door and walked into a wide center hallway with warm wooden plank floors and a maple bench against the wall under a row of hooks. She removed her coat and bonnet, hanging them from one of the hooks, and motioned for Sarah to do the same.

Sarah hung up her outer clothes and brushed her skirt down even though it didn't need it. There was nothing to be nervous about . . .

Well, there was, really, but she couldn't let that fact hold her back from what she'd come here to do. The newborn testing was too important to give way to her qualms.

"The clinic waiting room," Leah said quietly. She gestured to a long room on the right. An Amish couple sat in a pair of rocking chairs, the woman holding a small child in her lap. The pair looked up and nodded, seeming at home in this setting.

As they should be. The room was furnished with sturdy wooden pieces that looked as if they'd been made by an Amish craftsman, and the walls had been painted a soothing cream color. One corner of the room had been fitted up as a play area with a child-size table and chairs and a box of toys.

"This is very nice. It looks welcoming, not like a clinic at all."

Leah smiled slightly. "The first time I came here, the waiting room was lined with plastic chairs in bright colors and the walls covered with so many posters it made me dizzy. Now it's more comfortable, especially for the Amish patients, I think."

Sarah nodded. She would guess that Leah might have had something to do with the changes, but she didn't ask, knowing Leah would not want to sound prideful.

"The examining rooms are behind the waiting room," Leah said. "This whole side of the building is for treating patients, and on the other side, all the research is being done." She crossed the hall to a door that must lead into that other world. "One day the things they learn here may keep our children safe from genetic diseases. That's my prayer."

"Mine also," Sarah said, liking Leah more each time she saw her. "Even now, such progress is being made in treatment that would have seemed impossible ten or fifteen years ago. The earlier treatment is started, the better the outcome for the child."

Leah nodded, opening the door. "And the better we're able to educate the parents and prepare them for the future, too."

Sarah followed her into the research area, her tension ratcheting up even higher. This area was far different from the waiting room. Offices and labs opened onto the tiled, pale-green hallway down which Leah led her. Various people were bent over machines she couldn't begin to guess the purpose of.

For the most part, the researchers were so intent on their jobs that they didn't take notice of them. One white-coated woman glanced away from her computer, nodding to Leah in a friendly manner. Clearly Leah was at home in both worlds.

An Englischman came striding down the hall, frowning down at some sort of cell phone in his hand. He looked up, saw them, and broke into a smile.

"Leah!" He reached them and threw his arms around Leah in a hug. "I didn't know you were coming today. This is a nice surprise."

Sarah fought to control her expression at the embrace.

It was not her business to judge Leah's relationship with this man.

Leah detached herself from his grasp, straightening her apron, smiling. "Sarah, this impetuous person is one of the researchers I work with—Johnny Kile. Johnny is Rachel Brand's twin brother. Johnny, I want you to meet Sarah Mast, Emma Stoltzfus's niece."

So the man was both Rachel's brother and a medical researcher. Today was full of surprises, but that certainly explained his greeting to Leah. They must have been friends since childhood.

"Wie bist du heit," she said. "I am pleased to meet you. I know your sister."

Johnny's smile reminded her of Rachel's, and she saw the strong resemblance now that she knew.

"Welcome, Sarah. Has Leah talked you into helping her with the information gathering?"

"Ach, no," Leah said. "I should have explained myself better. Sarah is a midwife, just come to serve us in Pleasant Valley."

Something changed in Johnny's expression at the words—that indefinable look of someone who disapproved but would be polite. His sister, Rachel, was pregnant. Maybe he thought she would be better off going to a doctor than a midwife.

"She is here to meet with Dr. Brandenmyer today about newborn testing," Leah explained. "Will you let him know we are here?"

Johnny nodded, going to a phone on a nearby desk. While he did that, Leah set the black case she carried on the desk and took out a folder.

"I'll be giving my findings to someone who will enter them into the computer," she said. "When you are finished talking with Dr. Brandenmyer, I'll be around here someplace. Or ask anyone."

Sarah surreptitiously wiped her hands on her skirt. "I won't be long. I'm sure Dr. Brandenmyer is a very busy person."

When the man himself loped down the hall a few minutes later, that sense was confirmed. Dr. Brandenmyer had a lean, intelligent face, a pair of piercing eyes, and an air of knowing everything about everyone around him.

"So this is the new midwife." He greeted Sarah with a look that seemed to go right through her. "I was just talking to Dr. O'Neill about you."

Sarah blinked at the mention of the physician she'd worked with in Ohio. "I hope he is well."

"Fine, fine." He smiled. "He thinks very highly of you, you know."

So Dr. Brandenmyer had been checking up on her. She couldn't blame him for that. She could only be relieved that the report had been favorable.

"I enjoyed very much working with him. He cares deeply about his patients."

He nodded. "That comes through, doesn't it?" He glanced at Johnny and Leah. "You'll excuse us, won't you? I'd like to show the clinic area to Mrs. Mast."

The walk across to the clinic side didn't take long, but Dr. Brandenmyer used that time to turn Sarah's mind inside out, learning her opinions on every subject related to childbirth. He nodded gravely when she talked about the importance of having newborns tested.

"That's an important step. Even though we don't yet have a cure, the diseases can be managed much more effectively if we know about the situation from the beginning."

"Ja, that's so. I feel that every Amish baby should be tested automatically, regardless of whether a disease has been found in the family. It's such a simple thing to do, and it can save so much wondering and heartache."

Sarah paused, distracted. The young Amish woman she'd seen in the waiting room stood in the hallway, hesitating by the door to a treatment room. Sarah's heart clenched. She knew the emotion the woman attempted to hide. Fear. She was afraid of whatever came next.

She shouldn't interfere, but she couldn't just walk away, either. She went to the young woman, touching her arm gently.

"Are you all right? Do you need help?"

At the sound of Pennsylvania Dutch speech, the young woman turned to Sarah, relief relaxing her taut features.

"I have to have an ultrasound." She pronounced the English word carefully, hand cradling her belly in a gesture of protection. "I haven't had one before. What if it hurts my baby?"

"No, no, it won't do that. My name is Sarah. What is yours?"

"Naomi. Naomi Haus." She flushed slightly. "I'm sorry if I'm being foolish."

"It's never foolish to say when something bothers you. The person who gives you the test is just going to run an instrument across your belly. It doesn't hurt, and it will give the doctor an image of your baby."

"Will it see if something is wrong with my baby?" Naomi's eyes filled with tears.

Sarah glanced at Dr. Brandenmyer, afraid of seeing disapproval there. But he was watching them with understanding warmth in his eyes. He nodded, as if saying that she should answer.

"The ultrasound shows some problems, but not everything," she said cautiously, not knowing what Naomi's doctor might suspect. "I promise you that it won't harm your baby."

"Mrs. Haus, would it make you feel better to have Mrs. Mast come in with you for the ultrasound?" Dr. Brandenmyer asked.

"Oh, ja." Relief flooded Naomi's face. "I would like that if . . . if you don't mind." She looked at Sarah.

"I would be happy to." Sarah put her arm around the woman.

Dr. Brandenmyer nodded toward the exam room. "Thank

you," he said quietly. "You have a noticing heart. That's a rare gift."

When Sarah came back out a few minutes later, she was surprised to find Dr. Brandenmyer waiting. "Thank you for letting me go in with Naomi. I don't want to delay you . . ."

"Not at all." He detoured to a nearby counter and picked up a stack of business cards, which he handed to Sarah. "Count on us to process the tests for you. And don't hesitate to get in touch if you have any concerns. We'll be happy to consult with you."

For a moment she couldn't speak. "Denke," she said softly. "I'm wonderful glad you are willing to work with me."

Dr. Brandenmyer glanced at a man walking toward them—fairly young, dressed in ordinary Englisch clothes, not a doctor's or researcher's coat. "Here's someone you should meet, if you haven't already."

The man stopped, obviously acquainted with Dr. Brandenmyer. "Thank you for the tour. You have a great facility here."

Dr. Brandenmyer nodded, probably used to hearing that from visitors. "I'd like to introduce you two, since Mrs. Mast is from your area. Sarah, this is Dr. Thomas Mitchell. Dr. Mitchell, Sarah Mast. She's in the midwife practice in Pleasant Valley."

Sarah's breath caught. So this was the man everyone said was opposed to midwives. Somehow she'd expected someone older and set in his ways. Dr. Mitchell couldn't be much more than thirty, with an unlined face that made him look even younger.

For a moment the man just stared at her, his gaze icy. Then, without acknowledging her, he turned to Dr. Brandenmyer. "I didn't realize you had midwives working here."

Dr. Brandenmyer's eyebrows lifted. "We don't yet, but I hope we will, eventually. We're discussing doing the prenatal and newborn testing for Mrs. Mast's clients."

"I see." Dr. Mitchell clipped off the words. "Frankly, that surprises me. Thank you for inviting me to visit. It's been interesting." He gave Dr. Brandenmyer a meaningless smile, turned, and walked away, still without acknowledging Sarah.

Dr. Brandenmyer waited until the door had closed behind him, and then he blew out a breath. "Well, that was unfortunate. Have you had dealings with the man?"

"No. But I did hear that he has spoken out against midwives. I'm sorry if my being here has created an uncomfortable situation for you."

"Nonsense. I'd say Dr. Mitchell is the one who should be sorry. Still, I'm sure you sometimes encounter medical personnel who will give you problems. But the good that you do for your clients makes the trouble worthwhile, doesn't it?"

"Ja," she said, feeling as if she'd found an understanding friend. "It does."

Chapter Eight

"Finished my side," Benjamin said, flourishing his hammer. "Hurry up, slowpoke."

Nathan just grinned. "It's more important to do it right than to do it fast." He drove the last nail into the window molding.

"Let's have a look." Aaron decided he'd best interrupt before they started bickering, although truth to tell, his brothers had been getting on very well since Molly arrived. The past few days had been marked by harmony all around.

He checked out the molding, not that he needed to. He knew Nathan would see that it was done right. He slid his hand along the joins, noting how smoothly Nathan had fitted the pieces together, and felt a glow of something that might have been pride. His brother was a born carpenter, it seemed.

"Gut work. See how much of the next one you can do before we break for middaagesse."

Nathan nodded. "Can't believe it is Friday already. This week has gone by in a hurry."

"I hear they're working on the school Christmas program already." Benjamin sounded a little wistful. It hadn't been that long since the Christmas program was the highlight of his year. "We'll take Molly, ja?"

"Sure thing." Aaron stood for a moment, hands on his hips, surveying the work to be done. The finishing would take much of next week, most likely, but the end was in sight.

He'd not be seeing so much of Sarah Mast then. That was what he wanted, wasn't it?

He settled down to mitering the corners of the baseboard, taking his time, making it right. Maybe the thing was that Sarah had turned out to be a real person to him, not just a midwife. She was a woman with qualities he admired. He'd not soon forget her courage and strength that day at the pond.

But she was a midwife, and with Molly here, he couldn't forget that, either. He frowned down at the corner he was cutting, thinking about that conversation with Molly the night she'd arrived.

She hadn't brought up the subject of seeing a doctor or a midwife since then, and that chafed at him. Little as he knew about it, he thought she should be making that decision.

Why would she even consider having a midwife deliver the baby? She was old enough to remember what happened to Mammi. She of all people should understand why he felt the way he did.

"Someone's coming." Benjamin leaned over to peer out the window. "It's Molly."

"What is she doing here?" He glanced from Nathan to Benjamin, looking for a sign that they knew something of this unannounced visit. They both seemed as surprised as he was. But not as wary.

Molly tapped on the door frame and held up a basket. "I brought you some lunch. Help me up, already."

Benjamin moved, but Aaron beat him to it. He took the

basket, handing it to his brother, and lifted Molly into the room.

"You should wait until we have the steps built," Benjamin said, grinning at her. "Or we could rig up the block and tackle from the hayloft."

Molly took a playful swipe at him. "Mind your manners, or I won't give you any of the food I brought."

Aaron's jaw tightened. "I told you that Emma gives us our lunch. There was no need for you to come here."

"Ach, I must have forgotten." Molly evaded his eyes. "I'll just add what I brought to whatever Emma is fixing."

"Molly—"

But he was too late. She'd already gone through into the house, carrying her basket.

Not that he could have stopped her anyway. Molly seldom argued about things—she just went her own way, no matter what anyone said. The thought sent a chill down his back.

He knew perfectly well she hadn't come because she thought she should bring them lunch. She'd come to see Sarah for herself.

Through the window he could see the two of them in the kitchen, setting food on the table, talking and laughing as if they were old friends. They were, in a way, but that didn't make the situation any better. It made it worse. Molly might feel that she was slighting Sarah by going to someone else for the baby's birth.

By the time Sarah called them in to lunch, he'd built up a head of steam. At least he knew well enough to keep hold on it.

"You go on." He gestured his brothers toward the door. "I just want to finish this one piece before I quit."

Nathan opened his mouth as if to argue, took a second look at Aaron's face, and followed his younger brother into the house. The door closed on the women's chatter and the sound of laughter.

Gut. He drove a nail into place with a bit too much effort.

"Aaron?"

He froze at the sound of Sarah's voice. He'd assumed she was in the house with the others. He'd been wrong.

He picked up another finishing nail. "I'll be in soon. Just go ahead without me." He kept his eyes focused on the work.

Sarah moved, but not away from him. Toward him. She came to a stop next to him, and he could glimpse the fold of her skirt in the corner of his eye.

"Will you tell me what's wrong?"

He took a hasty blow with the hammer and missed the nail completely. Luckily he missed his finger as well.

"Nothing's wrong."

Her silence told him she wasn't buying that. Sarah seemed to have a way of knowing too much about his feelings. He didn't like that. Although he had to admit that in some circumstances that might be . . .

Maybe it was best not to let his thoughts stray in that direction.

"Molly didn't come over to bring us lunch. She came because she wanted an excuse to see you."

It was unfortunate that he knew he sounded like a sulky child.

"Molly doesn't need an excuse to see me. We are old friends." She hadn't moved, but it almost seemed as if she were closer to him, the way her voice warmed.

"I don't think she came only to renew your friendship."

"What's wrong—" She stopped, and he saw her hand tighten against her skirt. "I see. You are afraid that Molly will want a midwife to deliver her baby."

Afraid. The word echoed in his mind. That was exactly right. He was afraid.

Sarah reached out, as if to touch his shoulder, but then let her hand fall back against her skirt. "She's your little sister. It's natural that you would worry about her."

"You agree there's reason to worry." He jumped on her words, turning to look up at her.

She smiled, but her eyes were troubled. "As far as I know, your sister is a fine, healthy woman who's going to have a fine, healthy baby. So, no, I don't see a reason to worry, but you've been taking care of your brothers and sister most of your life. Of course you're concerned. That's what anyone would expect."

His mouth twisted in an attempt to smile. "I'm not sure Molly sees it that way."

"She knows you love her and want what's best for her." She smiled, and this time she did touch his shoulder . . . a light, caring movement that ended too soon.

"I don't think it's unreasonable to want her to see a doctor for this baby. I don't want to hurt your feelings, Sarah . . ."

She was already shaking her head. "My feelings don't have anything to do with it. This decision is for Molly and Jacob to make."

"That's what she said." He frowned down at his hand, clenched so tightly on the hammer that his knuckles were white. "Maybe it would be easier if Jacob were here. It's hard on a young couple, being separated at a time like this. She doesn't have him, so she depends on me. Does she expect me just to stop caring what she does?" He was crazy, to be talking about this to Sarah, of all people.

"No." Her voice was soft. "She expects you to let her grow up, Aaron. That's all. Just let her grow up."

Sarah set the bassinet next to the stove in Dora Schmidt's kitchen, running her fingers over the soft sheet to warm it. Soon it would cradle yet another new infant, following its brothers and sisters into a loving home.

True to Aunt Emma's prediction about the full moon, Dora had gone into labor early on Saturday. Sarah and Emma had arrived at noon in answer to a summons delivered by Dora's oldest boy, to find Dora mixing up a batch of jumble cookies with the younger children. With nothing else to do once things were prepared in the bedroom for the birth, they had joined in the baking.

Now, by midafternoon, Dora finally seemed ready to concentrate on the baby's arrival. She obviously preferred Emma's presence in the room to Sarah's, so Sarah kept herself busy while Emma attended to Dora's last stages of birth.

Foolish to mind that, she scolded herself, hand still on the bassinet. Naturally Dora would feel that way. In the meantime, her job was simply to help out—

"Sarah?" Dora's oldest girl, Ruth, hung over the banister, her face pinched. "Mammi says komm schnell. Komm!"

Her breath catching, Sarah hurried up the stairs and into the bedroom. Dora, on all fours on the bed, was pushing, her husband's hand covering hers. He looked as intent as she did. And Emma . . .

Emma should have been standing ready to ease the baby's passage into the world. Instead she sat on the edge of the bed, frowning a little as if wondering what she was doing there.

A fist seemed to clutch Sarah's heart. Something was wrong—something was very wrong with Emma.

But Dora's baby was crowning. First things first. She must focus on that. Gently she moved Aunt Emma to the rocking chair. Emma sat, docile as a child, her hands limp in her lap.

"Sarah," Dora gasped her name, eyes wide. "Emma, she—" Another contraction seized her, cutting off the words.

"Everything is all right. We'll take care of my aunt. Don't fret, now. This little one is almost ready to be in your arms." She bent over, her touch gentle. "The head is right here. Another push or two should do it."

"They always pop right out," Dora gasped. "This one, too."

"Sure will," she soothed, massaging to ease the passage

of the baby's head. And indeed, Dora knew what she was talking about. One more push, and the baby slipped into Sarah's waiting hands.

"A fine big girl," she said over the wails of the newborn. She suctioned the baby's mouth quickly and wrapped her in the warm blanket that lay ready. "Ach, look how beautiful she is."

For one precious moment she held new life in her arms, cherishing the soft bundle, hating to let go. This was why she was a midwife—this indescribable moment of seeing a child into the world.

She put the babe into Dora's waiting arms. Love and wonder transformed Dora's features, wiping away the fatigue. Eli bent close, his eyes wet with tears as he touched his daughter's tiny waving hand. Neither of them would even notice anything else for a while.

Dora put the baby to breast with the ease of long practice, and the infant latched on instantly. Dora obviously wouldn't need any coaching to breastfeed.

Another contraction, and the afterbirth was out. Sarah checked to be sure there was no tearing and went through the rest of the routine smoothly, talking as if nothing were wrong. But each time she looked at Aunt Emma, the puzzled expression was still on Emma's face.

Please, dear Father, help her. Show me what to do. She fought the trickle of panic.

Young Ruth turned into an efficient helper as soon as she knew her mother and the baby were all right. Together she and Sarah made Dora comfortable and changed the bedclothes, and Ruth brought the warm bassinet to put next to the bed.

"Your aunt . . ." The girl gave Emma a sidelong glance. "Is she all right?"

"She will be." *Please, God.* "I must get her to the doctor as soon as we have your mammi settled."

Eli, overhearing, nodded. "I've sent Daniel to call for

someone to drive you already. We'll be fine. My sister will be here soon to help."

"Gut. Denke."

He shook his head. "Thank the gut Lord you were here, too. We will pray for Emma."

Sarah would be praying, as well. She went to her aunt, wrapping a shawl gently around her. "Aunt Emma?"

Her aunt blinked a little, still frowning. Then recognition seemed to come back into her face. "Dora. The baby." She started to rise, but Sarah eased her back into the chair.

"It's all right. Dora and the baby are fine. A little girl."

"Gut, gut." Emma pressed her hand against her forehead. "I don't seem to remember. I feel all ferhoodled."

"I know." Sarah put her arm around her aunt's shoulders, trying to infuse her with warmth and strength. "We're going to see the doctor. We'll find out what the problem is."

Emma pulled away from her, some of the spirit coming back into her face. "I think I can decide for myself if I want to see a doctor."

The words bore an odd echo of Molly, saying that she would decide for herself how her baby was to be born. Molly was entering a new phase in her life, just as it seemed Aunt Emma was leaving one.

"Aunt Emma." Sarah knelt by the chair, taking both her aunt's hands in hers, holding her gaze by the force of will. "You seemed to black out right when Dora's baby was coming. If I hadn't been here, there'd have been no one to catch her."

"I don't—"

Sarah tightened her grip. "People depend on you, Aunt Emma. You can't let them down. You must let the doctor help you to be well again."

For a moment Emma held out. And then the lost look returned to her face. "Will I?"

Sarah took a shaky breath, knowing she couldn't promise. "I hope so. I pray so."

. . .

"*What* is taking them so long?" Aunt Emma plucked fretfully at the sheet covering her, twisting restlessly on the narrow bed in the emergency room cubicle. "They could have run the tests three times again already."

"I'm sure it won't be long." Sarah patted her aunt's hand, trying to keep her own worry out of her voice.

Aunt Emma stiffened, pulling away as she drew the sheet up to her chin. "It has already been too long. I told you I didn't need to come here. Get me my clothes."

"You don't want to leave before you've heard what the doctor has to say." Her aunt might sound angry, but Sarah knew only too well what the querulous tone concealed. Not anger. Fear.

The same fear edged along Sarah's nerves. She'd suspected, from the doctor's questions and his initial exam, what the trouble was. When he'd ordered a CAT scan and a blood-flow ultrasound, she'd been sure of what he suspected, at least.

Aunt Emma grabbed Sarah's hand with a bewildering switch of mood. "What is wrong with me, Sarah? Tell me."

She knew better than to answer that question. Besides, Aunt Emma had probably already figured it out but was loath to say the word. "We must wait for the test results, Aunt Emma. Just be a little patient . . ."

The curtain twitched, was jerked aside. But it wasn't the doctor she'd hoped to see. Instead her cousin Jonas surged inside, followed by his wife, Mary. "What is happening here? Mammi, are you all right? Why didn't you reach us sooner?"

This last was directed at Sarah, accompanied by an angry glare. She didn't blame him for his anger any more than she blamed his mother. They were both afraid.

"Ach, Jonas, don't be foolish." Mary slipped past him, giving Sarah a quick smile as she bent to press her cheek against Emma's. "How can anyone answer all those questions at once?" She held her mother-in-law's hand for a moment. "How are you?"

"All right. Ready to be out of here."

"We're waiting for the doctor to come back with the results of her tests," Sarah said, praying that Mary's calm good sense would rub off on Jonas. He and his mother were so much alike that they would make each other even more upset.

"What tests?" Jonas didn't show much sign of calming down. "How did this happen? We don't know anything."

Mary moved from patting her mother-in-law's hand to patting her husband's. "Sarah will tell us, if you'll settle down and let her."

That seemed to get through to him, and he subsided.

"We were at Eli and Dora Schmidt's house, delivering her baby. Aunt Emma had a little . . ." She hesitated over the word. "An episode. She became confused."

Sarah hoped he would be content with that much of an explanation. She didn't want to get into details in front of Aunt Emma.

"Out delivering a baby. Working too hard." Jonas chose to focus on that. "Mammi, if you'd come to live with us, this wouldn't—"

"Jonas, you don't know that." Mary interceded again. "It could still have happened. We must be grateful that Sarah was there with her, both for Mamm Emma's sake and the baby's."

"The baby." Emma repeated the words, and the anger faded from her eyes. "That baby is all right?" She looked at Sarah, pleading.

"The baby is fine," she said quickly. "A fine, strong baby girl. Dora and Eli are so pleased."

"Ach, that is so gut." Mary beamed. "I know they hoped for another girl this time after all those boys in a row, ain't so, Mamm Emma?"

Emma nodded, but she still wore a lost look that tore at Sarah's heart. "I let them down." Her voice caught on a sob.

Jonas moved to her side, taking her hand, all of his wrath washed away by her obvious distress. "Don't say that. You heard Sarah. Everyone is well." He struggled for a smile. "And so many people are here, out in the waiting room, wanting to hear about you. Bishop Mose and many others, praying for you."

Sarah edged back, letting Jonas and Mary take the places at either side of the bed. "Shall I go out and join them, then?"

"No, no." Emma looked frightened at the thought. "You must stay."

"Ja," Mary said, and Jonas gave what seemed a reluctant nod.

"If you want—" Sarah stopped, because someone else was entering the cubicle. The doctor, frowning down at the contents of a folder in his hands.

A chill settled into Sarah's heart. This would not be welcome news, she feared.

The doctor glanced from face to face, perhaps a little disconcerted by what might seem strange clothing to him. He focused on Emma. "Well, Mrs. Stoltzfus, I think we can say now what the problem is." He darted a quick glance at the others. "Do you want me to discuss it in private?"

"We are family," Jonas said quickly. "My mother—"

Emma cut him off with a gesture. "It is all right. You can speak with them here."

The doctor nodded, leaning an elbow against a piece of equipment and pushing his glasses into place. He was younger than Sarah had first thought, she realized. Perhaps the white coat and his tired expression made him seem older.

"We've determined that you suffered from a transient ischemic attack—what we call a TIA."

Emma didn't move for a moment. Her lips tightened. "A stroke, you mean."

"Not a full-fledged stroke," the doctor said quickly. "You had a fairly short period during which less blood than normal reached your brain. That's what caused the dizziness and confusion."

"Does that mean she will likely have a stroke?" Jonas clung tightly to Mary's hand.

"No, not necessarily. Most people who have strokes have had TIAs, but not everyone who has a TIA will go on to have a stroke." The doctor seemed to be relaxing a little now that the worst news had been delivered.

"Do I have to stay in the hospital?" Emma's tone betrayed her longing to be home.

"I don't think that's necessary. We'll give you a diet list to follow, and you'll need to be on medication. The nurse will bring you all of your instructions, and you should make an appointment with your regular physician as soon as possible." He pushed himself away, snapping the chart closed. "Any questions?"

There were dozens, but before Sarah could formulate even one, he had disappeared. A look at Emma's face convinced her not to pursue him. Her aunt needed time to absorb this news. She wouldn't be able to take in anything more now.

"I can go home?" Emma looked at her, questioning.

"Ja, you can. As soon as the nurse comes with instructions."

"Gut. I want to go home." She sat up, as if she were about to get out of bed.

"You must come to our house with us," Jonas declared. "We'll take care of you."

Emma glared at him. "I will go to my own home."

"Mamm, you can't—"

"Ja, I can."

The two of them wore expressions so equally stubborn that it was almost funny. A glance at Mary told Sarah that Emma's daughter-in-law saw it as well.

"Not now." She patted Jonas's arm. "Mamm Emma wants to be in her own home after a day like this. Sarah will be there with her. There's no need to make decisions all in a hurry."

"Ja, that's right," Sarah said, hoping her cousin would see the sense of his wife's comments. "Why don't you step outside and talk to those who are waiting, Jonas? We'll help your mamm get dressed."

He hesitated for a moment, and she feared he would continue the argument. But he nodded, bent over the bed to kiss his mother's cheek, and went out.

"There now." Mary brought the clothes from the hook on the wall. "Let's get you ready to go home. You'll sleep best in your own bed tonight."

With Sarah on one side and Mary on the other, they were able to get Emma dressed with little effort on her part. She was silent throughout, probably still processing everything she'd heard.

Sarah was settling the prayer kapp into place when Emma suddenly grasped her wrist.

"The baby—Dora Schmidt's baby. Did she have the baby?"

"Ja, she did." Sarah exchanged looks with Mary. "A healthy baby girl."

Emma's grip tightened. "You delivered her?"

Nothing but the truth would do. "Ja."

Tears filled Emma's eyes. "Useless." Her voice broke. "I am useless."

Chapter Nine

Aaron glanced at the basket tucked under the seat of the buggy as he drove up the lane to Emma's place on Saturday afternoon. Molly had handed him the basket with a string of instructions.

"Tell Sarah how sorry we are for her trouble. If you see Emma, be cheerful. And if Sarah needs anything at all, we will be happy to help. And don't say anything to upset them." At that point she'd hesitated. "Maybe I should go myself."

"You'll go nowhere but back inside." He'd turned her around and given her a little shove toward the door. "It's getting colder by the minute and coming on to snow soon if that sky is anything to go by."

Now, as he drew up to the hitching post and slid down from the buggy, his stomach tightened. Molly had probably been right—she'd have done this better than he would. She'd know the right words to say.

He pulled the basket from under the seat, feeling the warmth of the casserole it held. He'd find something to say, not that it would do much to ease Sarah and Emma's pain. He headed for the back door.

Sarah opened the door before he could knock. The smile she gave him couldn't quite erase the anxiety that shadowed her green eyes.

"Aaron. I didn't think to see you today. Komm in out of the cold."

He wiped his boots on the mat and stepped into the warmth of the kitchen. "Colder today than yesterday. Winter is setting in early for sure this year."

She nodded at the words, but he could see that her thoughts were elsewhere.

"Sarah, I'm sorry for your trouble." He almost reached for her hand, realized he still carried the basket, and gave it to her instead. "Molly sent this over for your supper. And she says that if there is anything at all that you need, just ask."

Tears shimmered in her eyes, hitting him with the impact of a blow. "Denke. Everyone has been so kind." She gestured toward the counter, crowded with casseroles and plastic containers.

He couldn't help but smile. "Feeding people is one way of saying we're sorry, ain't so?"

She nodded, lifting the towel Molly had put over her dish and peeping inside. "Ach, potpie, my aunt's favorite. We will have this today, for sure."

"I'll tell Molly." His fingers clenched. He had to ask how Emma was, but he dreaded upsetting Sarah. "Your aunt, is she . . ."

"She's resting." Sarah turned away to put the basket down, hiding her expression.

"I should leave, then. I don't want to disturb her." But he didn't want to walk away and leave Sarah with that bereft look in her eyes. "I was going to check the measurements for the cabinet doors, but if you think that will bother her . . ."

"No, no, that's all right." She turned toward him, fixing a

smile to her face with an obvious effort. "She won't even hear you." She opened the door to the addition, and he walked through. Somewhat to his surprise, she followed him.

He watched her, resting his hand on the cabinet. Even feeling as he had to begin with about this project, he could be confident that the work he'd done would last, serving generations to come. That was a satisfying thing about carpentry.

She stood for a moment, hugging her arms against the chill in the addition. "I thought you'd be asking me again if I'm sure I want you to finish the work. After all, you were right about Aunt Emma, ain't so?"

"I take no pleasure in that, Sarah." He looked at her gravely, trusting she knew he was sincere.

A faint color tinged her cheeks. "I know. I'm sorry. I shouldn't take my worry out on you."

"Is Emma so very bad?" Again he felt that impulse to touch her in comfort, and he repressed it.

"Not physically. But she is so depressed." Sarah lifted her hand in a helpless gesture. "I've never seen her this way. She is always so busy, so active. Now she just wants to sleep."

"I know she's grateful that you are here with her." It was the most reassuring thing he could think to say. "But this is not what you expected when you came to Pleasant Valley."

"No." She turned slowly, looking around the bare room as if she were seeing it the way she dreamed it would be. "I thought this would be a fresh start for me. That's why I sold my husband's share in the farm—so that I could invest in my future. So that I wouldn't be just helping Aunt Emma but actually be a partner to her. Now . . . well, now I don't know."

He studied her face. "You could have invested that money in your business in Ohio, ain't so? You already had a practice there."

"Ja. But there everyone saw me as . . . well, as my husband's widow. I didn't like feeling that people were sorry for me." She glanced at him, the pink in her cheeks deepening. "I sound sorry for myself, I think."

"No. Just honest." Maybe she deserved some honesty from him in return. "I know what you mean about those feelings. After Mamm died, I'd see folks looking at us that way—feeling sorry that our mamm was gone and our daad had turned to drink in his grief."

It wasn't as difficult as he'd thought to say the words. Sarah had a way of making you feel you could say anything to her.

She nodded, understanding in her face. "Knowing each other is part of the strength of being Amish, but maybe sometimes we wish folks didn't know so much."

"Ja." Again that impulse to touch her. "You have an understanding heart, Sarah Mast."

She was startled into a smile. "I have said too much, I'm afraid."

"No. Don't think that." He clasped her hand, just for an instant, and felt warmth travel clear to his heart.

Sarah drew in an audible breath. She felt it, too, then. He shouldn't—

She turned away, moving quickly to the window, giving them both breathing space. "Look. It is snowing." Delight pierced her voice. "Just look."

He went to stand next to her at the window, more aware of her nearness than of the scene outside. "You sound like a child, excited at the first flakes of snow coming down."

"It makes me feel like a child. Remember when you'd be sitting in the classroom, trying to concentrate, and suddenly you'd see that first snow of the winter starting to fall?"

He smiled in return, knowing that her Amish school had probably been just like his. "Ja. The teacher didn't even try to keep us in our seats at that." He shook his head. "Unfortunately, now that I'm a grown-up, the snow also makes me think of all the things that must be done before it gets too bad to work outside. We must get that phone shanty built for you right away."

Sarah blinked, looking at him without understanding. "The phone shanty? But Aunt Emma and I didn't even talk about putting one in yet."

"No? Maybe Emma didn't talk to you, but she spoke to Bishop Mose, and he agreed that you must have a phone for the midwife practice. I'm to build the shanty, just at the edge of the porch, and Joseph Beiler will do the wiring. He says he can rig up a battery-powered buzzer in the bedrooms, so you're sure to hear when someone calls."

She looked a little dazed at all of these arrangements. "But why didn't Aunt Emma say anything to me? I thought she didn't approve of the idea."

"Maybe she wanted to surprise you." He hesitated, not sure he should say more. "It seems to me that maybe your aunt was trying to show her confidence in you."

She looked up at him, eyes wide, face so close that he could see the tiny flecks of gold in the rich green of her eyes. "You think that?"

He knew what she was really asking, and he struggled to find an answer. "If I have doubts about midwives—well, you know why that is. But I see how much you care, and I would hate for you to give up."

"Denke, Aaron." Her voice was soft, and her lips trembled just a little. "Denke."

A longing to close the space between them flooded through him, startling him with its intensity. He wanted to hold her—

No. He couldn't let that happen. He took a careful step away from Sarah. "I'd better get those measurements done and get on home before the snow starts to stick." He yanked the tape from his pocket.

"Ja. I should check on my aunt." She turned away, not looking at him.

"Sarah . . ." He said her name without thinking, and then realized he really did have another thing he had to say. "I nearly forgot." Because he'd been so busy thinking of how close she was. "Molly is planning a little celebration for

Benjamin's sixteenth birthday on Wednesday. We would like you and your aunt to come for ice cream and cake after supper."

He would not let himself think about the fact that Emma would be back in the house where his mother died exactly sixteen years earlier. He couldn't.

"Denke. If Aunt Emma is well enough, we will be happy to come."

Sarah's words were what he expected. But her gaze—it seemed to go right through him. It seemed to see all the emotions he tried to hide, even from himself.

Sarah had managed to convince Aunt Emma to get up for supper—at least she hoped so. She glanced toward the stairwell as she warmed the chicken potpie on the stove. Aunt Emma didn't seem to be coming yet.

She bit her lip, praying she was doing the right thing in pushing her aunt to get out of bed. This inertia of hers was almost more frightening than the TIA itself. If Aunt Emma didn't discuss it with her family doctor, Sarah would have to.

She pulled out the lime gelatin salad Dora Schmidt had sent over, knowing it was one of Aunt Emma's favorites. As Sarah had said to Aaron, everyone had been so kind.

Aaron. She'd managed not to think about him for at least a couple of minutes. Maybe that was progress.

But now his strong-boned face, dark eyebrows drawn down, intense eyes questioning, shoved everything else from her thoughts. Questioning what? In those moments when they'd been so close that the air between them seemed to thin—had he been denying what he felt? Or rejecting her feelings?

She pressed her hands against her cheeks. They must be hot because she'd been bent over the stove. There wasn't any other reason.

At least Aaron had been almost encouraging about the

practice. Given his opinion of midwifery, that had been astonishing.

As for what he'd said about Aunt Emma and the phone shanty—well, she still could hardly believe her aunt would take such a step. She'd seemed so negative about a telephone the only time they'd spoken of the idea.

The sound of movement on the stairs alerted Sarah, and she took down bowls from the shelf. When her aunt entered the kitchen, she was ladling chicken potpie into them.

"Look what Molly sent over for our supper."

She fought to hold a cheerful facade over her anxiety. She'd never thought of Aunt Emma as old. But with her face drawn and her eyes lifeless, Emma looked every minute of her age.

"That was kind of her." Aunt Emma sat down heavily. "I'm not very hungry."

"Just have a little," Sarah said, sliding into her chair. She bowed her head for the silent prayer.

When the prayer was over, Aunt Emma sat staring down at the bowl.

"Try it." This was like urging a child to eat. Sarah took a spoonful herself. "Tastes a little different from yours, but gut."

The comparison pushed her aunt into tasting it. She nodded and then took another spoonful. Sarah's tension eased a little. Emma had to take an interest in something. She couldn't just lie there, staring at the wall.

"Molly is a fine cook," Emma said. "She had to learn early, with those boys to feed. She and Aaron had to do everything, sad to say. Their grossmutter helped when she could, but her health wasn't gut."

"Aaron talked Molly out of coming herself, since it was so cold out today. He brought an invitation to join them for ice cream and cake for Benjamin's birthday on Wednesday. It is hard to believe he'll be sixteen already. I think Aaron still looks on him as a little boy."

"Benjamin is starting his rumspringa." Now that she was eating, Aunt Emma kept on. "That will cause Aaron a few sleepless nights, ain't so?"

"I guess."

"So we are invited to his birthday, are we?" Aunt Emma looked at her with a spark of interest in her face. "I never have been invited before, so I'm thinking it must be because of you."

"I don't . . . I mean, I'm sure Molly is just being welcoming." Sarah didn't want to go anywhere near the subject of Aaron, but at least Aunt Emma looked alive again.

"Ach, I think it is Aaron who is glad you are here. I haven't missed all the excuses he finds to talk to you."

"Only because of the work." Her cheeks were hot again. If Aunt Emma thought that, what must other people be saying?

"You watch and see if I'm right. He'll make an excuse to talk to you at church tomorrow, he will."

"Don't go matchmaking," she warned, too pleased to hear Emma sounding like herself to shut down the topic. "If he comes near us at worship tomorrow, it will be to ask how you are."

Some of the animation faded from Emma's face. "I don't know. Maybe you had best plan to go alone."

To push, or not to push? Again, she didn't know the answer. "We'll see how you feel in the morning."

Aunt Emma nodded, but she seemed to be slipping back again into some quiet world of her own. Sarah sought desperately to find a way to hold her interest.

"You didn't tell me that you had talked to Bishop Mose about a telephone."

"Where did you hear about that?" Aunt Emma almost smiled. "Aaron, ain't so?"

"Ja, Aaron." But it didn't mean anything. "Why didn't you tell me? I thought you didn't want a phone." She stopped, not wanting to venture into an area where they might disagree.

"I thought about what everyone said, that night at dinner. It seemed to me that if everyone felt that way, maybe there was something in it after all." Emma did smile, the lines around her eyes crinkling so that she looked like herself again. "As for not telling you, I wanted it to be a surprise. I should have known better. There's no keeping secrets in Pleasant Valley."

Sarah reached across the table to clasp her aunt's hand. "Denke, Aunt Emma. You make me feel as if I really am your partner." It was an echo of what she'd said to Aaron.

Her aunt looked down, as if to hide her expression. "I wish that could be. But I see now that Jonas was right. I am too old to do this anymore."

Sarah's breath caught. "You don't mean you are closing the practice." Her dreams gone, all in a moment.

Aunt Emma looked at her in surprise. "Closing? No. Pleasant Valley cannot be left without a midwife. That midwife won't be me any longer. It will be you."

"But—" Sarah couldn't find the words to express the doubt, relief, and fear that fought inside her. "How can I? I can't do it alone."

Aunt Emma's hand tightened on hers. "You can. You will. God has given you a gift, Sarah. You must have confidence in that gift."

Sarah could only look at her, trembling between fear and hope. Aunt Emma had said what Sarah longed to hear. But how could she possibly do this alone?

"Everything looks fine." Sarah touched Anna Fisher's shoulder lightly, knowing that assurance was what Anna needed to hear. "Your little girl will have a baby sister or brother in about eight months. Are you having any morning sickness?"

"Not yet."

"Well, if you do, try drinking a cup of raspberry-leaf tea once a day. That will help."

Anna nodded, pressing her palm on her still-flat stomach. "You think I'm foolish to come in so early?"

"No, not at all." Sarah sank down in the chair across from the woman, clasping the hand she held out. "Your little girl's birth mamm dying so soon after she was born was such a sad experience. It's natural for you to be a bit apprehensive."

Sarah had heard some of Anna's story—of her flight from Pleasant Valley when she was just eighteen and her return three years later with the adopted child of her Englisch friend. Now she was well and truly settled back where she belonged, married to Samuel Fisher in early November and expecting a little one of her own already.

Anna nodded. "I tell myself it's foolish, but I needed to hear you say everything is all right." She hesitated, and Sarah sensed she had a still unspoken fear.

"What is it?" she asked gently.

"My sister-in-law Myra, Samuel's sister, has a Down syndrome child."

"I know." Sarah pictured the small, smiling face in her mind. "Of course you will be concerned, but that doesn't mean it will happen to you. We'll see to the tests at the appropriate time."

"Denke." Anna's eyes were suspiciously bright, as if tears lingered there. "My niece is a lovable, loving child. If it happens to us . . . well, it will be as God wills."

Sarah patted her hand again. There was little else she could say. "You have a gut head on your shoulders, Anna. I know you will not brood on this slight possibility."

"Right." Anna seemed to shed some of her apprehension. "You will deliver my babe, ain't so?"

"Ja." Time for the words she'd said to each client today. "You know about Aunt Emma's problems. She wants to turn her practice over to me." She could only hope her own doubts didn't show in her voice.

"You're all right?" Anna seemed to hear beyond the words.

Sarah blew out a breath. "I think so. I just . . . well, it's not what I expected when I came." Just a few weeks ago, but it seemed like a lifetime. "Always before I was in practice with other midwives. I had someone to consult, to turn to for advice."

"You can still do that, ja? Emma has a lifetime of experience."

"She does. But she has been so sad—" She shouldn't talk about her aunt, but she needed to, and somehow she had known since they first met that she and Anna would be friends. "She seems to feel so useless now. It's as if she's given up, and I don't know how to help her."

"I'm sorry." The clasp of Anna's hand was warm and comforting. "It's early days yet. And Emma is a strong woman."

"One of the strongest I've ever known." Sarah appreciated hearing someone else say what she believed.

"You have a gut head on your shoulders, too, Sarah. You won't let yourself brood on this."

Sarah had to smile at Anna quoting her own words back at her. "No, I won't. But I do wish I could find a way to show her how much she means to people."

Something sparked in Anna's eyes. "Will you and Emma be going to her son's next week for Christmas?"

"Maybe just for the day, depending on how Aunt Emma feels by then. She'd rather sleep in her own bed. Jonas's family will come to visit on Little Christmas, I think."

Christmas Day itself was a time to remember God's amazing gift of His son. The next day, Little Christmas or Second Christmas, was for visiting with family and friends.

"Why? What are you thinking?"

Anna shook her head, smiling. "Wait until I see if I can make it happen." She glanced at the door to the hall. "My Englisch friend Rosemary Welch is driving me today. She wants to talk with you, if you are willing."

"Ja, of course." She dismissed the question of Christmas from her mind. "Is your friend looking for a midwife?"

"Sort of." Anna sounded evasive. "Let me bring her in so that you can hear it from her."

Sarah nodded. Englisch women were not as likely as Amish to want a home or midwife-assisted birth, but it did happen. Her former practice had had several Englisch clients.

Anna disappeared into the hallway and reappeared a moment later, clasping the hand of her friend. Anna found it harder to guess the age of an Englisch woman than an Amish woman, but she'd guess the woman to be about Anna's age or maybe a few years older.

"Sarah, this is my friend and neighbor Rosemary. She is expecting in March."

"Wilkom, Rosemary." Sarah waved to a seat. "How can I help you?"

The woman looked around curiously as she sat down. "I'd never even known anybody who had a midwife for her baby's birth before I came here. It seems like most of my Amish friends prefer it."

As always, it took Sarah a moment to adjust her mind to the quicker tempo of English speech. Then she nodded. "We are more likely, I think, to see childbirth as something natural rather than as a medical procedure."

Rosemary nodded eagerly. "That's exactly what I've been thinking. I mean, I'd begun to think we'd never have a baby. We'd been trying forever, and I figured . . . Well, anyway, just when I'd given up, it happened." Her face was transfigured by the look Sarah cherished . . . the sheer, astonished love for an unborn child.

"And you think you might want to have a midwife attend the birth."

"Well, I started reading up on it and talking to people. It seems like such a comforting, natural way of bringing a baby into the world." She smiled, running her hand over the bump under the loose sweater she wore. "I want the best for my baby."

"I would be happy to—"

"Well, it's not as simple as that." Rosemary interrupted her. "See, my husband . . . well, he's so nervous about this baby you wouldn't believe it. He's being way overprotective, and he insists on my seeing a doctor."

"Then—"

"I've heard that sometimes midwives and doctors work together." Rosemary rushed on, obviously intent on getting it all out. "Is that true?"

"Ja, that's so. In my practice in Ohio we did that. But here . . ."

"So I figured you could do that with my doctor," Rosemary said. "I'm seeing a doctor in Pleasant Valley. Dr. Mitchell."

Sarah took a breath, trying to think how best to say this. "Many doctors are willing to work with midwives, that's true. But I'm afraid that Dr. Mitchell may not be one of them." In fact, after their encounter at the clinic, she was sure of it. He'd made his disapproval clear enough. "I've heard from several people that he doesn't approve of midwives."

Rosemary's face fell. "I hoped . . . well, you could try, couldn't you? I mean, maybe if you talked to him and I talked to him, he'd come around. It's not as if I have any problems. So what do you say?" She sounded confident, but her gaze was pleading. "Please?"

Say no. That was what Sarah wanted to do—what every instinct urged her to do. She hadn't run into Dr. Mitchell since that day at the clinic, and he hadn't approached her. Why stir the pot?

But there was the little matter of the promise she'd made to care for mothers and babies to the best of her ability. Aunt Emma's words about her gift echoed in her mind. How could she deny that for the sake of saving herself trouble?

She took a breath. "Ja. All right. I will try."

Chapter Ten

Sarah ended up going to the birthday celebration alone. After Aunt Emma's appointment with her doctor, she had come home silent and withdrawn. Jonas, who had gone with them to the appointment, had urged Sarah not to miss the party even though his mother didn't feel up to going.

Sarah didn't have any illusions about Jonas's reason for offering to stay with her aunt until she returned. He wanted another opportunity to try to convince Emma to move in with him.

Sarah understood only too well. Jonas loved his mother. He felt responsible for her. It wasn't his fault that he didn't understand her.

Not that she could say she was doing any better. As close as she felt to her aunt, she seemed unable to penetrate the shield Aunt Emma had put up.

Emma believed she was useless. Unless they found a way to convince her that wasn't true, Emma would be no happier at Jonas and Mary's than she would be anywhere else.

Lights glowed from the kitchen windows as Sarah approached the Miller house, and two other buggies were parked under the trees. Trying to banish her worries from her thoughts, she mounted the steps and rapped at the back door, smiling a little at the sound of voices and laughter inside.

The door swung wide, and Aaron seemed to fill the opening. He stepped back. Seeming to realize that a dish towel was tied around his waist, he pulled it free and tossed it over his shoulder. Obviously Aaron had been working in the kitchen.

"Sarah, wilkom. As you can tell, the others are already here." He glanced past her. "Your aunt didn't join you?"

"I'm bringing her apologies. She had her doctor's appointment this afternoon, and that tired her."

"I'm sorry. I'm sure Molly will want to send some cake home with you for her." He helped her with her coat, his big hands resting on her shoulders for just a moment before he turned to hang it from a peg in the back hallway.

She untied her bonnet. Had his face tightened a little when he asked about her aunt? Probably. Today might be the celebration of Benjamin's birth, but it was also the anniversary of the day his mother died—a death for which he still held Emma responsible.

Sarah couldn't quite repress a sigh. She longed to mend that situation, but how could she when neither of the two people most involved would talk about it?

"Is something wrong?" Aaron must have caught the sound. "Are you worried about leaving your aunt alone in the house?"

"She's not alone." She handed him the bonnet to hang atop the coat. "Jonas went with us to the doctor's appointment, and he'll spend some time with her while I'm here. I'm just . . . worried about her reaction to this situation."

He couldn't ignore that, not without being rude. He'd have to make some response. "She is still feeling low?"

"Ja. The doctor says there's no reason she can't live a normal life, but I don't think he understands. To her, normal is being useful. And right now, she feels completely useless."

She half expected Aaron to say that retirement was best for Emma and for the community. But he didn't. He looked down at her, face grave. "This puts a heavy burden on you, I know. I'm sorry for that."

The lump in her throat was unexpected. "Denke, Aaron." The words came out in hardly more than a whisper.

Aaron's hand came out, as if he would touch her in . . . what? Sympathy? Or something more?

"There you are." Molly appeared in the kitchen doorway. "Sarah, I'm so glad you are here. Komm, schnell. We're going to bring out the cake."

She followed Molly into the kitchen. Anna and Samuel were there with their little girl, as well as Rachel and Gideon Zook with their three youngsters. The children's excitement over the cake with its crown of candles seemed to vibrate in the air.

"Happy birthday, Benjamin." Sarah handed him the small gift she had brought from herself and Aunt Emma—a knitted muffler. "How does it feel to be sixteen?"

"Ach, all he can think about is his rumspringa, ain't so, Benjamin?" Nathan ruffled his younger brother's hair while Molly set the cake in front of him.

"Blow out all the candles now," Molly said. "Hurry, because these children want their cake before the ice cream melts."

Happy faces surrounded the table, with every one of them smiling. Except . . . except for the worry that darkened Aaron's eyes.

What was wrong with him? For a moment Sarah felt nothing but exasperation. Couldn't he just be happy over his brother's birthday?

But something had put that worry in Aaron's face. He might be a bit stubborn on some subjects, but she'd seen enough of him to know that he was a solid, sensible man. Would he be worried needlessly?

The cake was sliced and served around the table, and

Molly hustled back and forth from table to counter, making sure everyone had what they needed. The buzz of talk and laughter grew stronger.

Sarah slid from her seat, leaving her slab of cake half-eaten, and caught Molly's arm. "Why don't you sit down for a bit? It wears me out to watch you. I'll do whatever else needs doing."

"Ach, I'm fine." Dimples showed in Molly's cheeks. "You could fetch another stack of napkins for me though. They should be in the pantry, unless those boys have found some other place to hide them."

"I'll get them," she said. Following Molly's gesture, she rounded the corner.

Sure enough, there was the pantry, shelves lined with filled jars that were probably the gift of neighbors, since she didn't imagine three men living alone had put them up. But the pantry wasn't unoccupied. Aaron had one hand braced against a shelf, a brooding look on his face.

"I'm sorry." He'd probably come in here for some peace and quiet. "I . . . Molly sent me in search of napkins."

He managed a smile that didn't quite mask the sorrow in his eyes. "She must have given up on my finding them. She thinks we have some birthday napkins somewhere." A spasm that was probably involuntary crossed his face.

Sarah's heart seemed to cramp in response. "This is hard for you. I'm sorry."

Aaron looked toward the shelves, seeming to scan them, but she doubted he saw them. "We will celebrate Benjamin's birthday."

"Even if it brings back bad memories for you."

"Ja." For a moment his lips clamped shut. Then he shook his head. "You said to me once that if Benjamin was like anyone, it would be me."

"I think that is true." She sensed there was more coming and took a step nearer.

"Maybe. Maybe not. I worry . . ." He sucked in a breath,

as if he needed air to say this. "Our father started to drink after Mammi died. He was an alcoholic. He promised over and over again that he would quit. He never did."

"That doesn't mean—"

"You know what happens during rumspringa." Anger flared in his face, but it wasn't directed at her. "Sooner or later someone will show up with a case of beer. Or worse. Benjamin will try it. Sure he will. And what if he is like Daad, and can't stop? What then?"

Out in the kitchen there was light and laughter and teasing voices. But this small space seemed filled with Aaron's pain.

"You must stop thinking that way." She caught his arm, hard as a metal bar. "I understand why you do. Anybody would." Anybody who accepted the weight of responsibility the way Aaron did. "I have heard that alcoholism runs in families, too, but that doesn't mean Benjamin will be affected. Think about it, Aaron. The rest of you are all right."

"Even so . . ."

"Even so, you worry. I know. Have you talked to Benjamin about this?"

"No." He looked appalled. "How could I say that to him?"

"He's not a child anymore, Aaron." She felt his warmth through her hand on his sleeve. She tightened her grip. "Talk to him. Tell him what worries you, one man to another. Don't you think you owe him that?"

He studied her face, his eyes very dark. "I don't know. Maybe you are right. I'll think on it." He put his hand over hers, clasping it firmly. "You are a gut friend, Sarah. You—"

"Molly wants to know where the napkins—" Nathan cut off his words, probably because he saw them standing so close, hands touching.

Sarah stepped back, knowing her cheeks were scarlet, bumping into the shelf behind her so that the jars clinked together.

"Maybe you'll have better luck than we have." Aaron's

voice sounded almost normal. Almost. "We'll have to give everyone paper towels and be done with it."

"Ach, here they are." Nathan reached over Sarah's head and came down with a plastic package of napkins. "I'll give these to Molly. Don't—" He seemed to decide better than to say anything else. Instead he hurried out.

"I'd better go and finish my cake, or Molly will think I don't like it." Sarah hurried away, wishing she could plunge her face into a bucket of cold water to remove any trace of the embarrassment she felt.

What must Nathan be thinking? Worse, what must Aaron think?

No one seemed to have noticed that she'd been missing. She slipped into her seat, too aware of the fact that Aaron had entered the room after her. He moved around the table to the coffeepot, taking a long time about pouring himself a cup.

Molly took the chair next to her. "My little bruder is sixteen. I can't believe it. I remember the day he was born." A shadow crossed her clear eyes.

"A time of mixed feelings, I know."

Molly nodded. "I try not to think about that today. It's not fair to Benjamin." Her gaze rested fondly on her young brother.

"He's a fine boy."

"Ja." She smiled. "I hope my boppli turns out so well." She clasped Sarah's hand. "And that is something I wanted to ask you, Sarah. I have made up my mind. Will you deliver my baby?"

Her words seemed to ring out. Sarah didn't dare to look at Aaron for fear he had heard. But whether he had or not, there was only one answer she could give.

"Ja, Molly. I would be happy to."

She didn't want to look at Aaron, but she couldn't seem to help herself. He had heard. No doubt about that. He stared at her, and his face was dark with anger.

. . .

Sarah had to struggle to stay alert while she sat in the hard plastic chair in Dr. Mitchell's waiting room. She had promised Rosemary she'd talk to the doctor, and so she would, though she had no great hope of being successful.

It didn't help that she was so tired. Alice Straus's baby had decided to arrive in the middle of the night. The pounding on the front door had awakened her and Aunt Emma in the wee hours, and Sarah had rushed off, arriving just about in time to catch the baby. As Alice had said, she and William were old hands at this.

It was fortunate she had arranged for an Englisch driver to bring her to the doctor's office in town today, rather than relying on the horse and buggy. She'd probably have fallen asleep holding the lines, and Dolly would have taken her right back home again.

She shifted, trying to find a comfortable way to sit in the chair, aware of the curious stares of the elderly Englisch couple who sat across from her. Keeping her gaze fixed on her hands, folded in her lap, she tried to ignore their gaping. Surely, living in Pleasant Valley, they'd seen Amish before.

The receptionist had called one person after another, ignoring her. Deliberately? Perhaps. The woman hadn't even tried to hide her astonishment when Sarah called.

Dr. Mitchell's office was in a converted storefront down the main street of town from Bishop Mose's harness shop. For just a moment she wished she'd consulted the bishop before taking this step. She'd value his advice on dealing with the Englisch doctor.

Or was she just hoping someone would give her a reason not to do this thing? If so, that would be cowardly. She had promised to devote herself to her mothers and babies. She couldn't back down because it was difficult or because Dr. Mitchell had clearly shown his distaste at their first meeting.

She stifled a yawn. She'd had a busy day seeing clients. Whatever fears she'd had that they would go elsewhere when they heard Aunt Emma was retiring had come to naught. In fact, the practice had begun to boom again.

One patient she'd expected hadn't turned up today. Had Aaron talked Molly out of coming to Sarah's practice so quickly?

She couldn't help but cringe away from the memory of those moments in Aaron's house when he'd looked at her with such open dislike. Only a short time earlier his gaze had carried a very different message.

She understood his feelings, but that didn't seem to ease the hurt. Coming as Molly's decision did, on the anniversary of his mother's death, it was no wonder he'd reacted badly when he'd heard Molly's words.

Maybe, if Aaron had talked Molly out of using Sarah's practice, that would be for the best. Whatever happened, she didn't want to be the cause of a breach between brother and sister.

As for the breach between her and Aaron . . . well, that had only widened. Her hands clenched each other tightly. For a few short minutes, alone with him, she'd felt closer to him than she had to any man since she and Levi had been newlyweds.

But a relationship with Aaron wasn't to be. She accepted that, didn't she?

"Mrs. Mast?" The receptionist raised her eyebrows as she said the name. "Doctor will see you now."

She rose, breathing a silent prayer for guidance, and followed the woman's gesture through the heavy door and on into an office. The door clicked shut behind her.

Dr. Mitchell couldn't have helped hearing her enter, but he didn't look up from the papers he studied. Was he really that engrossed, or was this a not-so-subtle attempt to put her in her place?

If so, he truly didn't understand the Amish. For them, humility was a way of life.

The breathing space gave her an opportunity to take in the room. The wall behind his desk was lined with sturdy oak bookshelves, but the desk itself was a metal and laminate affair that looked as if it had been put together in half an hour with a screwdriver. The end wall bore a line-up of framed certificates with various seals bearing witness to his accomplishments.

Dr. Mitchell looked up finally, pushing a pair of round glasses into place. She was struck again by how young he was. Usually it was the older doctors, used to hospital deliveries, who opposed midwives and home births.

"Mrs. Mast. The midwife." He said the word as if it left a bad taste in his mouth. She had to remind herself that he undoubtedly wanted what he thought was best for his patients.

She nodded. "We met at the clinic."

Ignoring the reminder, he waved a hand toward the chair across the desk from his seat. "Sit down."

She took the chair he indicated, tension rising. He would, she thought, not make this easy. "You may know that my aunt, Emma Stoltzfus, has been midwife to the Amish of Pleasant Valley for many years. I have recently come to join her."

"I've heard." His lips tightened. "What brings you to see me?"

She took a breath, organizing her thoughts. "Before I came here, I was in a group practice in Ohio. We were fortunate enough to work with a local doctor who was sympathetic to home births—"

He cut her off with an abrupt gesture. "I don't know what you were used to there, but here in Pennsylvania, only registered nurse-midwives are recognized. Obviously you're not that, and even if you were, I would still say that the proper place for a woman to give birth is in a hospital with qualified medical personnel in attendance." His face had reddened as he spoke, and he clutched the pen in his hand so tightly she thought it might snap.

"I understand your position," she said, trying to keep her tone even. "I wouldn't ask, but Rosemary Welch has requested that I speak with you. She would like to have a midwife-attended birth, and she hoped we might work together to make that happen."

The pen snapped, pieces flying across the desk. Dr. Mitchell shoved his chair back, shooting to his feet.

"Understand this. I would never allow a patient of mine to be treated by an ignorant, untrained woman whose only claim to know anything comes from an apprenticeship to someone who knows as little as she does."

"Dr. Mitchell, lay midwives are accepted—"

He pointed to the door. "I don't have anything more to say. If you ever go near one of my patients again, I'll have the law on you. Now get out of my office."

Aaron stayed on after he sent Nathan and Benjamin home, tinkering with the latch on a cabinet door. He had to talk to Sarah. According to Emma, Sarah had an errand in town but would be back soon. He'd wait.

He checked the latch again, opening and closing the door several times, as if his world depended upon it working smoothly. The new rooms were nearly done. Sarah could start moving furniture into them in a day or two. Then it just remained to put up the telephone shanty, and there'd be no reason for him to see much of Sarah.

Good. It was past time to put some distance between them, especially after what had happened last night.

He took a cloth and began wiping down the door that Benj had sanded. It wasn't, he supposed, really fair to blame Sarah for Molly's decision to have a midwife. Molly had decided, and Molly was as stubborn—well, as stubborn as he was.

After everyone had gone home he'd tried to talk some sense into his sister. Molly had listened patiently to all he'd had to say, but that didn't change anything. She wanted Sarah to deliver her baby.

He realized he was rubbing the door hard enough to take

another layer of wood off it. Molly wanted him to forget about Mammi. She expected that he'd go through that again . . .

He steered his thoughts carefully away from that direction. He couldn't give Molly orders anymore. And he couldn't persuade her. The only other choice was to get Sarah to back out.

How likely was that? Probably not very likely. Sarah gave an impression of quiet, of gentleness, but on some subjects she could be steel. He had a feeling this was one of them.

He heard the sound of a car in the lane, and his fingers tightened on the soft rag he held. Sarah must be home.

The car stopped; the car door closed. He heard her light voice thanking Ben, the Englischer who drove folks to places they couldn't go easily by buggy.

In a moment the back door to the house shut. He could hear a murmur of voices in the kitchen, probably Emma telling her that he wanted a word. The door opened, and she came in.

The careful speech he'd been rehearsing vanished from his mind at the sight of her. Most people might not notice, but he'd seen enough of Sarah in recent weeks to recognize the strain that pressed lines around her eyes and tightened her lips.

"Was ist letz?"

Her startled gaze met his. "What makes you think something is wrong?"

"I know," he said simply. Right or wrong, he couldn't deny that he knew. And he cared.

She put one hand up to rub her temple, as if her head ached. "I had to go and see the new doctor in town. It didn't go well."

"The doctor . . ." Concern clutched his heart. "Are you ill?"

"Ach, no, nothing like that. An Englisch friend of Anna's wanted me to ask Dr. Mitchell if he would be willing to cooperate with me in giving her a home birth. He was not open to the idea."

"I've heard that he doesn't approve of midwives." And when he'd heard it, he'd agreed with the doctor, sight unseen.

"'Doesn't approve' is a mild way of putting it. He wouldn't even listen to what I've done before."

Sarah paced to the window and back again, and Aaron suspected that she'd forgotten who she was talking to. She just needed to release her frustration.

"Our practice in Ohio often worked with a physician in just such circumstances, but Dr. Mitchell wouldn't listen to me. He practically threw me out of his office."

Aaron couldn't repress a spasm of anger at the man for his rudeness. "Sarah, you must be careful. You can't make an enemy of someone like him."

She focused on him then, and her chin came up slightly. "I must do what is best for my clients."

That touched a match to his worry for Molly. "I suppose that's what you are telling yourself about my sister."

She blinked at the change of subject. "Molly asked me to deliver her baby. I didn't go to her. Besides, she didn't come today. I thought that meant you'd talked her out of it."

"I tried." He plunged on, not wanting to see the pain in her eyes. "You must know why I tried. But Molly is stubborn as the day is long. She kept saying it's her decision."

"Isn't it?" She gazed directly at him, a challenge in those green eyes.

He shook his head, trying to shake off his suspicion that she was right. He turned away, because this would be easier if he didn't have to look at her.

"Sixteen years ago my mother died because she wanted a midwife." He turned back to her. "Your aunt. Do you think I have forgotten that? Could ever forget that?"

"Aaron, you can't know—"

He spun and grabbed her hands, willing her to stop. "That morning she was laughing, joking about how soon the baby would come and whether it would be a boy or a girl." The memory came back, as vivid as if it had happened yesterday. "She put her hand on my face. She said she knew I'd be the best big brother, whether it was a boy or a girl." His voice broke, and he thought his heart was breaking, too. "By the next morning she was gone."

"I'm so sorry." Sarah put her hands on his arms, and he could feel the care flowing from her, through her hands into his very skin, it seemed.

Into his heart.

He looked at her, feeling as if he were sinking into the softness of her eyes. So much caring. So much gentleness.

He lifted his hand, almost before the thought formed. Touched her cheek, finding the skin just as soft as he'd imagined. Her gaze was startled, aware, her eyes darkening as she gazed at him. Her lips parted on a breath. He bent toward her, drawn irresistibly closer. He wanted, he needed . . .

No. He couldn't. He took a step back, shaken at what he'd almost done, and saw the same reaction in her face.

"I'm sorry. I shouldn't have . . ."

She shook her head. "Don't blame yourself. It was my fault, too."

"I have feelings for you, Sarah." He took another step back. "That does not change anything. Molly is still—" He hesitated.

"What about Molly?" Her voice was strained.

The sound hurt him. But he couldn't let it hold him back.

"Molly won't change her mind. But you can refuse to accept her."

Sarah grew pale, her eyes wide in a strained face. "I can't do that."

He stood for a moment. Waiting. Hoping. But she didn't speak.

"Then we don't have anything to talk about." He grabbed his coat and strode out, away from her.

Chapter Eleven

The work frolic and grocery shower at the home of Eli and Dora Schmidt was in full swing by the time Sarah arrived on Saturday. She'd hoped to convince Aunt Emma to come, feeling the outing would do her good, but without success.

Handing the buggy over to one of the young boys who was responsible for taking care of them, Sarah carried her heavy grocery bags into the kitchen.

The room was filled with an assortment of women and children, the women talking as they scrubbed down cabinets, the children either clinging to their skirts or playing with a box of blocks in the corner.

Sarah felt instantly at home. The grocery shower was an institution, held whenever one of the Leit suffered from financial problems. Each new arrival would bring bags filled with groceries, until the family had enough to carry them through the crisis.

Eli had broken his arm while trying to repair his barn roof right after Dora had given birth, so a work frolic was a fine way to clean Dora's house, finish the repairs Eli had been making to his barn, and enjoy being together, all at the same time.

Ruth, Dora's oldest daughter, relieved Sarah of the bags, greeting her with a warm smile. "Denke, Sarah. It is so gut of you."

"This is from my aunt, also. Two loaves of her applesauce bread are on the top."

"That is so kind of her. And of you." Dora slipped away from the knot of women to embrace Sarah. "How is she? I have been praying for her."

Was it her imagination, or did the chatter quiet now, as if everyone wanted to hear her answer?

"She is doing a little better now. I'll tell her you asked about her. Now tell me how that beautiful baby is doing."

It wasn't that she wanted to hide the truth, but given the way talk went around the Amish community, she didn't want to say anything that might be blown out of proportion by busy tongues.

"Ach, she's a gut baby, chust like all the rest. She eats, she sleeps, she wets." Dora beamed. "She is sleeping now, but she'll be up for a feeding before long, so you can see her then. You're staying, aren't you?"

"Ja, just put me to work." Sarah handed Ruth her coat and bonnet.

"Komm, join us." Leah Glick lifted a stack of plates down from a cabinet shelf. "We can use an extra pair of hands."

"For sure." Anna added her voice to her sister's. "At least we get to work inside, not out in the cold." She nodded toward the kitchen window.

A group of men clustered around the barn. It didn't take a second glance for Sarah to recognize Aaron's tall figure on a ladder. She looked away again quickly.

She hadn't talked with Aaron since that difficult moment when she'd refused his demand that she not accept Molly as a patient. If he had his way, it would probably be a long time before she spoke to him again.

"If Eli hadn't been so foolish, trying to do the repairs to the barn roof himself, he wouldn't have that broken arm." Dora sounded more than a little exasperated with her spouse. "I told him and told him to hire the Miller brothers for that job, yet nothing would do but that he must try to save money by doing it himself."

Barbara Beiler looked up from the oven she was scrubbing. "Well, now he's getting it done free already."

"I doubt he thought it was a gut exchange for a broken arm," Anna said, a little tartly.

"Sarah, I think you know most everyone, don't you?" Leah must be used to intervening tactfully between her sister and sister-in-law. "You know Anna and Barbara, and my other sister-in-law, Myra."

Sarah nodded, smiling at the young woman. Myra's brother, Samuel, she reminded herself, was married to Anna. Aunt Emma could detail all the intertwined family relationships back through the generations. Sarah was just beginning to sort some of them out.

"So, Sarah." Barbara shut the oven door with a satisfied bang. "Are you and Emma ready for all the company you'll be getting for Second Christmas?"

Silence greeted the words as everyone else seemed to join Sarah in staring at her.

"What?" Barbara's cheeks flushed. "What's wrong?"

"That's supposed to be a secret, remember?" Leah sounded a bit put out with her talkative sister-in-law.

"Ach, I remember that. But chust from Emma, ain't so?"

"We weren't going to tell Sarah, either." Leah gave Sarah an apologetic smile. "But maybe it's just as well for you to know."

"Know what?" Nothing to worry about, was it? Second Christmas, the day after the solemn celebration of Christ's birth, was traditionally a time for visiting with friends and relatives, sharing the joy of the season.

"We thought it sounded as if Emma needed a little pick-me-up," Leah said. "So we've been passing the word for folks to stop by that day, especially anyone whose baby she delivered."

Barbara chuckled. "That includes most everyone in the valley, I'd say. I'm sorry if I spilled the beans, Sarah. But maybe you'd just as soon know if a houseful of people is coming."

"I . . . I think that's best." She could hardly talk around the lump in her throat. "That is so gut of you." She clasped Leah's hand in gratitude.

Leah shook her head. "It was Anna's idea to begin with. The rest of us have just helped to pass the word. But if you think it will be too much for Emma . . ." She let that trail off, waiting for an answer.

"I think it will be exactly what she needs." Sarah looked around the kitchen, her heart swelling. "You are all so kind."

The silence was broken by a wail that seemed to punctuate her words. Soft chuckles came from the women.

"The boppli agrees," Dora said. She turned as if to go for the infant, but her daughter pushed her gently into the rocking chair.

"I'll get her, Mammi." Ruth hurried from the kitchen, and her light steps sounded on the stairs. With plenty of people around to care for a new baby, the little one would never be left to cry. Ruth came back a moment later with a small bundle in her arms.

"Let Sarah see how she's growing," Dora said, waving her hand toward Sarah.

Smiling, Ruth put the baby in Sarah's arms.

Sarah snuggled the small, warm infant close to her. The babe's redness had faded, leaving her with skin as soft and sweet as a peach. The little one's hand waved, and then latched onto Sarah's apron.

Sarah nuzzled the small head, inhaling the scent of baby. The infant responded by turning her head, seeking the milk Sarah couldn't provide. Her heart seemed to squeeze.

"Ach, Sarah, you should have a houseful of babies of your own," Barbara said.

There it was—the thing she didn't want to talk about. But obviously she had to, and maybe it was best to get it over with. "My husband and I were never able to have a baby. We wanted to, but I never got pregnant. The doctors couldn't find anything wrong, but it just . . . never happened."

She could sense their feelings—sympathy, curiosity, pity.

"Like my Englisch friend Rosemary," Anna burst in, obviously trying to spare her any embarrassment. "She and her husband were married for six years with no babies, and just when she'd given up, she's pregnant."

"We are so happy for her." Quiet Myra spoke up, surprising Sarah. "Rosemary has been such a gut neighbor to us."

Leah nodded. "She mentioned to me that you might be helping with the birth, Sarah."

No doubt Leah hadn't intended to put her on the spot, but she had. Sarah took a breath, trying not to picture Dr. Mitchell's face suffused with anger.

"I'm afraid that didn't work out. Rosemary hoped I'd be able to cooperate with her doctor, as our practice in Ohio did." She said the words carefully, mindful that at least one of these women was Dr. Mitchell's patient. "But the doctor here didn't wish to do so."

"Dr. Mitchell says lay midwives are ignorant amateurs who shouldn't be allowed anywhere near a pregnant woman." Mary Esch said the words defiantly, putting a protective hand across her belly.

Someone inhaled sharply. Sarah felt as if she'd been slapped. She tried to come up with something, anything, to say that would ease the tension in the room.

Mary looked around the kitchen. "Well, it's true. That's what he says. And I'll have a real doctor deliver my baby, not—"

"Mary." Leah's voice held a command. "That is your right, for sure. But you might have a little respect for those of us who don't share your belief."

Mary looked abashed for a moment. Obviously she, like many others, held their former teacher in respect. Then she turned away, reaching for her coat. "I'll be going now. My doctor doesn't want me to spend too much time on my feet these days." She swept out of the kitchen, and the door slammed behind her.

"Don't listen to her," Anna said quickly. "Mary always has the rough side of her tongue for anyone who doesn't agree with her."

"She's also waited a long time to get pregnant," Leah said, as if trying to be fair. "I'm sure she's just speaking out of her concern over being pregnant at her age."

"You were in your thirties when you got pregnant," Anna said, her voice tart. "It didn't turn you into a shrew."

"Anna, that's unkind," Leah chided her sister.

"Well, she wasn't very kind to Sarah."

"It's all right," Sarah said quickly. "I understand her feeling. Obviously Dr. Mitchell views childbirth as a medical procedure. I don't agree when it's a healthy mother and a normal birth, but doctors are invaluable when something goes wrong."

"Certainly Dr. Brandenmyer does gut work," Leah said, as if trying to steer the conversation into less controversial territory. "And he approves of midwives. It's too bad he's not closer. Anna's friend could go to him."

"At least then Sarah wouldn't cause problems by talking to him," Barbara said.

Once again she was the recipient of several stern looks from her sisters-in-law.

"Well, it's true," Barbara said. "People are talking about Sarah's visit to Dr. Mitchell."

Sarah felt as if a pit had opened up at her feet. "I didn't know." The words sounded lost, and she tried to make her voice firm. "What are they saying?"

"I'm sure—" Leah began.

Barbara swept on. "Some folks are saying you shouldn't have caused problems for us with the doctor, and because of an Englisch woman, besides. We're better off not to get involved."

For a moment Sarah couldn't speak. This was one of the risks she'd taken when she'd agreed to see Dr. Mitchell—the risk that her own people might hold it against her.

"I made a promise when I became a midwife," she said. "A promise always to do my best for every mother and baby. Every one, not just Amish."

Leah and Anna nodded, obviously agreeing. That was what she'd expect of them. But some of the others didn't look so supportive.

Her heart sank. She'd been trying to do her duty, but it seemed she'd caused problems instead.

"*Ach,* this little one is certainly active." Sarah held the stethoscope against Molly's abdomen and watched it bounce at her baby's vigorous kicking.

Molly laughed, her face lighting with joy. "For sure. Do you think that means it's a boy?"

"I wouldn't count on anything from the strength of the kicks," Sarah cautioned. "I've known some pretty lively little girls, haven't you?"

"Ja." Molly's smile didn't fade, and she pressed her palm against the kick. "There now, little one. I love you just as much whether you're a boy or a girl. But I do wish you'd let me sleep once in a while."

"Babies always seem most active when mamms are trying to rest." Sarah had a piercing wish to feel that for herself. "You know that if it should ever happen that you don't feel the baby kicking for several hours, you should let me know right away."

"Ja, the midwife in Indiana said the same." Molly sighed. "She had a partnership with a doctor there. I wish you had . . ." She flushed. "Well, you know what I mean. It would ease Aaron's mind, I think."

"I wish it could be that way, too." She pushed thoughts

of Dr. Mitchell away. "But if you'd feel more comfortable going to a doctor . . ."

"No, no." Molly clasped her hand in a quick grip. "I know what I want, ain't so? I was just thinking of Aaron, that's all."

"He worries about you. That's natural." Sarah tried to keep her voice noncommittal.

"I hope he hasn't been giving you a hard time about it." There was a question in Molly's voice—a question Sarah didn't intend to answer.

"Everything is fine." She patted Molly's shoulder.

There was no point in telling Molly about her worries. She had Aaron angry with her for treating his sister and a sizable portion of the church community unhappy that she'd caused problems with the doctor over an Englischer. Instead of moving the practice forward, she seemed to be losing ground.

But that was not Molly's worry. "And all is well with you, too. This boppli will be here soon. You have everything ready?"

"Ja." Molly swung her legs off the bed. "I wish my Jacob could be here for the birth, but he can't take time off and then spend it sitting around waiting for me to go into labor."

"It's hard for you, being apart at a time like this with only letters to share what's happening." That seemed to happen too often these days, as young men had to travel farther to find work.

"It is hard." Molly's lips trembled a bit. "But this job in Wisconsin will earn him enough money to come back home and settle down for good. We're going to build a house and stay right here then."

"I'm glad. And meanwhile you have Aaron and Nathan and Benjamin. That's probably enough men to have worrying about you."

"For sure." Molly's eyes danced. "One or another of them is always looking at me like they expect me to explode."

"It's gut for them," Sarah said. "They'll appreciate you

more." She'd almost said they'd appreciate their mammi more, but stopped herself just in time.

Molly nodded, glancing around the birthing room where Sarah had started seeing patients even though it wasn't completely set up yet. "You know, I think it will be best if I come here for the birth. It might . . . well, save Aaron some worries."

He wouldn't have to relive his mammi's death in the same home, in other words. "Ja, I think that's a fine idea."

Molly hesitated for a moment. "You know why Aaron feels as he does, don't you?"

"I know about your mother's dying when Benjamin was born. You're not letting that worry you, are you? Because there's no reason . . ."

"No, no." Molly waved that away. "I just wanted you to understand about Aaron. I wouldn't want you to dislike him because of his attitude."

"Don't worry. I don't dislike him." In fact, she liked him far more than she could admit, not that the liking could ever lead to anything.

"Gut." Molly straightened her skirt and pinned her apron into place. "Aaron's such a gut man, always caring and responsible, as if he really were the daadi." She was silent for a moment, apparently thinking of her father.

Sarah was silent as well, not knowing what to say. The Miller children had had a difficult time of it.

Molly seemed to shrug off her dismal thoughts. "Anyway, I am thinking it is high time Aaron let go a bit. Nathan and I are grown, and Benjamin well on his way. It's time Aaron was thinking of marrying and having a family of his own."

If that was a hint, all Sarah could do was ignore it. Naturally that was what his family would want for Aaron—a woman who could give him babies of his own.

When she didn't respond, Molly gave a little shrug. "But now he's letting himself get all worried about Benjamin's rumspringa. Ach, the two of them seem determined to misunderstand each other."

"Maybe that's because they're too much alike," Sarah suggested, glad to get onto safer ground.

"Probably so." Molly blew out a breath. "Benjamin went to his first singing on Sunday night, and what must he do but stay out later than Aaron told him. So of course the two of them argued, with neither of them listening to the other one, until I was ready to knock their heads together."

Sarah had to smile at the thought of Molly tackling her two tall brothers. She probably wouldn't hesitate. "That might not be a bad idea."

Molly laughed. "If I try it, I'll tell them you told me to do it."

Sarah smiled in return, but her heart was heavy. It sounded as if, in his concern for his little brother, Aaron was pushing the boy toward exactly the kind of behavior he feared.

She couldn't do anything about it. She couldn't break his confidence in order to tell Molly. And she herself was certainly the last person on earth he'd listen to.

Molly gave her an impulsive hug. "Denke, Sarah. You make me feel better just talking to you. I'd best chase down those brothers of mine and go home, so you can have your supper."

"I'll see you next week, then, since you are into your last month now. And if you'd rather I come to your place, just let me know. There's no reason why you need to go out in the cold."

Sarah began tidying away the blood pressure cuff and stethoscope, and pulling the sheet off the bed. It made as good an excuse as any to avoid going into the hall with Molly and seeing her brothers.

Molly went out. Sarah heard the rumble of male voices. Footsteps. And the sound of the door closing.

She let out a sigh. Gut. Aaron was gone. She could come out now.

She stepped into the hallway and stopped. Aaron hadn't left. He stood there, staring at her.

. . .

Aaron's heart jolted when he saw the swift, unguarded look in Sarah's eyes before she masked it with her usual placid smile. "Aaron. I thought you had left with Molly."

"I'm sorry. I didn't mean to startle you. I just wanted to speak with you for a bit."

Concern entered her face at that. She probably thought he'd come to argue with her again, and that shamed him.

"I thought we should have a walk-through of the work," he said quickly. "Just to see if there's anything else that you'd like to have us do."

"Ja, that would be fine." The tightness around her lips eased. "From what I've seen, the work looks excellent." She stood back, gesturing him through the doorway to the first room, where she'd been meeting with Molly.

"We always want to look at it with the client, just to be sure. Sometimes there might be some little change that will make it better."

Averting his eyes from the hospital-type bed that was already set up, he crossed the room and opened the closet door. It seemed Sarah had already put some things on the shelves. "Is the size of the shelves working out all right?"

"Just fine." She patted a stack of crisp white sheets. "I started filling the closet last night. That makes me feel as if we're taking a step forward." Some faint shadow crossed her face at that, making him wonder what had caused it.

That was not his concern, he reminded himself. His job was nearly finished here. And despite the purpose to which the rooms would be put, he couldn't help being pleased with the work they'd done. It was satisfying, building something that would last.

Sarah turned away from the closet to glance around the room, painted in a soft off-white. "Really, Aaron, the addition turned out so well. I wish everyone in the valley could see it."

He nodded. She was thinking about her practice, no doubt, and not his workmanship, but that was as it should be.

"You'll be having a gut portion of the valley here on Friday, I understand."

"Ja. Leah and Anna set that up." A faint flush colored her clear skin. "They have been so kind."

Did she say that about him when she spoke to someone else? Not likely.

"Maybe you should try to have the rest of the furniture in the rooms by then. If you leave the doors open, it will be natural enough for folks to walk through and check them out. And you know they'll spread the word fast enough."

A spark of excitement lit her face. "That would be gut. You're right. But Jonas isn't coming until Saturday to bring down the other furniture we're going to use from the attic."

"We'll do it, if you want. I can bring the boys over tomorrow to take care of it."

Her eyes widened in surprise. "That's kind of you."

He shrugged, embarrassed by her gratitude and a bit ashamed that she had cause to be surprised that he'd help out.

"Molly will like seeing what it's going to look like when she has her babe here." He couldn't help the edge that came to his voice.

Sarah's eyebrows lifted. "Given how you feel about it, I'm surprised you want to do anything to help."

Naturally she'd force him to say more than he wanted to. His jaw tightened, but he forced the words out.

"When I was bringing her over here today, Molly thanked me. She thanked me for not interfering with how she wanted to have her boppli. She said she knew how hard it was for me, so that made it all the more valuable to her that I didn't interfere." His lips twisted. "You can imagine how that made me feel."

"Ja," Sarah said softly, and her face was tender with sympathy. She had every right to be angry with him, but she wasn't.

"I sat out here waiting for her." He jerked a nod at the rocking chairs in the hallway. "I thought about that." He blew out a breath. "And I knew she was right. I have gut reasons for feeling as I do, but I had no right to interfere with her decision. And no right at all to try to pressure you, Sarah. I'm sorry for that."

"I understand." Her eyes warmed in a smile. "You've taken care of your siblings all these years, and now they're growing up. It's hard to let them go."

"Ja." He thought of Benjamin coming in Sunday night a full hour after he was supposed to. "Sometimes it's impossible. Benjamin . . ." He stopped, not wanting to talk about it with Sarah, of all people.

"What about Benjamin?"

"Nothing." He clipped the word off. "Maybe we'd best check out the phone shanty, if there's nothing you want changed in here."

She looked at him for a long moment, concern in her eyes. Then she turned without a word and took down a heavy shawl to put around her.

He followed her the length of the back porch to the small frame building they'd built to house the telephone. He shouldn't have cut her off, but he didn't want to listen to her saying he was wrong in the way he dealt with Benjamin.

"You won't have to get your feet wet this way," he said, swinging the door open. "You'll need to stop by the telephone office or call them to set up the service. Joseph Beiler says to tell you he'll come by next week to put in a buzzer system."

"That is kind of him. I thought . . ." She stopped.

"You thought what?" For sure it was something about him.

"I thought maybe you'd be opposed to having the phone here."

That surprised him. Did she really think he was that negative?

"Why? We have a phone for our business. I'm sure you'll not be standing out here in the cold chatting instead of paying attention to your work."

The way he'd caught Benjamin using the shop phone to call his girl. His lips tightened. That boy was determined to test every boundary to the limit.

"Aaron? Is something wrong?"

His face must have given him away. "No." He clipped off the word. "Well, then, I guess the job is done here now."

"Ja, of course. You are ready to be paid. How much do I owe you?"

Now he'd made her think he was asking for money. It seemed he could say nothing right to this woman.

"I wasn't asking to be paid now, Sarah. There's no hurry about that."

Her jaw seemed to tighten. "The job is finished, and it's only right that you receive your pay. How much do I owe you?"

Harassed, he shook his head. "I haven't figured out the bill yet."

"Perhaps you could do that tonight."

"Fine." He snapped off the word, not sure whether he felt more exasperated with her or with himself. "I'll do that and bring it when we come tomorrow to move the furniture."

"You don't need to—"

"I said we'd do it, and we will. We'll come by tomorrow."

And now he was insisting on seeing Sarah again when he'd just been telling himself that it was gut the job was done so he'd not be seeing so much of her. Seemed where Sarah was concerned, he just couldn't win.

Chapter Twelve

Aaron and his brothers had come and gone early the next morning, carrying furniture down from the attic and moving it from place to place until she was satisfied. Even then, Sarah found herself so excited that she couldn't leave well enough alone in the new rooms.

She made up the beds, spreading one of Aunt Emma's handmade quilts over each. She polished the small tables and rocking chairs they'd put in each room and fussed over the arrangements of equipment and supplies until everything was stored, linens on their shelves, their array of herbs and tinctures on another. The windows shone, their white shades pulled down to exactly the same level.

Now . . . all they needed were clients, the women who would give birth in these rooms. Hopefully there would be enough women that she could actually make a living at the practice.

She thought of the money she'd paid to Aaron that morning, and uncertainty gripped her. The practice seemed to be picking up recently, but was it enough? If Aunt Emma did decide to move in with Jonas, what then? Sarah probably couldn't afford to buy this house, and yet, wasn't it partially hers already, with the investment she'd made in the birthing rooms? She was going on faith and the agreement she'd made with Aunt Emma, but would Jonas see it that way?

A sweet aroma drifted through the air, tickling her nose and drawing her toward the kitchen. She got there in time to see Aunt Emma sliding a cookie sheet out of the oven.

"What are you doing, Aunt Emma? I thought you were resting."

"Ach, I realized what day it is. Goodness, Sarah, you should have reminded me."

Sarah shook her head. "You'll have to remind me. What day is it?"

Aunt Emma wasn't mixing up the days again, was she? But her expression said she was sure of herself, and her eyes snapped with an energy Sarah hadn't seen enough of lately.

"The Christmas program at the school is this afternoon." Aunt Emma slid snickerdoodles onto a cooling rack. "I always bake plenty of snickerdoodles. Half the valley will be there for sure."

Relief swept through Sarah. Aunt Emma was right and sounding more like herself every minute, too.

"I didn't remember, and I know we said we'd be there." She crossed the kitchen, pushing her sleeves back. "I'll help. Shall I stir up another batch?"

"Ja, best do that." Her aunt slid a second pan from the oven, and the air filled with the scent of cinnamon sugar. "Doing their program always seems to make the children hungry."

"Everything makes children hungry, it seems to me." Sarah measured sugar into an earthenware bowl. "It will be nice to see a program here. How many of them do you suppose you've attended?"

"Ach, too many to count, for sure. It was seeing Aaron and his brothers here that made me remember the day. I've seen all three of them in Christmas programs, and Molly, too, of course."

"I'd guess Aaron knew his part perfectly," Sarah said, stirring the dough.

"You'd guess right. I remember when Nathan forgot his lines. Aaron looked embarrassed for him, but Nathan just smiled and made something up."

"It's a forgiving audience, ready to clap for anything."

Sarah had vivid memories of being so nervous she'd been convinced she'd never remember what to say. The annual Christmas program was a tradition in every Amish school, and she'd guess some of the same poems and skits were used year after year in school after school. That didn't make them any less meaningful.

"Aaron was always the serious one, even before his mother died." Aunt Emma paused, hands covered with dough. "More so, afterward, of course."

Sarah hesitated, the question she wanted to ask trembling on her lips. No, not just wanted. Needed to know. She needed to understand what really happened when Aaron's mother died, especially now that Molly was her patient.

Please, Lord. Let me do this right.

"I don't want to bring up unhappy memories for you, Aunt Emma. But I am concerned about Aaron's attitude, especially now that Molly is coming to us for her baby's birth. Please, will you tell me about what happened when Benjamin was born?"

She held her breath.

Aunt Emma was still for a long moment, face averted. She blew out an audible breath. "I never thought I would tell this, not to anyone. But I think now you are right. Having Molly coming here changes everything."

"I think so, too." Sarah murmured a silent prayer that she'd know how to respond.

Her aunt wiped her hands slowly on a towel, over and over. "You will have to know, so that you can deal with

Aaron for the best." She pulled out one of the chairs and sat down heavily. "Komm. Sit with me."

Sarah slid into the chair next to her, suddenly cold. Whatever she heard would change things, for good or ill.

"You asked me before. I got angry." Emma's face seemed to draw against the bone. "Maybe because I still felt guilty after all these years."

Sarah's heart cramped. "Guilty?" She barely whispered the word.

"I should have seen."

"Seen what?"

Aunt Emma's gaze seemed focused on the past. She shook her head slightly, as if to clear her vision. "To begin with, everything went fine. No problems. Benjamin came out easy, rosy and perfect." She paused, the lines in her face deepening. "Then Miriam started bleeding. I knew right away it was bad."

Sarah nodded. That was the midwife's worst nightmare—something suddenly going wrong in what had been a casebook delivery. "You sent for help."

"Ja, of course. I did what I could for Miriam and told her husband to hurry to the nearest phone." She gripped Sarah's hand, painfully tight. "There were not so many sixteen years ago as there are now. I heard him rushing out, calling to Aaron to get the horse and buggy. I heard the buggy go down the lane. And then . . . nothing. He didn't come back. The paramedics didn't come. Finally I sent Aaron running to the nearest neighbors to tell them to send for help. By the time help came, it was too late."

Emma's eyes were dry, but her face was ashen. She'd probably cried all her tears over this unhappiness years ago.

"Aaron's father?" Sarah thought she knew, but she needed to hear it.

"One of the neighbors found him, eventually. In the buggy, asleep." Her face twisted, but she clung to her control. "I should have seen that he'd been drinking. I should have realized, should have sent Aaron—"

"Don't, Aunt Emma." Sarah's words were edged with tears. "Don't. How could you have known?" Her heart twisted. No wonder Aaron's father had drunk himself to death. "But Aaron . . ."

"He's never known the truth of it." Emma straightened. "We agreed that the children shouldn't know. They'd just lost their mother. They probably didn't even know about their father's drinking. How could they face the thought that their father had been to blame?"

"So you let them blame you."

Aunt Emma's face smoothed out, as if she'd found serenity with that burden. "Better for them to blame me, if they had to, than their own father."

"I guess so." But Sarah said the words hesitantly. Was that the right thing? Or would it be better for Aaron to know the truth, no matter how hard?

"I pray so." Aunt Emma shook her head. "The poor man still drank himself into an early grave. But I did what seemed right at the time, even if it was hard. That's all any of us can do."

Sarah nodded, an image of Aaron's face filling her mind. He'd done what he thought was right, too, giving up his own life to be both mother and father to his siblings. Would that have been easier or harder if he'd known the truth? She'd never know.

The schoolhouse was filled to bursting with all the people who'd come to see the children's Christmas program . . . one of the few times of the year when the children actually performed for anyone. Sarah stood against the wall, but Aunt Emma had a seat where she could easily see.

Thank the gut Lord Emma had decided to attend. Surely that meant she was feeling better, didn't it? At the moment she was watching intently as the first and second graders spelled out the word *Christmas* with a simple rhyme for each letter. Aunt Emma had probably delivered most of the children, and she watched them with such pleasure that she seemed more herself.

Gut, Sarah thought again. Especially since they were going to Jonas's house tomorrow for Christmas, and he was sure to renew his plea for his mother to move in with them. That seemed to him a logical step, with Aunt Emma's other two sons clear out in Nebraska now.

But was it? *Please, Father, guide me to the right answer.*

The youngest children were succeeded by the oldest, doing a skit about the signs of Christmas. Out in Ohio, she'd been used to having few visible signs of Christmas among the Amish, but it was a little different here in Pennsylvania, with its strong Pennsylvania Dutch traditions. Most houses seemed to have a few greens and candles, and even the schoolhouse had greens in each window and stars dangling from the chalkboard molding.

She shifted position a little. Whatever Emma decided about her future, Sarah would support her, but still, she couldn't help feeling a little apprehension. If Jonas persuaded her to sell the house . . .

She wouldn't let her thoughts stray in that direction. Sufficient unto the day were the troubles thereof. At the moment her main trouble was the fact that Aaron stood almost directly opposite her across the room, and her heart gave a little jolt each time their eyes met.

Enough, she scolded herself. It doesn't mean anything. It can't. But still, the feelings were there, ready to spring to life each time their gazes crossed.

She focused firmly on the children and kept her eyes on them until they'd finished.

Loud applause greeted the final act. Beaming, the little actors and actresses either waved to parents and grandparents or peeked from behind siblings, depending on how brave they were.

"Oh, that was just wonderful." Sarah turned to find Rosemary standing next to her. Correctly interpreting Sarah's surprise, she smiled. "Anna invited me to come. I've never attended one of these Christmas programs before. To think they do the whole thing in English, even the little ones."

"It is a tribute to their teacher." Sarah hesitated, not sure whether to bring up the subject. Still, it had to be on Rosemary's mind, as it was on hers. "I'm glad to see you. I wanted to say again how sorry I am that things didn't work out with Dr. Mitchell."

"He's more stubborn about it than I'd expected," Rosemary said. "But I haven't given up. I'll talk to him about it again at my next appointment."

"I don't think that will do any gut." And it might do a great deal of harm, especially if Dr. Mitchell thought Sarah had put her up to it. "Maybe it would be best just to leave things be."

"Nonsense." Rosemary swept that typically Amish response away. "I don't give up easily, you know." She spun with a quick movement. "There's Anna waving at me. I'd better get some refreshments. I'm always hungry these days."

Sarah watched her go, thinking of all she should have said. It was often that way with the Englisch. They talked fast, acted fast. Unfortunately, in this instance Rosemary's quick talk might set Dr. Mitchell's back up still more.

Sarah took a step, thinking she'd get refreshments for Aunt Emma, but she seemed well blocked in by young scholars greeting their parents with question after question about how they'd liked the program. She needn't have worried, anyway. Rachel was handing Emma a filled plate and a cup of punch.

Sarah settled back against the wall and watched as Rachel Zook's children swarmed all over her and Gideon, talking a mile a minute. Rachel listened, hugged, said all the right things. Her gaze met Sarah's over the children's heads, and she slipped away from their clamor to greet her.

"Ach, those kinder are so excited I think they will never settle down." She fanned her flushed face with one hand. "Gideon can deal with them for a while."

"They did a wonderful gut job with their parts," Sarah said. "You look as if you should sit down for a while instead of standing here talking to me."

"I'm fine," Rachel said. "I won't stay long, but I wanted to let you know that everything is set for Second Christmas. There's nothing at all for you to worry about, because Anna and I have it arranged, even down to the boys to tend the horses."

"That is ser gut of you, Rachel. That will cheer Aunt Emma up as nothing else could, I think."

Rachel squeezed her hand. "You look as if you could use some cheering, as well. You've had more worries than you expected when you came here, ain't so?"

"Ja. Still, it will work out as God wills, I know." Sarah did know that, which meant she should stop all the futile worrying she did . . . an easier thing to tell herself than to do.

Rachel's children claimed her attention again, and Sarah edged her way through the crowd toward her aunt. A group of scholars swirled around her like an eddy in a stream, diverting her, and she found herself in the midst of the Miller family.

Molly greeted her with a warm smile. "Happy Christmas, Sarah. It always feels like Christmas to me once I've seen the children's program."

Sarah nodded. "They were wonderful gut," she said, giving the expected response. She smiled at Benjamin. "You can remember better than I can what it was like, I guess."

Apparently that was the wrong thing to say, because Benjamin stiffened. "I'm well past my scholar days, even if some people don't seem to remember that." The fulminating glance he sent toward his oldest brother left no doubt in her mind who he meant.

Aaron's face was tight as he surveyed his young brother. "You were rude to Sarah, answering that way. Apologize."

Rebellion flared in Benjamin's eyes, but before he could speak, Nathan threw a heavy arm across his shoulders.

"Komm, we'll bring everyone some punch before it's all," Nathan said, using the typical Pennsylvania Dutch expression. "And a few cookies, too."

"I'm sorry for my brother's ill manners, Sarah." Aaron seemed set on apologizing, though it would be better forgotten.

"It's nothing," she said quickly. "I take it you and Benjamin are on the outs at the moment."

Again, she thought, and saw by Molly's expression that she was thinking the same.

"Ach, the foolish boy thinks he should spend Christmas Day at Louise's house," Molly said. "He'll forget it soon enough, if we just ignore it. After all, it's not as if Louise's parents would even invite him. They think Louise is too young to become serious about anyone."

"As Benjamin is," Aaron growled, clearly not ready to regard the situation lightly.

"Now, Aaron, the boy knows that at heart," Molly said. "Least said, soonest mended. Goodness, Nathan was just as foolish. Remember when he thought he'd go off to New York to celebrate New Year's Eve? Boys that age are always coming up with silly ideas they know perfectly well they can't do. I'm sure Sarah would agree with me."

Molly seemed determined to put her on the spot. Sarah shook her head.

"I don't think Aaron needs my opinion on the subject." And she had no desire to have him glaring at her again.

Instead, he smiled at her with a warmth she was sure was only momentary. No matter—it still made her heart turn over.

"You'd be wrong about that, Sarah. I do value your gut opinion."

Her heart wasn't just turning over. It was melting in a silly puddle of warmth. Silly or not, she may as well admit the truth, just to herself. She was falling in love with this man.

It was crazy, and it could never lead to anything but heartache, but it was true. She loved him.

Aaron made one last try at getting out of going to Emma's as he climbed into the buggy on Friday. "It looks like this snow might start to stick. Maybe we'd be better off to stay home."

Nathan gave him a surprised look, while Benjamin, still nursing a grudge, stared off into the distance.

Molly waved off that objection as she had all the rest. "Nonsense. We're just going down the road. We could walk home if we had to. Now stop making excuses, and let's get going."

He got in and picked up the lines, clucking to the horse. "You boss your Jacob around like that, do you?"

"Jacob doesn't try my patience with silly arguments," Molly said, her voice tart. "You know as well as I do that Emma would be hurt if we didn't show up today. Besides, that would be like advertising to the whole valley that you hold a grudge against her."

"Ja," Nathan pitched in. "You'll have the bishop komm to call at that, ain't so?"

"Aaron thinks he knows better that anyone. Even the bishop."

Benjamin's words might have been just brotherly insults had it not been for the edge in his voice. Aaron had to bite his tongue to hold back a retort. The boy was trying his nerves these days.

He managed, for Molly's sake. Or maybe for Sarah's. He knew well enough what she thought of the situation.

For just an instant he saw her face the way it had been in the moment he'd said her opinion mattered to him . . . soft, surprised, wide-eyed.

What he'd said had been true enough, but he'd never

intended to let it out of his mouth. What had possessed him to say that? He must be crazy.

Molly was chattering away about all the buggies turning in at Emma's, and he managed, he hoped, to sound normal as he answered and joined the procession up the lane to the house. When they reached the back door, several teenage boys, laughing and jostling each other, were waiting to take care of the horses. Without a word, Benjamin jumped out and joined them.

Well, maybe that was for the best. Trying to keep the boy by his side would be futile. The worst that could happen today was some horseplay that accompanied the horse tending, especially on a day like this. Even as he assisted Molly up the steps to the porch he saw a snowball fly through the air.

The house was as crowded as he'd expected, judging from the number of buggies outside. People flowed through the dining room, where food constantly appeared as each person arrived, to the living room, where Emma sat in a rocker, Jonas standing by her side. The doors to the two new rooms stood open, accommodating the overflow.

The line moved slowly toward Emma, and he had a moment of panic. Could he really congratulate Emma on her years of service to the community?

He spotted Louise's parents ahead of them, but Louise was not in sight.

"Maybe I should go check on Benjamin," he muttered.

Molly clasped his arm in an unyielding grip. "You'll do no such thing. He's not a four-year-old, Aaron. Leave him alone."

"I wish he were still four. He was easier to handle then."

"Only because you have so much trouble letting him grow up." Molly gave him a direct look that reminded him of Mammi. "He is growing up, Aaron, like it or not. It's time to let him do so."

He was saved the trouble of answering by the approach of Sarah and Jonas's wife, who were working their way down the line, greeting newcomers, urging people to eat. He could hear Sarah answering someone's question about the new rooms, explaining their purpose, praising him for the fine work he'd done on them.

She meant well, but he'd just as soon not be linked in everyone's mind with the birthing rooms. Too late for that now.

Gideon, Rachel's husband, worked his way free of a cluster of women who seemed to be discussing childbirth. He gripped Aaron's arm with a look of relief.

"Aaron, just the person I need. I've left some cases of soda on the back porch to stay cold, but Rachel is insisting they be brought in, along with glasses she thinks they stored in the pantry. Can you give me a hand?"

"Sure thing." Glancing past Gideon, he spotted Rachel in the dining room, directing her helpers as they arranged food and replenished trays. "Never argue with a woman who's on a mission."

"Ach, you're right about that." Gideon led the way through the crowd to the kitchen. "Rachel's the sweetest-tempered woman in the world, but when she's in charge of something, you'd best hop to."

Aaron managed to suppress a laugh. Everyone knew how happy Rachel and Gideon were, having found love so unexpectedly after the loss of their first loves. The new baby would just round out their joy.

The kitchen, thankfully, was free of people at the moment. Gid gestured vaguely toward the porch. "If you'll get the soda, I'll search for the glasses."

Aaron headed for the back door as Gideon vanished around the corner into the pantry. Maybe the shock of cold air would get rid of the feelings that roiled inside him.

The cases of soda were stacked against the wall of the house. He picked up two and backed into the kitchen, letting the door swing shut.

"How many do you want, Gideon?"

"I'm not Gideon, but I'd say that's probably enough," Sarah said.

He turned slowly, trying not to betray any emotion at all when he looked at her and knowing that was probably useless. Sarah seemed able to see right through him.

"Sarah. There's a wonderful-gut turnout today, for sure."

"Ja." Sarah's expression bloomed with a smile so warm it would surely melt the snow outside. "Aunt Emma is so happy. She never suspected a thing, and she was just overwhelmed when people started arriving. It's such a tribute to her work."

That was the last thing he wanted to talk about. "How was your Christmas Day? You and Emma went to Jonas's house, ja?"

She nodded, face clouding a little. "It was lovely to observe the day with them."

"But—"

She smiled ruefully. "Ach, all right. Ja, Jonas tried to persuade his mother to move in with them and sell this house."

"And what did Emma say to that?"

"That she would think on it." Sarah gazed at the kitchen wall, but he knew she was seeing what lay beyond—the two new birthing rooms that seemed to represent a fresh start for her.

"If Emma did sell . . ." The thought hit him and wouldn't let go. If Emma sold out, Sarah might give up her practice. She'd be free to do anything, including marry again.

"Ach, nothing is going to happen very soon." Sarah made an obvious effort to shake off her concerns. "Don't worry. We'll still be here when Molly has her baby."

"Ja." He wouldn't pretend to be happy with the arrangements.

"The telephone goes in this coming week. By the time Molly goes into labor, it will only be steps away." She came closer to him, putting her hand on his arm as she looked up in his face. He seemed to feel that touch through every cell of his body. "Aaron, I promise you, at the least sign of trouble, I'll call the paramedics. They can be here in minutes."

His muscles froze. Sarah snatched her hand away as if she felt it.

"Help would be closer than that if she would just go to the hospital to have this baby."

"That isn't the birth Molly wants," she reminded him.

"You don't need to tell me that." He bit back any other words that might spill out. Just a moment ago he'd been indulging in ridiculous daydreams. Thinking that if Emma sold the house, Sarah might be free to give up her practice. Free to marry again.

He knew what he was really thinking. That this was a woman he could love, except for the one thing she'd never give up.

"Excuse me." He turned, groping for the door handle. "I'll . . . I should bring in some more of the soda." He slid out, closing the door behind him, and took a deep breath of cold air. It didn't help. Maybe nothing would.

Chapter Thirteen

Sarah stood there for a long moment after Aaron went out, fists clenched, breath ragged. There was too much between them, and at the same time, not enough.

Feelings—they had plenty of those. She knew she wasn't imagining that Aaron felt something for her. Unfortunately, those feelings were all tangled up with his pain over the way his mother died.

She bit her lip. If only she could tell him the story Aunt Emma had told her. Her aunt hadn't asked her to keep silent, but even so, how could she tell him? Aunt Emma, those nameless others in the church who'd known about what his father had done . . . they'd all agreed it was best that Aaron and his siblings be protected from that knowledge. She couldn't go against their wisdom.

"Aaron?" Gideon pushed through the door and looked around. "I thought Aaron was in here."

"He went out . . . I think he went outside to get something. I must see if Rachel needs any help." She hurried into the front of the house, not wanting to see the curiosity in Gideon's face.

"Denke." Aunt Emma was standing in the middle of the living room, everyone silent around her. Tears shimmered in her eyes. "You are all so gut to komm here today. You have made me feel wonderful gut about the years I have spent with you."

Sarah's breath caught. Those words almost sounded like a prelude to Aunt Emma saying she was leaving.

But she didn't. She thanked the community, she glanced around the room, naming those at whose births she had assisted, and she made more than one person wipe away a tear. But she didn't say that she was leaving.

Still, the worry wasn't over. Sooner or later Aunt Emma would want to make a change. Ideally, by then Sarah would be in a position to buy the house from her, maybe even to bring in another midwife to assist her. But how soon would that be?

Someone spoke to her, and she wiped her worries away so that she could nod and smile and urge people to eat. There would be time enough later to think about the future. Maybe, after today, Aunt Emma would be ready to talk about what that might hold.

Sarah was urging a big serving of peaches-and-cream cake on Bishop Mose when she heard a vaguely familiar voice behind her.

"I don't know where Louise has gotten to. I thought she was with her sisters."

Sarah turned to catch a glimpse of Louise Buckholtz's mother, looking fretfully around the crowded rooms. After her daughter's plunge into the icy pond, Louise's mother was probably more than a little cautious about her.

"Ach, she's here somewhere," her husband responded. "We'll find her when it's time to leave."

A trickle of worry ran along Sarah's skin. Louise was nowhere to be seen. Neither was Benjamin, and the other boys who'd been helping outside had come in to get warmed up. Besides that, Aaron hadn't reappeared.

Sarah worked her way through the crowd to the kitchen. The ones she wanted weren't there, either, but a cluster of teenagers had gathered around the table, talking and laughing. They looked up when she entered.

"Does anyone know where Louise Buckholtz is? Her mother is looking for her."

Silence, but a few looks were exchanged. She understood. They didn't want to tell on one of their own. Well, she wouldn't force the issue. Louise and Benjamin weren't in the house. That meant they were either snuggling in one of the empty buggies or in the stable.

She went quickly to the back hall and took down a thick shawl. Louise and Benjamin's behavior wasn't her concern, as she was sure Aaron would be quick to point out to her. Still, she'd felt a bond with the two of them since the incident at the pond.

Outside, she crossed to the long line of buggies and began walking along it, her feet making no noise on the soft snow. She saw no one, and the snow, falling more rapidly now, seemed to blanket any sound.

She'd nearly reached the end of the row when she heard voices, coming not from one of the buggies but from the structure beyond. Apprehension building, she went quickly through ankle-deep snow to the barn. The door was shoved back a foot or so. The voice she heard was Aaron's, and it was angry.

She pushed the door farther, its scrape interrupting his words, and stepped inside.

It was fairly evident that Aaron had burst in upon Louise and Benjamin. They had probably been snuggling on that conveniently placed hay bale, smooching, to judge by Louise's flushed cheeks.

"Louise, there you are." Sarah forced her voice to a calm cheerfulness that she didn't feel, not daring to look at

Aaron as she crossed to the girl. "Your mamm is looking for you. Maybe you'd best go and see what she wants."

She put her arm around the girl's waist, urging her toward the door, afraid Louise was about to make the situation worse by being defiant. But Louise was obviously upset and embarrassed, and she clasped Sarah's hand gratefully.

"Denke, Sarah. You are right. I should go to my mamm." She dared a look at Benjamin. "I will see you later, Benj."

Benjamin didn't bother to reply. His fists were clenched against his sides, and he was glaring at his brother. The two of them wore such similar expressions that it would have been laughable if they weren't both so on edge.

Sarah saw the girl out the door and paused. She'd give a lot to go with Louise and let the Miller brothers fight this out for themselves. But the thought of Molly stopped her. At this stage of her pregnancy, the last thing Molly needed was more family stress. For her sake, if not theirs, Sarah would have to try to intervene.

She'd never be able to move Aaron, but Benjamin might be an easier proposition. She went to him, taking his arm in a grip he couldn't ignore.

"Komm, Benjamin. All the helpers have gone inside to eat before getting busy again when folks start to leave."

He drew back against her grasp. "My brother and I—"

"Can talk later," she finished for him. "The way it's snowing, there's not much time before everyone will decide to head for home. Komm, you're needed."

He held out against her for another moment. Then he gave a quick nod and strode out of the barn.

Now for Aaron.

Please, Lord, let me say the right thing to him.

She turned to face Aaron, meeting a look so thunderous that it made her quake inside.

"I suppose you had a reason for interfering in family business that doesn't concern you." His voice was heavy with sarcasm.

"My reason is to keep you from making a mountain out

of a molehill," she said, with a briskness she didn't know she owned. "Those two will do nothing more than steal a kiss or two, like any teenagers, unless you convince them otherwise."

"*Me* convince *them*." He took a stride toward her so that he loomed over her, his face dark with anger. "Don't you mean you? You're the one who acted as if their behavior was perfectly natural, sneaking out here alone together."

"Komm, Aaron." She fought to keep her voice light. "All of us did the same when we were that age and fancied ourselves in love. And if no one started making us feel like star-crossed lovers, we quickly found out the truth for ourselves."

"I'm afraid I was too busy taking care of my brothers and sister to do any such thing when I was that age."

The words were a reminder of what lay between them. She fought the longing to tell him the truth about what had happened when Benjamin was born. But if it were to be done, it couldn't be like this, blurted out because he was angry with her.

"Most of us did. That's what rumspringa is for, figuring out who you're meant to be with for the rest of your life." The thought of Levi made her heart wince, but she went steadily on. "My daad always says his beard went completely white when the three of us hit rumspringa within two years of each other. But whatever he felt, he managed to make us believe that he trusted us. And we felt we had to live up to that trust."

Aaron shook his head, frowning, like a horse shaking off flies. "How can I trust Benjamin when he does something like this, sneaking off with a girl? Should I just act as if it's nothing?"

"No, of course not. You should talk to him calmly, not when you're angry. Help him to see that he must protect Louise by not giving anyone cause to gossip about her. He will respond when he knows you trust him." She prayed she was right, for all their sakes.

"Will he?" The anger faded slowly from his face, leaving

concern and worry in its place. "Once he was the little bruder I loved and protected. But as he grew, it seemed a gap came between us. Now—now I just don't seem to know him."

She couldn't help responding to the lost note in his deep voice. She put her hand on his arm, longing to comfort him. "One thing I know for certain sure is that making Benjamin feel you don't trust him could push him straight into the thing you fear."

Aaron took a breath so deep it made his chest heave. "You make it sound easy. Trust him. But it seems every time I speak to him he flares up at me."

He looked down, seemed to realize she was touching him, and put his hand over hers. His was warm and hard from the work he did, but gentle, too. Her breath caught.

"You . . . You have to try." Just as she had to try to gather her scrambled thoughts. "Maybe, when you look at him, you could picture that little bruder who tagged along after you. Don't tell me he didn't, because I wouldn't believe it."

"Ach, those were the times when he thought his big brother could do no wrong. They are gone, I think."

At least he wasn't angry anymore. But he was holding her hand with such tenderness and speaking so softly that her foolish heart was tumbling over itself.

"Just try, Aaron. For Molly's sake, as well. She'll do better if she's not worrying about the two of you, ain't so?"

"How is it you understand my family so well, Sarah?" His fingers tightened on hers, and she looked up to find his face very close. "How is it you understand me?"

"I . . . I don't . . ." Whatever words she might say were lost in the intensity of his gaze, and her heart swelled until she thought it would burst. Aaron's eyes darkened. A pulse beat at his temple. And then he lowered his head and kissed her.

The world narrowed to the strong circle of his arms. All she could hear was the steady beat of his heart against her palm on his chest. She couldn't feel the chill of the air for the warmth that flowed from him.

Then he pulled back, taking a quick step away from her.

He looked . . . confused, as if he didn't quite know what had just happened.

"I shouldn't—" He stopped, shook his head, started again. "I'm sorry." He smiled a little, lifting his hand to run his fingers along her cheek in a feather-light caress. "I can't chide Benjamin for smooching in the barn when I'm doing the same thing, can I?"

She couldn't think of a single thing to say. Thank goodness Aaron didn't seem to expect anything. He just cupped his hand under her elbow and led her toward the door.

Aaron propped the latest copy of the Amish weekly newspaper up in front of him and leaned back in his chair, feigning a relaxation he didn't feel. Molly didn't seem to notice, in any event. She sat across from him in the rocking chair, sewing at some tiny baby garment, a soft, secret smile on her face. The old house was quiet except for the rhythmic sound of her rocking and the crackle of the fire he'd started in the fireplace when they got home.

He tried to concentrate on the printed page and failed completely. The events of the day were too powerful to shut out. He could pull a book from the bookcase at his elbow, but he probably wouldn't be able to concentrate on that, either, even though some of those books were like old friends.

Benjamin had stayed out of his sight since that encounter in the stable, which was just as well. Aaron needed time to think before he talked to the boy.

And he needed to avoid thinking about what had happened between him and Sarah.

"Well?" Molly said. "You might as well put down that newspaper and stop pretending you're reading it. Talk to me about it, whatever it is."

He took his time folding the paper and putting it into the basket beside his chair. But Molly still looked at him, eyebrows arched, face questioning.

"How do you know something happened? Did Benjamin

come to you about it?" He couldn't help the way his voice sharpened on the question. If the boy was trying to drag Molly in between them—

"Ach, how could I not guess? Benjamin and Louise disappeared from view, then you and Sarah. And then Louise comes back in looking like a scalded cat."

"I'm sorry about that." His fingers tightened on the arms of the chair. "Sarah tried to treat her as if everything was fine, but Louise was upset." He had upset the girl—that was the truth of the matter.

His reaction to finding them together had clouded his common sense. He'd been fortunate that Sarah had come in when she had, though he hadn't appreciated that at the time.

"Well?" Molly's foot tapped. "Are you going to tell me or do I have to guess?"

"Just what you thought happened. Benjamin and Louise had sneaked away from the rest of the kids. They were smooching in the barn when I found them."

"Well, at least he had sense enough to meet her someplace out of the cold," Molly said.

Aaron glared at her. "He shouldn't have been meeting her anyplace. Don't tell me you condone sneaking around."

Molly considered that, head tilted. "No, I don't, but I'm not exactly surprised. They're young, and they fancy themselves in love."

Aaron shifted his gaze away from her. "You sound like Sarah. That's just about what she said."

"I thought Sarah figured into this story someplace. What did she do?"

"She came in on us before I had a chance to say much." He blew out a breath. "All right, I admit it. That was gut, because she kept me from saying all the wrong things. She talked to Louise as if nothing was wrong, saying her mother was looking for her."

"That was clever of her," Molly said. "If you'd had your way, you'd probably have reduced the girl to tears, and then where would we be?"

She was right, little though he wanted to admit it. "Maybe Louise should be doing a bit of crying," he muttered.

"Ja, and I'll bet she did, but not in public, where everyone would see and be talking about it." Molly was briskly practical. "Komm, now, Aaron. Don't you think Jacob and I slipped away for some snuggling now and then? The only difference is that you didn't catch us."

He ran his hand through his hair, frustrated. "You women are ganging up on me. And Jacob's lucky I didn't catch you."

Molly chuckled. "He knows it." She leaned across the space between them to put her hand on his wrist. "Ach, Aaron, don't be so hard on Benjamin. I know you think you had to be a parent to the rest of us, but you didn't treat Nathan that way. You probably don't know half of what he's gotten up to."

"I can trust Nathan not to cross the line."

"That's because Nathan is like you." She patted his hand and then sat back. "Benjamin isn't."

His hands curled slowly. "Benjamin is more like Daad."

She considered that silently for a moment. "I suppose he is, in personality. That doesn't mean he has to make Daadi's mistakes."

"He won't if I can help it." Aaron had promised Mammi he'd look after the young ones. He couldn't let her down.

"Aaron . . ." Distress filled Molly's voice. "Don't push him away from you while you're trying."

"You sure you and Sarah didn't get together on this? That's what she said, too."

Molly stroked her belly, seemingly without being aware she was doing it. "Sarah is a wise woman, I think. And a gut one, too." She gave him a speculative look. "It sounds like you're getting to know her pretty well, ain't so?"

The memory of that kiss brought a wave of heat to his cheeks. "Don't start matchmaking already. I'm not looking for a wife."

"You should be." She rapped the words out, sounding

like Mammi when she was exasperated with his stubbornness over something. “What are you waiting for, Aaron? I could understand that you didn’t want to burden someone else with us when we were young, not that there weren’t plenty of women who’d have taken us on for the sake of marrying you.”

“That’s not—”

“But it’s different now.” She swept on, not letting him interrupt. “I’m married, Nathan’s grown and will probably marry in the next year or two. Benjamin’s halfway to being a man. It’s time you thought about a life of your own.”

“Maybe I will.” He seemed to feel Sarah’s soft lips again. But how could he think of anything serious with Sarah, feeling as he did about her profession? “But if I do, I won’t let you know until it’s all set, little sister.”

That made her chuckle. “Don’t you want my advice?”

“I’ll handle any courting I do by myself, thanks.”

The back door rattled, announcing that Nathan and Benjamin were home. Molly rose, gathering up her sewing.

“You need a little privacy to talk to Benjamin. Just remember what I said.” Her eyes twinkled. “And what Sarah said.”

She went out, and he heard her saying good night to her brothers. A moment later Benjamin came in, fists clenched, every line of his body stiff, defensive.

“Molly said you wanted to talk to me.”

He nodded. “Ja, I think we should talk. Sit down, why don’t you?”

“I’ll stand.” Benjamin took up a position in the center of the hooked rug Mammi had made, legs spread stiffly.

Aaron’s throat seemed to close. How had he let such a chasm grow between himself and his little brother? Never mind that Benjamin constantly found new ways to exasperate him. He was the older brother—it was up to him to behave like an adult.

He took a breath, knowing what should come first. “I’m afraid I might have scared Louise this afternoon.” He kept his voice even with an effort. "I'm sorry for that. Will you tell her so? She'd probably rather I not mention it to her."

Benjamin blinked. Clearly that wasn't what he'd expected. "I . . . I . . . Ja, I will tell her so."

"I reacted without thinking when I found you." *How could you be so thoughtless?* That was what he wanted to say.

But Sarah had been right. It wouldn't lead to any good result. He seemed to hear her soft voice in his heart.

"I don't need to tell you that you shouldn't have gone off to the barn with Louise. I think you know that."

"We just wanted to be alone a little bit, that's all." Anger edged his voice. "You don't have to make it sound like we . . . we were doing something wrong."

"I know you weren't." He hesitated. "I know, too, that you wouldn't want to do anything that might make folks talk."

"I don't care what they say. Bunch of blabbermauls, always talking about other people."

Aaron took hold of his temper with both hands. "Folks do talk. It's only natural. You might not care what they say about you, but there's Louise to consider. Like it or not, folks are harder on a girl's reputation. You care about Louise, ja?"

Benjamin nodded, the mulish look lingering. "Ja. We care about each other. You wouldn't understand."

Every generation must surely say that to the one ahead of it. It made Aaron feel old.

"I understand caring. Loving." He said the word deliberately. "It means putting the other person's well-being ahead of your own. I trust you to do that for Louise. That's all I wanted to say." Or at least, it was all he thought it safe to say.

"It is?" Surprise chased the wariness from Benjamin's face.

"Ja." Aaron managed a smile as he rose. "I'm going up to bed. Will you take care of the lights and locking up?"

Benjamin nodded, the surprise lingering in his eyes. "Ja. I will. Good night, Aaron."

"Sleep well." At least they were saying good night without any slammed doors or shouted words.

That was a step in the right direction, wasn't it? Aaron just wished he really trusted his little brother as much as Molly and Sarah seemed to think he should.

Sarah put one jar after another on the pantry shelves the day after the celebration. Rachel, Anna, and Leah had insisted on staying to do all the cleanup yesterday, determined not to leave until every last dish had been washed and dried and put back in its proper place.

Sarah had persuaded them to leave the gifts for her to take care of, saying Aunt Emma would want to look at them all again. Given the time of year, most people had brought the bounty of their gardens.

Each canning jar bore a label identifying its contents, but not the name of the woman who'd preserved it. That would be prideful.

Still, Aunt Emma, knowing her people as well as she did, hadn't had any trouble identifying the giver. Sarah slid a quart jar of applesauce into place. That was probably from Dora Schmidt. Dora had talked about how bountiful their crop of McIntosh apples had been that year.

Sarah paused, hand on the shelf, knowing perfectly well what she was doing. She was occupying herself with these thoughts to block out the memory that had haunted her dreams and disturbed her sleep last night—the memory of Aaron's kiss.

She pressed her palms over her eyes, as if to shut out the image in her mind. Anyone would think it was the first time she'd been kissed, already. It wasn't, and she wasn't a teenager anymore, caught up in rumspringa. At her age, a kiss should mean more. Did mean more.

But it couldn't mean more, not with Aaron. Too much stood between them. Even if he knew the truth about his mother's death, that wouldn't change things. He'd still disapprove of the work to which she'd dedicated her life. To say nothing of the burden if she didn't have children.

No, she was right to plan a life of singleness. She wouldn't go through the pain again of disappointing the man she loved, and God had given her useful work to do. No one could ask for more.

Her heart seemed to hurt in her chest. She couldn't deny the longing, but she would take refuge in obedience, doing the work God had set for her.

"Sarah, what are you doing? The canned meat goes over there." Aunt Emma bustled into the pantry, taking a jar from her hand.

"Sorry. I wasn't thinking." Sarah glanced cautiously at her aunt. Last night Aunt Emma had been a bit happy, a bit tearful, emotions all mixed together. Today all her defenses seemed to be up again . . . her voice tart, her lips set in a firm line.

"Is something wrong?" Sarah ventured the question, not sure she wanted to hear the answer.

"Wrong? What could be wrong with wanting to have things arranged properly on the shelves? What if I came in here in the dark and couldn't . . . couldn't . . ." Her face crumpled suddenly, tears not far away. "Ach, Sarah, I'm sorry. I'm that ferhoodled after yesterday that I don't know what I'm saying."

"I'm sorry. Was it too much for you? They only meant to be kind."

Aunt Emma's mouth worked for a moment, as if she wanted to hold back the words. "They were saying I'm done, ain't so? That my useful days are over."

Carefully, carefully. Sarah wasn't sure she knew the right words here.

"I don't think it was that," she said slowly, feeling her way. "I think they wanted to express their love and caring after learning about your health problems."

"Maybe so." Aunt Emma's expression smoothed a little, but something still clouded her eyes. "But even if that's not why they did it, it's true enough. After what happened with Dora's baby, no one will trust me to deliver their baby. I might as well give up." A desolate note sounded in her voice.

Sarah understood. Who better than she to know that drive to be useful?

"Aunt Emma, you shouldn't think that way. I'm sure—"

"You don't need to worry about the house," her aunt interrupted, suddenly decisive. "I told Jonas this last night. I'm signing the property over to you for the midwife practice."

Sarah's breath caught. "But . . . you can't. It should go to your boys. I'm only your niece."

"You are a daughter to me." Aunt Emma clasped her hand firmly. "You must know that. Your mamm always knew I felt that way. She was glad to share you with me. That's why you came to visit so often when you were little—because your mamm knew how I felt."

Sarah's eyes filled with tears. "I know she never grudged the time I spent with you or the fact that I wanted to be like you."

"Well, then, it's settled." Aunt Emma patted her hand with a return to her usual briskness.

Sarah couldn't just leave it at that. "But your sons . . ."

"My boys will do as I tell them. Besides, they all received a gut start from their father and me when they went out on their own. They don't expect more."

Sarah wasn't so sure of that, but there wasn't much she could do about it. And she had to try to do something about Aunt Emma's feeling of uselessness.

"I'm grateful." She fought to keep her voice from wavering. "I'll be happy if I'm half the midwife you are. But you mustn't give up just because of one problem. You're doing well on the new medication, and I'm here to back you up. There's no reason you can't go on. Just maybe cut back a little."

But Emma was shaking her head. "I want to believe that, I do. But I can't. I can't."

"Please, Aunt Emma—" Sarah stopped. Probably they both heard the sound at the same time. A buggy pulling up, wheels creaking against the two inches of fresh snow on the lane.

Aunt Emma rubbed a clear spot in the fog on the pantry window. "It's John and Charlotte Zug. Judging by the look on Charlotte's face, you're going to have the first new baby in the birthing center."

"We," Sarah corrected. "We are."

Chapter Fourteen

Several hours later Charlotte's boy arrived, lusty and red-faced, with a minimum of fuss and bother. Sarah put him in his mammi's arms gently, touching his head with its soft fuzz of blond hair.

"Ach, he is beautiful, ain't so?" The mother beamed, brushing her lips lightly on her son's little fingers.

Her husband bent over them, his smile wide enough to split his face, it seemed. He'd been smiling since the first glimpse of his son, and he'd even wanted to cut the cord once it stopped pulsating.

"Ja, indeed he is." Sarah couldn't help the lump in her throat. Indeed, she hoped she never stopped feeling that way at a new life. "Now we'll get you all cleaned up, and I'll see to getting you some soup and tea."

She could stand a little something herself. It had been a while.

She'd hoped, after their talk, that Aunt Emma would participate in the birth, at least spelling her from time to time, but Emma had disappeared upstairs.

Sarah pressed her lips together. She had to help Aunt Emma over this obstacle, but how?

She turned toward the kitchen but spun back when the front door swung open.

Ruth, Dora Schmidt's oldest girl, hurried in, stamping snow off her shoes. "My mamm says to tell you that our neighbor, Sadie Stolzfus, is in labor, and Mammi heard about Charlotte, too, so she sent me to help you." The girl's blue eyes grew anxious. "That is all right? I helped you when my mamm's baby came."

"That's wonderful gut of you both, Ruth." With Aunt Emma hiding out upstairs, she'd need an extra pair of hands with another mammi coming in soon. "There's a pot of chicken soup on the stove. Will you fix a tray for Charlotte with soup, tea, maybe some bread and butter? I'll have to get the other room ready."

"Ja, sure thing." Ruth slipped her heavy coat off, her face alight with enthusiasm. "I'll help any way you need. I'll do that right away. What did Charlotte have?"

"A fine, strong boy." Sarah liked the energy and enthusiasm the girl brought in with her. "Maybe you can hold him when you take the tray in."

"I'd like that." Ruth disappeared into the kitchen.

Sarah let out a relieved breath. Like most Amish girls of sixteen, Ruth knew her way around a kitchen. If called on, she could probably produce a full dinner for ten or twelve. She could be trusted to handle the light supper a new mommy needed.

Sarah went quickly into the other room to put fresh sheets on the bed. Once things were ready, perhaps she'd get a few minutes to rest before Sadie arrived.

But that wasn't to be. No sooner had she finished the room and checked on Charlotte and her babe than a buggy was pulling up outside.

She hurried to open the door for the new arrivals. "Wilkom, Sadie. Thomas. I heard from Ruth Schmidt that you were on your way."

Sadie paused in the hallway to catch her breath for a contraction, and Sarah automatically started timing. Thomas held his wife's hand, looking as if he'd rather be anywhere else.

"There." Sadie blew out a breath. "Ja, Dora told me she was sending Ruth over to help. Ruth's a gut girl. She won't let you down."

Like Aunt Emma, Sarah thought, and then was ashamed of herself. Emma wasn't letting her down, but maybe she was letting herself down with this loss of confidence.

"Let's get you settled." Sarah led the way to the birthing room, but another contraction hit before Sadie even sat down. Sarah rubbed Sadie's back, timing her, until it passed.

"Goodness, you didn't komm any too soon, ain't so?"

Sadie looked faintly embarrassed. "I wanted to finish up some things at home before I came. You know how it is."

She did indeed. She'd seen it often enough, especially with those who already had a couple of young ones at home, like Sadie. "Well, this boppli isn't going to take too long, so we'd best get ready to catch him or her."

The next hour flew by so quickly that Sarah barely had time to pop in to Charlotte's room and make sure all was well there. Sadie's baby seemed determined to get into the world as quickly as possible.

Then, as sometimes happened, everything slowed down. Sadie twisted on the bed, trying to get comfortable. "Why isn't it time to push yet? Is something wrong?" Alarm filled her voice and showed in Thomas's face.

"Nothing is wrong," Sarah soothed. She double-checked the baby's heartbeat and took a quick look. "The baby is fine. Just rest for a few minutes and try to relax between the contractions."

"The other two came so fast when I was at this point. I don't understand." Sadie was alarming herself and tensing up, sure to make matters worse, not better.

Sarah took her hands, gripping them firmly so that Sadie looked at her. "Listen now, Sadie. Each boppli is different, ain't so? I think this one is a little bigger than your last two, so he or she might take a bit more work. But you can do it. I'm going to massage you with oil so hopefully you won't have any tearing. And Thomas is going to rub your back and talk to you."

She gave Thomas a commanding stare. His face was pale, but he nodded and moved closer to his wife, beginning to rub her lower back. "Listen to Sarah. She knows what's what. We'll have a nice big baby soon."

Sarah nodded at him encouragingly. She worked the tight muscles, easing the opening, praying there would be no tearing to deal with. She reached for the warm compresses she'd prepared, hoping that would do the trick.

"Maybe a boy." Sadie panted. "Maybe a boy this time."

"Or a big girl," Thomas said. "Either one is gut."

Another contraction hit, and Sadie breathed her way through it. Suddenly her expression changed. "Sarah, I'm wanting to push. Is the baby coming?"

A quick check showed her the baby's head was crowning. "On the way. Put your hand here, and you can feel the baby's head." She guided Sadie's fingers to touch the top of the head, loving the awe on the woman's face.

The door opened behind her. Ruth looked excited. "Sarah, Anna Simon is here. She says she's in labor."

Anna was a first-time mother, inclined to be nervous. This might be nothing. Or it might be that all three babies had decided to arrive before the new year. Sarah took a step toward the door, but a groan from Sadie had her spinning around again. She grabbed Ruth's arm.

"Go upstairs and get my aunt. I don't care what you have to do, just get her down here to see to Anna. Sadie's baby is coming now."

Ruth gave a quick nod and fairly flew out the door. Sarah heard rapid steps going up as she reached Sadie. No time for anything else now. She'd just have to pray that Emma knew where her duty lay.

"Push now, Sadie. Your boppli is on its way."

A few more minutes, and once more she was holding precious new life in her hands. "A baby boy," she said over the newborn's thin wail, putting the babe on his mamm's chest. "Just what you need with those two little girls at home, ain't so?"

"A boy?" Joy suffused Sadie's face. "Ach, Thomas, look at our little son."

For a moment Sarah thought Thomas was going to celebrate by passing out. She slid a straight chair close to the bed, and he flopped into it, touching his new son.

"A son," he whispered. "A fine, strong little boy."

Ruth popped back in, smiling at the sight. "Your aunt is with Anna, and I just checked on Charlotte. Shall I help you make Sadie comfortable?"

"You are a blessing, Ruth. That's just what I need."

They worked together companionably. The placenta came on a contraction as soon as Sadie put the baby to breast. Sarah checked it, explaining softly to Ruth what she looked for in the afterbirth. The girl was interested, no doubt about that.

The same expression was on Ruth's face that must be on hers. Perhaps Sarah was watching another birth . . . the birth of a future midwife.

Once Sadie and her babe had been cleaned up and settled comfortably, Ruth disappeared into the kitchen again without being told.

Sarah slipped quietly into the room they used for meeting with patients. Anna lay propped up on the bed, with her young husband sitting on the extreme edge of the rocking chair. Emma sat beside the bed, holding Anna's hand, talking softly, calmly, with every fiber of her being assuring the young woman that she was safe.

Something that had been tense inside Sarah began to ease. Aunt Emma still had a place here, a useful role to play. Please God that she realized it.

The next three days passed in a blur of endless laundry, cooking, serving meals, helping Anna with breastfeeding, tending to three new members of the Amish community. By the time Anna and her husband left, their little girl wrapped up snugly against the cold, Sarah was ready to collapse.

She went back into the living room, where Aunt Emma had already claimed her familiar rocker. Sarah slid into the opposite chair, feeling the tiredness in her very bones.

"Now that's being a midwife," Aunt Emma said, her voice filled with satisfaction. "Three babies arriving in a mite over twenty-four hours . . . I think that's a record. I'll have to look it up."

Sarah smiled, also satisfied. "Do that when we get a minute."

"Ach, we should have a little time before the next one, ain't so? That would be Molly, and she's not due for another two weeks."

Sarah rocked tiredly. "According to the calendar. But as you told me when I was just starting out, babies don't look at the calendar."

Aunt Emma chuckled. "That's right." She was silent for a moment, but she looked content. "That girl of Dora's . . . I think we'll make a midwife out of her, ain't so?"

We, she'd said. Sarah smiled, meeting her aunt's gaze with one full of understanding. They didn't need to say more . . . it was all there between them: the craft God had called them to, the pleasure of working together, the hope and joy of passing their gift on to another young woman, with each generation building on the last.

"Ja," she said softly. "We will make a fine midwife of her."

Aunt Emma stretched, stifling a yawn as she picked up her book to update her records. "You should get some rest, but Molly is coming for her checkup today."

Sarah nodded, rubbing the back of her neck. "It's all right. I'll go to bed early tonight for sure."

"Maybe Aaron will bring her," Emma said, her voice carefully casual. "We haven't seen him so much since the work is finished. You'll be glad to visit with him a bit, ja?"

Sarah gave her a warning look. "You aren't matchmaking, are you?"

Emma spread her hands wide, as if disclaiming any such intention. "I know you think you don't want to marry again. That doesn't mean Aaron can't be your friend."

She couldn't meet her aunt's eyes. "I don't think—"

"Sarah Mast." Aunt Emma sat bolt upright. "Is something going on with you and Aaron already, and you haven't told me?"

"I . . . We . . ." She stopped, started again. "I think we both feel attracted to each other." Who was she trying to fool? Herself? It wasn't attraction she felt for Aaron Miller. It was love. "But there's too much standing between us to ever get serious."

The joy vanished from her aunt's face, and the lines grew deeper. "You mean that he blames me for his mammi's death. But I told you how that was." She was silent for a moment, brooding. "We thought we were right at the time, not telling him. But now . . . maybe now he should know the truth." She looked at Sarah, her face troubled. "What do you think?"

"I don't know." She'd struggled in prayer with that question ever since Aunt Emma had told her what had happened. How could she tell him something that must make his feelings for his father even worse? And how could she do it out of some selfish need to remove the barrier between them?

She shook her head, rubbing away the lines that had formed between her brows. "I don't know, and that's the truth. I've been praying about it. I just hope God shows me what is right, because I don't know."

Sarah rubbed her mittened hands together and stamped her feet, trying to warm up. She wasn't quite sure what she was doing at this sled-riding party at Aaron's when she really wanted to be home catching up on her missed sleep, except that both Molly and Benjamin had urged her to come.

Aaron's seconding of their invitation had been polite, no more, seeming to reestablish the boundaries between them that had been shattered the day he kissed her.

Still, it was Benjamin's group of teenagers they were entertaining, and having an extra female adult around was appropriate. Molly certainly ought not to be standing out in the cold, watching the kids sail down the trail in the snow the Miller brothers had made on the hill behind the house.

It was a magical sight, she had to admit. They'd set up torches along the path, and the sleds swooped down, the kids' shrieks and laughter shattering the cold silence of the night.

Nathan, grinning, ran up to her, clapping his hands together as if for warmth. "Sarah, you need a break. Go in the kitchen with Molly and have some hot chocolate already. We can manage things out here."

"Maybe I will." She felt a wave of gratitude toward Nathan, who at least cared how she was doing. After the briefest of greetings Aaron had stationed himself on the hill, as far away from her as possible.

"Give me a shout if you need me."

He nodded, grinning, and ran off to help the kids who'd just spilled from an overloaded sled.

The blast of warm air welcomed her into the kitchen, and her breath caught. Molly stood, hands braced against the sink, in the classic posture of a woman caught in the middle of a contraction.

"Molly?" Sarah slipped off her coat and crossed the kitchen.

"Ach, Sarah. I'm fine." Molly straightened, smiling. "It's nothing. Just Braxton Hicks contractions."

"Are you sure?" Molly's baby wasn't due for a good two weeks, but even first babies sometimes came early.

"Ja. Don't say anything to Aaron. He's already hovering over me like a broody hen."

"I won't." Sarah patted Molly's shoulder. "But you sit down for a bit. I'm taking a hot chocolate break. Will you have some, too?"

At Molly's nod Sarah poured mugs for both of them and sat down across from Molly at the kitchen table. She took a cautious sip and felt the warmth move through her. "Gut."

Molly nodded. "I keep sampling it while I make it. Soon I'll need a crane to get out of my chair."

"It's not that bad. You look just as you should." Indeed, Molly had the glow that first-time mothers so often did at this stage—as if her happiness was too great to contain. "I hope you're not overdoing it, putting on this party for the kids."

"Ach, it's nothing. All I had to do was make the hot chocolate. They brought the rest of the stuff." She waved a hand toward the counter, stacked with all the unhealthy snack foods dear to the hearts of teenagers.

"Benjamin looks happy." She'd seen him sailing down the hill on a sled with Louise, both bundled up against the cold and laughing.

Molly nodded. "I understand you gave Aaron some gut advice about our little bruder." She smiled, not quite looking at Sarah.

Not another matchmaker—was it so obvious that she had feelings for Aaron? Sarah tried to keep her tone casual. "Ach, I remember too well what it was like when each of my bruders hit sixteen. Daadi always said he had to keep rebuilding trust each time one of us broke it, until finally it took."

"It's what I said to Aaron myself, but I think he needed to hear it from someone other than his sister. Someone he admires, like you."

That was getting too close for comfort. Sarah rose, taking her mug with her. "I'd best go back to my duties, and this will keep my fingers warm. Denke, Molly. And if those contractions become regular . . ."

"I will get in touch with you." Molly looked a bit disappointed, maybe because Sarah was so unwilling to talk about Aaron.

But she couldn't confide in anyone about her feelings for Aaron, and certainly not in his sister. Snuggling into her coat and scarf, she went back outside.

The volume of noise had grown, if anything, and she suspected that some of the sleds tipped over on purpose, not by accident. Nathan spotted her and jogged over.

"Sarah, komm. You must have one ride down the hill, at least."

She shook her head, smiling at him. He was as enthusiastic as the younger ones were. "No, I don't think so."

"Ja, Sarah, please. It's such fun." Louise gave a shy smile, holding out her hand.

"Komm, Sarah." Benjamin took the mug from her and set it on the porch rail. "Just once, anyway."

Laughing, she let them tug her up the hill. She wasn't too old to enjoy a sled ride, was she? And it was nice to feel that these young people accepted her.

They reached the top, and someone pushed a sled into position. She climbed on, tightening her scarf, feeling ridiculously young for just a moment. Nathan held the sled steady until she was settled. Then he turned away.

"You go with Sarah, Aaron."

She glimpsed Aaron shake his head, but then the sled started moving on the trail made icy by all the ones that had gone down already. Aaron muttered something, grabbed for the sled, and hopped on behind her. For an instant they wobbled, off balance, headed for a snow bank. Sarah gulped an icy breath, but Aaron got both legs up, feet on the steering bar, and guided the sled onto the path.

They picked up speed, the trees whizzing past, the air cold on her cheeks. Aaron's arms, strong and steady, went around her, securing her. The world became suspended, and only they were real, swooping down the hill, close against each other, sailing through the night.

Too soon they reached the bottom, tumbling off. Aaron

still cradled her close, his cheek pressed against hers. The love she felt for him seemed to explode in her chest, as if her heart had shattered into pieces.

She scrambled to her feet, trying to smile. She couldn't let him see, couldn't let him know.

"Denke, Aaron." The words came out in a whisper, and she cleared her throat, striving for normalcy. "I feared for a minute I'd have to go down solo."

"You're all right?" His fingers brushed her cheek in a feather-light touch. "Nathan was as heedless as one of Benjamin's friends."

"I'm fine." But she couldn't hold on to her calm facade much longer. "I . . . I must help Molly with the food." She turned and hurried to the house, forcing herself not to run.

She hoped she had fooled Aaron. Certainly she didn't fool Molly, who saw her face the instant she came through the door.

"Sarah, was ist letz? What's wrong?" Molly came quickly to put a comforting arm around her.

"Nothing." But her voice choked on the word.

"It's Aaron, isn't it?" Molly led her to a chair and sat down next to her. "I knew it. I knew you had feelings for each other."

Sarah shook her head. It was too late now to pretend that Aaron meant nothing to her, obviously. She mopped away a stray tear and straightened.

"I think that I am the only one foolish enough to feel something, Molly. And you must say nothing to Aaron about this."

"But why?" Molly bent toward her, her expression earnest. "You two would be so gut for each other. I'm sure he cares for you."

"No." Sarah had to stop this before Molly said something to Aaron and made the whole situation unbearable. "You're wrong. And even if he did feel something, your mammi's death . . ."

She let that trail off. It was impossible to get anywhere this way.

"You mean because Aaron blames Emma for Mammi's dying that way." Molly sounded composed, as if she'd come to terms with this long ago.

Sarah pressed her fingers against her forehead, trying to stop the pounding that had begun there. "He can't forgive, and I can't explain—"

She stopped, aghast at what she'd almost blurted out.

There was a heavy step in the hallway, and Aaron stood in the door, hands pressed against the frame as if to hold himself back.

"What do you mean? What can't you explain?" His voice rasped with a harshness she'd never heard from him.

Sarah groped for strength. "Nothing." She fought to keep her voice calm. "Nothing."

He crossed the space between them in two long strides. "Tell me, Sarah. If there is something about my mother's death, I have the right to know it."

She shook her head, helpless against the tide of his anger.

"It's something about Daadi, isn't it?" Molly's face was pale, but she seemed composed. "I always thought there was something."

Sarah took a deep breath. She'd prayed that the Lord would guide her in this decision. She hadn't expected that His answer would come in this way, but perhaps it had. Walking away from this was now impossible.

Aaron leaned over her, one hand on the back of her chair, the other planted firmly on the table. She couldn't look at him, so she looked at his hand instead—taut, hard, the tendons standing out as if he strained against something.

This would be difficult, no matter how she told the story. It was best just to get it out as quickly as she could.

"My aunt finally told me what happened that day. Everything was fine until after Benjamin was born. Then things went wrong, and your mamm started bleeding. Aunt Emma knew right away that she needed to go to the hospital. She sent your father to call for the ambulance."

She stopped, as if a hand had clutched her throat. How could she say the rest of it?

"He . . ." Aaron sounded puzzled, shaking his head. "He went . . . I remember that. I harnessed up the horse for him, and he went."

"He didn't bring help." Sarah said the words flatly. Just get it out. "By the time Aunt Emma realized no one was coming and sent you to the neighboring house to ask for help, it was too late."

"What happened to him?" Aaron's voice was harsh.

"One of the neighbors found him asleep in the buggy. He'd been drinking." She hesitated. "Aunt Emma has blamed herself ever since, thinking she somehow should have known he'd been drinking, but she didn't."

Aaron shook his head again, anger battling grief and doubt in his eyes. "No. That can't be. He didn't start drinking until after Mamm died. He was grieving, and he turned to that—" He stopped, probably because she was shaking her head.

"I'm sorry. Maybe you didn't recognize it, but he was drunk that night."

"Why?" The question burst out of him. "If this is so, why didn't we ever know?"

Oh, Aaron. Her heart hurt for him.

"You had just lost your mamm. They didn't want to put that burden on you as well. They agreed to be silent."

"They had no right." The doubt was gone from his voice now, leaving only the grief and anger.

Her heart sank. Knowing the truth hadn't mended Aaron's feelings. It had only turned them in a different direction.

She rose, putting her hand on his arm in a gesture meant to comfort. His muscles were rigid, unyielding. He couldn't accept comfort from her.

"They meant it for the best, Aaron. Don't you see that? They didn't want you children to turn away from the only parent you had left. Please . . ."

She let that die away. Nothing she said would help now. He and Molly both needed time to accept the truth.

She turned and went quickly out the door.

Aaron was vaguely aware of Sarah's departure. He looked at Molly, afraid of what he might see, but she seemed calm enough.

"She shouldn't have told that in front of you," he said.

"You didn't give her much choice." Molly moved, seemingly at random, and sat down heavily in the rocking chair. "It's not Sarah's fault."

His heart seemed to clutch. He remembered Mammi sitting in that chair in the days before Benjamin's birth, knitting something small and white—a bootie, maybe.

"If it's true . . ." He couldn't go on. Everything he thought he'd known had been turned on its head.

"It is true," Molly said, her voice flat. "We both knew that the moment Sarah said the words. Daadi was never the same after Mamm died. He probably blamed himself."

"So he drank even more." Aaron's anger spurted out.

"Don't, Aaron." Molly shook her head tiredly. "They're both gone now, and being angry doesn't help anyone. The only thing to do now is to forgive."

He wanted to say that he couldn't help the anger. But wasn't that what Daad would have said about the drinking? That he couldn't help it?

The shrieks and laughter from outside seemed to be louder. Molly glanced toward the window.

"I'll see to them," he said quickly. "Why don't you go on to bed? This has been enough for you to deal with. The kids can get their own snacks."

Molly made a shooing motion with her hand. "Go. See what's going on. We'll talk later."

He stepped outside, pausing for a moment on the porch, praying that the cold air would clear his head. He needed a bit of clarity right now.

The kids had grown more boisterous, for sure. Nathan wasn't much of a deterrent. He was too close to them in age and not settled himself yet.

Aaron went down the steps. Sure enough, the volume of noise lowered the minute the kids saw him. He nodded to Nathan.

"Let's start getting them inside for something to eat. It's time to wind this down, I think."

Nathan grinned. "Nobody wants to stop on a night like this. But I'll try." He jerked his head toward the lane. "I see Sarah is leaving."

Aaron followed his gaze to where Sarah adjusted the harness on the buggy horse. He went quickly to her, not giving himself a chance to think about it. He caught the strap and pulled it through.

"Shouldn't one of the boys be taking care of this?"

He'd make this sound normal if it killed him. Molly was right. None of this was Sarah's fault. And as for those moments when he'd held her close in his arms . . . well, maybe he'd best not think of that.

"They're too busy having fun to disturb them," Sarah said. She swung the lines into place, her face turned away from his.

She started to climb up, but he stopped her with a hand on her arm. She shook her head.

"I'm sorry, Aaron. I shouldn't have . . ."

"You were right to tell us," he said quickly. Even through his own haze of pain, he could see that she'd hurt herself, too, in the telling.

"I don't know." She turned, looking into his face as if searching for something there. "Aunt Emma just told me about it a few days ago, and I've been praying for guidance ever since."

His hand closed over hers, and he felt the warmth of her comfort. "You did right. The truth is always best, ain't so?"

"I hope." Doubt clouded the clear green of her eyes, but it couldn't dim the caring.

He wanted to draw her into his arms. He wanted to hold her close and let her comfort him.

But that wouldn't be fair to her. He helped her up into the buggy.

"Denke, Sarah. For everything."

She nodded, lifted the lines, and clucked to the horse, moving down the lane away from him.

He didn't have time to think about it. Tonight, of all nights, when they had all Benjamin's friends here. Still, if they hadn't been here, if he hadn't taken that sled ride with Sarah, maybe the truth wouldn't have come out.

When he returned to the kitchen, it was full of kids, all talking and eating. The din seemed enough to rattle the windows. He didn't know how Molly managed to keep smiling, let alone stay on her feet.

He guided her gently into the rocking chair and took over, making sure everyone had enough to eat and drink while praying they'd soon get tired and go home.

Finally it was over. Nathan and Benjamin went out to see the last stragglers off. Aaron glanced around the kitchen, relieved to see that the girls had cleaned most everything up before they left.

"No more now." He headed Molly off before she could reach the sink. "We'll finish the rest, and in the morning you can tell us we did it wrong. Now go off to bed."

"Bed sounds gut." Benjamin came in ahead of Nathan, yawning ostentatiously, and headed for the stairs.

"Not you," Aaron said quickly. "It's Molly who must go to bed. Thank her for all she did, and you can help me wash up these cups."

"Can't we leave them until morning?" Benjamin clung to the doorframe, as if reluctant to let go.

"No, we can't." It was hard to remain patient with the boy at times like this. "Komm, tell your sister good night."

Benjamin crossed the kitchen slowly, not looking at Aaron. He leaned toward Molly to accept her hug. Aaron caught a whiff of his breath, and it was as if the boy had slapped him full in the face.

He grabbed Benjamin's arm, spinning him around. "You've been drinking." He seemed to be drowning in a flood of painful memories. "Admit it! You've been drinking!"

Benjamin looked away. "I don't—"

"Don't lie to us. We can smell the beer on your breath. Where did you get it?" His stomach churned. "Is this the first time?"

"All right." Benjamin yanked himself free. "You don't have to make such a big thing of it. I just had a beer. So what? Lots of guys have a beer once in a while."

Lots of guys didn't have a father who'd been an alcoholic. The words were on his tongue, but he couldn't say them.

"Where did you get it?" he asked again.

Benjamin shrugged. "One of the guys brought a six-pack. That's all. I don't know what you're getting so excited about. I'm not drunk."

"You were drinking." Like Daadi. "You let someone bring beer to our house."

"I didn't tell him to." Benjamin's expression turned sulky. "It's not like I planned it. But he had it, and everyone would think I was a little kid if I didn't have a taste."

"You can't—"

"You think I'm like Daadi." Benj's temper flared, and he fairly shouted the words. "You think I'm like Daadi, and you hate me for it." He spun and ran from the room.

Chapter Fifteen

When Aaron came down to breakfast the next morning, Benjamin wasn't there. He sent a questioning glance toward Molly, who was ladling oatmeal into a serving bowl.

"I thought I'd let Benjamin sleep a little longer this morning," she said. "It was a late night."

"Ja." The word was heavy with regret. He should not have let anger get the better of him. Engaging in a shouting match with his young brother was not the way to help Benjamin toward maturity.

Aaron's chair scraped. He sat, bowing his head for the silent prayer.

The prayer ended. Nathan scooped oatmeal into his bowl and reached for the brown sugar. "Your oatmeal always tastes better than when I make it, Molly. I don't know why. I make it the way you showed me."

Aaron appreciated the effort Nathan made to sound as if this were any normal morning. Nothing would be gained by going over last night's events, surely.

"That's because Molly watches the oatmeal while it cooks, instead of letting it boil and stick like some people do," Aaron said.

Nathan grinned, his good nature unimpaired, and spooned oatmeal into his mouth. "You could take over the cooking," he mumbled around the oatmeal.

Molly swatted at him with a dish towel. "Don't talk with your mouth full. Don't you remember any of the manners I taught you? It's no wonder you don't have a steady girl yet."

"I'm just taking my time about picking one out," he said. "I want to be sure I do it right, like your Jacob did."

Molly smiled, passing him a bowl of scrambled eggs. "My Jacob knew what he wanted from the time he was sixteen already."

"You mean he knew what he wanted as soon as you decided for him, ain't so?"

Molly withdrew the bowl. "You sure you want breakfast this morning?"

"All right, all right, I give." He held up his hands in surrender. "Jacob knew you were the one for him from the minute he clapped eyes on you."

Aaron listened to his siblings' good-natured kidding with half his attention as he nursed a mug of coffee. He must have slept some last night, but it didn't feel that way. He wasn't sure whether he'd spent more time thinking about Benjamin's drinking or Sarah's unexpected revelation. Or about Sarah herself.

Too bad all that thinking hadn't resulted in any major breakthroughs. All he knew for sure was that he had to talk to Benjamin seriously, and not when the two of them were like powder kegs ready to explode.

Nathan finally stood up, giving Aaron a questioning look. "You ready?"

"I want to talk to Molly for a bit. You go ahead and get started."

Nathan nodded, grabbed his jacket from its hook, and

headed out the back door. He'd have the workshop warmed up by the time Aaron got there.

Aaron looked at Molly, lifting his eyebrows. "Did you tell Nathan what Sarah said about Daad?"

She shook her head. "That's for you to do, I think. You're the head of the family."

"I haven't been doing that any too well lately." He stared down at the cooling coffee in his mug, as if he might find an answer there. "What happened with Benj and the drinking . . . it's exactly what I've been worried about, and yet I still wasn't prepared."

"I'm not sure how you would prepare for that. I'm worried about him, too," Molly said, her voice soft. "Maybe especially after what Sarah told us last night."

"Ja." He was silent for a moment, trying to still the pain. "It's hard—trying to adjust to the truth being so very different from what I've thought it was all these years."

Molly nodded, her usually merry face grave. "I was young enough not to notice a lot, or maybe not to understand what I did see. I just knew that I'd soon have a new baby sister or brother." She smiled just a little. "Don't tell Benjamin, but I was hoping for a sister."

"I won't tell him." Would he have been less worried if the child had been a girl? Maybe, but it was impossible to say.

"You were up most of the night." Molly reached across the table to clasp his hand. "I heard you pacing."

"I'm sorry if I disturbed you. You need your rest."

"Ach, how could I sleep? I just kept going over it and over it. Like you."

"I've remembered a little more, I think." He gripped her hand. "It's all mixed up in my mind—what Sarah said, what I believed, what I think I remember. All the signs were there—I don't know why I didn't piece it together myself."

"You wouldn't have wanted to believe it. I wouldn't, either. Somehow it was easier to excuse Daadi's drinking when we thought it was caused by grief. But it was guilt."

"I think so." He frowned down at their clasped hands. "Maybe we shouldn't tell Nathan and Benjamin."

Her hand jerked in his. "Isn't the truth always better?"

"I know that's what I said last night. But I don't want Nathan and Benjamin to feel the anger I do."

"Ach, Aaron, you must not be angry. You certainly can't blame Emma or anyone else who hid the truth from us. Poor Emma. She must have known all these years that you blamed her, and she bore it because she thought it was better for you."

That sliced straight to his heart. "For Emma to do that . . . somehow I must make things right with her."

"Ja, you will want to, but I think Emma does not expect anything from you. She's a woman who always does what she thinks is right." She paused. "Sarah is like her in that respect."

His jaw tightened. Sarah had let herself in for pain in her effort to help him.

"None of us has the right to be angry," Molly said earnestly, clasping his hand. "What happened is God's will. We have to accept that. We have to forgive, if we want to be forgiven."

He swallowed, throat muscles working. His little sister had learned wisdom, it seemed.

"I know. But it is hard." He squeezed her hand and then released it. "Now maybe I'd best try to put that forgiveness into action. I'll tell Benjamin I'm sorry for my anger last night. That's a beginning, ain't so?"

Molly nodded, smiling. "I'll go up with you. It's time that lazybones was out of bed."

They walked up the stairs together. His heart was a little less heavy, it seemed, for having talked everything over with Molly. He would miss her if she went back to Indiana.

Benjamin's door was closed. He tapped lightly, then opened it and looked inside. "Benjamin?"

The bed was empty, the coverlet so smooth it was impossible that anyone had slept in it. Benjamin was gone.

Sarah followed Aunt Emma into the township fire hall the morning after the sled-riding, trying to stifle a yawn. She'd had too little sleep last night, worrying and wondering about whether she'd done the right thing in telling Aaron about his father. Finally, surrendering the situation once more to the Lord, she had fallen asleep at last.

But it was just as well that Aunt Emma had booked them to help with crafts for the spring volunteer-fire-company benefit. The work would keep her thoughts from useless worry.

Women of the community, mostly Amish but some Englisch, met together twice a month through the winter to create items to sell. It was one of the events that brought Amish and Englisch together in Pleasant Valley.

It might be cold outside, but inside the cement-block building was warm and alive with the buzz of women's voices and the aroma of coffee and baking.

"Sticky buns," Aunt Emma said with satisfaction, hanging her coat and bonnet on the row of hooks along the wall. She glanced toward the pass-through into the kitchen. "Florence Burkhalter is in charge of refreshments today, and she always makes the best sticky buns."

Sarah hung her things up, too. "I think I'd better do some work before I indulge in something so rich." It was impossible to resist completely the sweet, sticky rolls. In the meantime, she'd enjoy the smell.

Aunt Emma nodded, smiling as she glanced around the room. She looked more like her old self every day, and Sarah rejoiced in that. She'd enjoy this outing, especially since it was such a gut cause.

Amish or Englisch, everyone in Pleasant Valley benefited from the fire company. Although Amish volunteers couldn't drive the truck, they did every other job related to the fire company, knowing their houses and barns were as likely as anyone else's to need saving, and their elderly and children as much in need of the rescue squad.

"Pitch in anywhere," Aunt Emma directed, picking up the bag that carried her quilting supplies. "I'll be working on the quilt."

Sarah nodded, knowing her aunt meant anything except the project stretched over a large frame in the corner. By a kind of unspoken consent, only the most skilled, experienced quilters joined that group, creating works of art that would bring buyers from as far away as New England to bid on them at the spring sale.

Aunt Emma trotted off to the corner. Sarah paused for a moment to see her warmly welcomed, and then she made her way toward the table where Rachel and Leah were working, greeting other people along the way. She didn't know everyone yet, of course, but someday she would.

"Leah." She nodded. "And Rachel. How are you feeling?"

"Gut, gut." Rachel smoothed her hand over the front of her dress. "Lots of kicking going on since Mammi is sitting still. Joseph is hoping so much for a little bruder."

"Perhaps Gideon wants a boy, as well," Leah said.

"Gideon wishes only for a healthy boppli," Rachel said. "As I do."

"Ja," Sarah said softly. That was what they all prayed for with each pregnancy. "What are you working on?"

"Crocheted and knitted baby shawls," Leah said, pushing several balls of soft pastel yarn toward her. "They go very fast at the sale, so we can surely use another pair of hands."

Sarah sat down. "This I can do. Aunt Emma wouldn't let me near the quilting frame."

Rachel chuckled. "Ach, no, they are most particular about that."

"Everyone is having a gut time, it seems." Sarah began casting stitches on. "It looks like every family in the valley is represented here."

"Not all, I suppose, but most," Leah said. "Some people would rather give money than time, but this"—she glanced around the busy room—"I would not want to give this up."

Community. That was what Leah meant. It was almost a tangible presence in the room.

Across the room the door opened, letting in a blast of cold air, along with two women. Anna and Rosemary, her Englisch friend.

In a moment the two women had made their way through the tables to them. Leah reached out to pat her little sister, as if still reminding herself that Anna was home to stay.

"You came. And Rosemary, how nice to see you." Leah's English was perfect, Sarah noticed, probably a result of all the years she'd spent teaching. "Will you help us with the baby shawls?"

Anna and Rosemary exchanged a glance as they sat down, and Sarah thought the Englisch woman looked upset.

"Rosemary? Is something wrong?" Sarah leaned toward the woman. Rosemary had been blooming with her pregnancy when she'd come by the house. Now she seemed distressed.

"I . . ." Rosemary paused, as if not sure how to go on. "Anna said you'd be here today. I just have to talk to you." She came to a halt again.

Sarah reached toward her, wanting to reassure her. "Of course, Rosemary." Her mind raced. Some problem with the baby?

Please, Father, don't let it be that, when they've waited so long.

Rosemary's eyes brimmed with tears. "I shouldn't have done it. I know that now. I should have listened to you. Richard didn't want me to say anything, but I just went ahead, and now look what's happened."

Leah and Rachel exchanged puzzled looks. "We don't understand," Leah said. "What did you do, Rosemary?"

Anna patted her friend's hand. "It's all right. Just tell Sarah what happened."

Rosemary took a breath, seeming to compose herself. "Yesterday I had my appointment with Dr. Mitchell. I know you said it would do no good to talk to him again, but I just had to try. I thought I could persuade him to cooperate with you on my baby's birth."

Sarah had a sudden image of Dr. Mitchell, face red with barely suppressed anger. "It's all right," she managed to say. "I understand your feelings."

A tear spilled over, and Rosemary wiped it away. "I tried. But Dr. Mitchell seems so completely unreasonable where midwives are concerned. He became very angry. I wouldn't have imagined he could be like that."

She could, Sarah thought but didn't say.

"Luckily Richard was with me," Rosemary said. "I'd have just dissolved in tears." She managed a watery smile. "But Richard was incensed. He decided then and there that we should change doctors. So we're going over to the clinic in Fostertown. It's a drive, but it's better than the alternative."

"I'm glad." Sarah patted her hand. "Really, Rosemary. I'm sure you'll be happy with your care there. I have been so impressed with Dr. Brandenmyer's clinic."

"Yes, yes, I know I will be." Rosemary's tears threatened to overflow again. "But that's not the bad part."

Her voice rose, and Sarah was conscious of a hush falling over the other women as they realized something was wrong.

"Dr. Mitchell was so angry. And he blamed you, Sarah. He blamed you for his losing me as a patient, said you'd interfered in his practice. I tried to explain, but he wouldn't listen, not even to Richard. He said he'd thought about shutting down your aunt when he first came here, but he'd heard she was retiring. But now you're here to take her place, and he's determined to put you out of business."

For a moment Sarah felt as if she couldn't breathe. The words rang in her head. Could he do it? Would he really try?

The silence in the room was as tangible as the sense of

community had been earlier. Then a low buzz of conversation broke out again.

Sarah knew who they were talking about now. They were talking about her. About the trouble she'd brought on the midwife practice, on all of Pleasant Valley.

Could she rely on them to stand by her? A cold hand seemed to grip her heart. She didn't know.

The drive home passed mostly in silence. Sarah stole a glance at her aunt as she turned into the lane, but Aunt Emma's expression revealed nothing.

She must have been as aware as Sarah was of the whispers and speculation making their way around the crowded room. For the Englisch, it would probably be a matter of minor interest, with sides being taken according to how each person felt about midwives.

For the Amish, the situation was far more complicated. To have an Englisch doctor threaten to close down an Amish midwife practice would naturally bring in conflicted emotions—memories of times past when the Amish had been persecuted by their neighbors, fears of a strain put on other Amish businesses by the prejudice that could result, concern that Amish women would have their childbirth choice taken away.

Sarah's throat tightened with the tears she wanted to shed. What must Aunt Emma be thinking? That she had brought Sarah here, entrusted her precious practice to Sarah, only to see it destroyed by Sarah's actions.

She drew up at the back door, as always, to let Aunt Emma down. Impulsively, before her aunt could move, she turned to her, grasping her arm.

"Please, Aunt Emma. Talk to me. I have brought a terrible thing down on everything you built, and I don't know how—"

"Ach, there's no need for such grieving." Aunt Emma's

first look of surprise changed instantly to one of caring. "I'm not blaming you for what has happened."

Sarah couldn't accept absolution so easily. "If I hadn't come here, this wouldn't have happened."

"If you hadn't come, I might have lost a mother and baby entrusted to my care. I can never forget that, and you mustn't, either." She clasped both of Sarah's hands in hers. "Sarah, Sarah, the only thing you did was put the patient's interest ahead of your own."

"You'd have been wise enough to handle Dr. Mitchell better, I think." Sarah struggled to blink back tears. "Was I wrong to go to him?"

Aunt Emma's gaze slid away from hers. "I don't know, and that's the truth. We already knew his answer would probably be no, from all we'd heard from other folks. When the woman asked you . . ."

"An Englisch woman. There are those who are saying I shouldn't have put the practice in danger for an outsider."

"Well, then, they're wrong." Her voice suddenly stronger, Aunt Emma squeezed Sarah's hands, meeting her gaze again. "Ach, I know that well enough. Our gift as midwives is for any woman who comes to us, Amish or Englisch."

Sarah searched her face. "Just answer me this. Would you have gone to Dr. Mitchell?"

Aunt Emma was silent for a long moment, and Sarah knew that her answer would be the truth. Finally she sighed. "Probably not. But it's done now, and we'll stand together and face whatever trouble comes."

"You deserve to have things a little easier now." Sarah's voice broke with the pain. "That's what I wanted to give you."

"That's what I thought I wanted. All I thought I *could* want from my life after the stroke." Her aunt's smile erased years from her face. "You and all those babies showed me I was wrong. I still have something to give. And I still have a duty to do what is right, no matter the cost." She pressed her cheek briefly against Sarah's. "Now stop worrying. We will do what we have to, and in the end, it will be in the hands of God."

"Ja." Sarah closed her eyes for a second, searching for strength. "You are right. It will be His will."

There was no resignation in the thought. Just comfort, and the knowledge that whatever happened, God would use it for His purposes.

Aunt Emma climbed down, heading toward the porch. The horse, recognizing that his day was nearly over, trotted toward the stable without her needing to touch the lines.

"There, now." A few minutes later Sarah was rubbing the horse down, talking as she did so. "You've had a cold day, but now you're in."

She led him into the stall, and he headed for the hay rack. She checked to be sure the water hadn't frozen in the bucket. May as well do the feeding now, since the afternoon was nearly gone, and the outside chores would be finished.

Sarah took a step toward the feed barrel and then stopped. That almost sounded like a footstep in the hay loft. Probably an animal, seeking warmth, but—

"Is somebody there?" she called, feeling a bit foolish.

Answering footsteps. She looked up to see Benjamin looking down at her.

"Benjamin! What on earth are you doing up there?" Her mind scrambled for logical answers and found none.

"I . . . I'm sorry, Sarah. I saw you were not here." He climbed down the ladder and stood before her, his gaze not quite meeting hers. "I'll get out of your way."

"Wait." She clasped his hand to stop him. It felt like ice in her grip. "You're half-frozen already. Komm. We'll go in the house and get you warmed up."

"I don't want . . ." He hesitated, shot her a glance, and looked away again.

Sarah had seen that look before, on her younger brothers' faces when they'd gotten themselves into some sort of mischief that they didn't want to confess but couldn't see their way clear of.

"Explanations later," she said briskly, tugging him toward the door. "We'll get you warm first, and then we can talk about the trouble, whatever it is."

He pulled back, just for an instant. He could yank his way free of her easily enough, but he didn't attempt that.

"Why do you think I'm in trouble? Has Aaron been talking to you?"

Trouble with his big brother, then. "I haven't seen Aaron." She smiled, patting his arm. "But I have two younger brothers who always came to me when they were in a fix. I know the signs." She tugged again. "Komm, schnell."

Seeming to give in, he walked along quietly beside her. She glanced at his face once, to find him looking across the field to where smoke rose from the chimney of his own home, something almost tragic in his eyes.

Well, at sixteen you always thought your current problem was the worst thing that had ever happened. Not that she'd say that to Benjamin. He'd only be offended if she didn't take it seriously, whatever it was.

Chapter Sixteen

Aunt Emma turned from the stove when they entered together, giving Sarah a questioning look.

"Benjamin needs to warm up a bit before he goes on home," she said, keeping her voice light. "Komm, sit here by the stove." She piloted him to the chair closest to the heat. Poor boy did look half-frozen.

"I have some vegetable beef soup heating already," Aunt Emma said. "It will be ready in a moment. Sarah, why don't you fix Benjamin a mug of hot chocolate? The water is warm already. I thought we'd enjoy that after driving home in the cold."

She went on chattering cheerfully, her words filling up the silence with a sound as gentle and welcome as the crackling of a fire on the hearth. By the time Benjamin had shed his jacket and stretched out his hands to the stove, Aunt Emma was filling a bowl with the steaming soup.

"There, now," she said, setting it in front of him. "I believe I'll take a little rest before supper, Sarah."

Her glance conveyed volumes. *Talk to him,* it said.

Sarah nodded. “Gut idea.” *I’ll try.*

They heard Aunt Emma’s footsteps go heavily up the stairs. Sarah poured the hot chocolate into mugs and sat down opposite Benjamin. “Better now?”

He nodded, seeming to inhale the soup. “Don’t know when I’ve been so cold.”

“Do you want to tell me what you were doing in the stable?”

He frowned down at the mug of cocoa. “I . . . I stayed at a friend’s house last night. His daad insisted on driving me home, but . . . but I had him drop me off here. Said I’d walk the rest of the way.”

He seemed to run out of words.

“But you didn’t go on home.”

No response.

“Is it maybe that you weren’t ready to see them yet? Or you were trying to think what to say to them?” She kept her voice even, not judging.

Benjamin shot her a look. “You sure you didn’t talk to Aaron today?”

“I didn’t see any of your family today.” She’d been busy with her own concerns. She brushed away the weight of worry about Dr. Mitchell and concentrated on the troubled boy in front of her. “But I think maybe I can guess that you had a quarrel with someone at home.”

“Aaron.” His jaw clamped on the name, and she thought that was all he’d say. Then the words burst out of him, rushing pell-mell like a boulder rolling downhill. “I know I did wrong, but it wasn’t my idea. One of the older guys brought a six-pack to the party. He called me over, offered me some. How could I say no?”

He looked very young, and very vulnerable. So he’d had something to drink, and obviously Aaron had found out. It was the worst thing Benjamin could do in Aaron’s eyes, and coming on top of learning the truth about his mother’s death, it must have been devastating.

Her silence must have done what words would not, because Benjamin shifted uneasily in his chair. "Well, I guess I should have said no. But it's not so bad, is it? Lots of guys drink a beer now and then. Some of the girls, even. Aaron didn't need to act like I'd broken every one of the commandments."

"Benjamin . . ." She took a breath, praying silently for guidance. "I don't think you could expect him to like it, could you?"

His mouth worked. "I know. And it was the first party I ever gave. He and Molly—they'll probably think I should never have another one. But Aaron was so . . . I've never seen him like that."

"If I were making a guess, I'd say that Aaron said more than he intended to in the heat of the moment." She chose her words as if she were picking her way across the icy pond. Benjamin should know what Aaron feared, but it wasn't her place to tell him. "I'm afraid he was already upset by . . . by something I said to him. I imagine when you see him, he'll be wanting to be friends again. Like you."

"Do you think so?"

"Ja, I do." She patted his arm, rising. "I'll get you some more soup. You must be hungry if you've been hanging around here all afternoon."

"Denke, Sarah. But I'd better start walking. It'll be dark soon."

"You don't need to walk. I can—" She stopped, hearing the sound of a horse and buggy approaching the house. She went to the window and peered out.

"It's Aaron." Had he come because he knew Benjamin was here? Or for some other reason? Last night had been . . . complicated. She wasn't sure she was ready to talk to him again already.

Benjamin's spoon clattered on the table. "How did he know I'm here?"

"I can't even guess, but he's here now, so you won't have

to walk home." She tried to sound as if it were any ordinary visit. "I'll just step out and speak to him while you get your coat on."

Hurrying a little, Sarah wrapped her shawl around her and went outside with no clear idea in mind of what she would say to Aaron. She just knew she couldn't let the two brothers meet without at least trying to mend the breach between them.

Aaron jumped down from the buggy and strode toward her, a frown darkening his face. "Benjamin—is he here? Matthew Kile said he dropped him off here hours ago."

"Ja, he's in the kitchen."

The frown deepened, if possible. "You should have sent him home."

She would not let herself respond in anger to his tone. "I found him not half an hour ago, hiding in the barn. He'd been there for hours, and he was half-frozen. I brought him inside and gave him something hot to eat."

He had the grace to look ashamed at his hasty words. "I'm sorry, Sarah. I didn't mean to imply that you were hiding him from us. We've just been so worried. Molly is nearly out of her mind with wondering what happened to him, and I . . ."

He didn't finish, but she knew the rest of it, because she knew him. "And you have been blaming yourself."

"Ja." The muscles in his jaw clenched visibly. "I suppose he told you what he did."

"He told me he'd had some beer, ja. One of the older boys brought it to the party."

"He told you that? He wouldn't answer when I asked where he'd gotten it."

"Why do you think that is?" *Oh, Aaron, stop and think about this.* Her heart ached for him, trying so hard to do the right thing for his siblings.

His lips firmed, and for a moment she thought he wouldn't answer. Then he gave a small shake of his head.

"Because I was yelling at him, I suppose. Because I

went through the roof when I knew he'd been drinking. You know why, Sarah."

"Ja," she said softly. "I know. But Benjamin doesn't. Don't you think you should tell him?"

"No." He pushed that thought away with both hands. "I can't. I can't let him feel what I do about our father."

"But if he doesn't know why you feel so strongly about it, how will he understand?"

He looked at her, eyes tortured, and his pain pierced her heart. "I can't, Sarah. Somehow I must keep him from following our father's path, but I can't tell him what happened the day he was born. There must be another way."

"If there is, I think it does not involve shouting at him." She tried to smile, hoping to take any sting out of the words.

"I know." He reached out, clasping her cold hands between his, warming them. "You're a gut friend to us, Sarah. It wonders me that you're willing to be bothered, as much trouble as we are."

She knew the answer to that, but she couldn't share it with him. "We're neighbors. That's reason enough."

The cold wind ruffled the shawl, and a shiver went through her. Aaron rubbed his hand on her arm.

"You're the one who's frozen, standing out here talking. Komm, let's go in. I promise I won't shout at Benj for causing us so much worry."

She nodded, turning to mount the steps, very aware of him close behind her as they went into the house.

"Here is Aaron," she said cheerfully when they reached the kitchen. "Ready to give you a ride home."

Benjamin froze, it seemed, looking at his big brother with wide, vulnerable eyes. "Aaron? I . . . I'm sorry." His voice was uncertain.

Aaron crossed the kitchen in a few quick strides and pulled his younger brother into a hug, holding him for a moment. He ruffled Benjamin's hair. "We've been worried about you." His voice was rough with emotion. "Let's go home. Molly won't be content until she sees you."

Sarah watched them go, tears trembling on her lashes.

Please, Father. Help them to understand each other. Please.

The worship service had ended, and Sarah stood with Anna and Rachel. She felt a surge of gratitude toward them. She'd been nervous when she and Aunt Emma arrived for worship this morning, sure that her troubles had been the main topic of conversation among the Pleasant Valley Amish for the past two days.

She wouldn't have been overly surprised if people had kept their distance this morning. Perhaps some did, but Rachel, Anna, and Leah had more than made up for that by drawing her instantly into their circle.

She'd sat between Anna and Rachel during the service, with Leah behind them at the end of a pew, convinced that she'd be taking her small daughter out at some point during the three-hour service. Little Rachel had surprised her mammi by getting through the service, but they'd gone out quickly afterward in search of a bathroom.

"It's gut to see your aunt looking so well." Rachel nodded toward Emma, who was chatting with a few of her oldest friends. Around them, men and boys worked at transforming the large shed that had served as their sanctuary into a dining area where everyone would be fed.

"She has been better the past couple of days." Sarah hesitated, but if she couldn't talk openly about it to these two, then with who? "I feared she'd be devastated by Dr. Mitchell's threats, but the trouble seems to have revived her instead."

"Ja, our Emma has always been a fighter," Rachel said.

Anna nodded. "She's never hesitated to say what she thinks to women who don't follow her rules during pregnancy or fathers who don't think newborn testing is necessary. A prejudiced young doctor isn't going to scare her."

The words were comforting. "You're right. But still, I wish I hadn't caused this trouble."

"You didn't, and that's what I've said to anyone who dared say different to me." Anna squeezed her hand. "Rosemary has been blaming herself, too, for bringing it up, but it seems to me Dr. Mitchell is the one in the wrong. He doesn't have the right to tell us how we should have our babies." Anna looked like a bit of a fighter herself.

"That's true," Rachel said. She ran her hand over her belly. "I want you and Emma to deliver this baby, no one else. I'm not going to a hospital with strangers and machines and unfamiliar ideas."

Sarah managed a smile. "You make me feel better, you two. But I know there are those who don't agree. And that's their right, too."

Anna looked as if she were going to burst into speech on that subject, but Rachel put a calming hand on her arm.

"Have you heard anything more?" she asked, her voice low.

"Not a thing. I keep feeling as if something's about to fall on me."

"Maybe it's just talk," Rachel said. "Maybe Dr. Mitchell spoke out of anger and has thought the better of it."

"I hope so." But there was no conviction in Anna's voice.

Rachel patted Sarah's arm. "We are all praying about it already."

"Denke." There seemed to be a lump in her throat.

Rachel turned. "Ach, there is Aaron. I want to ask him how Molly is doing."

It looked as if Aaron had been headed toward the door, but he veered in their direction when Rachel waved.

He nodded at their greetings, looking distracted. "I'm going home to check on Molly. Nathan and Benjamin will stay for lunch." He managed a smile. "Those two never pass up food, that's certain sure."

"We won't hold you up, then, but we wanted to know how Molly is." Rachel smiled. "No one blames her for not coming out on such a cold morning at this time."

"Ja, that's it." Aaron seemed relieved at having so handy a reason provided for him. "She just . . ." He stopped as two boys carrying a table moved between them. Touching Sarah's elbow, he drew her back out of their path, and her breath caught at the protective gesture.

"You're sure Molly is well?" She took advantage of their momentary isolation to ask the question.

His brow furrowed. "I don't know. She says it's just that her back aches too much to sit on a bench for three hours, but . . ." He let that trail off, sounding like a man unwilling to venture too far into the particulars of pregnancy.

"I'll be glad to stop by the house on our way home," she offered.

"Ja, that would be wonderful gut." Relief smoothed his forehead. "You don't need to tell her I was worried."

She had to smile. "I won't." She paused, wondering if she could ask about Benjamin.

"I am grateful to you for your kindness to Benjamin," he said, making it unnecessary to ask. "I think he is ashamed of what happened, especially causing us such worry when we realized he'd been out all night."

"I didn't do anything, but I'm glad if things are better between you."

"You did a great deal," he said, his voice firm. "It wasn't a coincidence that Benjamin hid out in your barn. He trusts you. He wanted to talk to you."

"When I look at him, I see my own little bruders." A smile curved her lips, chasing away some of the worry that had been hanging over her. "They were always in and out of mischief and coming to me with their troubles. I wasn't trying to interfere."

Or had she been? Certainly she'd felt it would have been disastrous if Aaron had gone in to Benjamin in an unforgiving mood.

"It's not interfering when it comes from a friend." His fingers brushed hers, hidden by the fold of her skirt so that no one would see. "If you . . ."

His words trailed off, and he looked toward the door, frowning.

Sarah followed the direction of his gaze. Her breath seemed cut off, as if she'd fallen and had the wind knocked out of her. Bishop Mose stood near the door, talking to the man who'd just entered. An Englisch man wearing a police uniform.

Silence spread through the space as people nudged one another, saw, and conversation stopped. Soon it was so quiet she could hear the low rumble of the man's voice as he spoke to the bishop.

"That is the township police chief." Anna whispered the words, moving next to Sarah.

A sign of support, that was what she meant by standing beside Sarah. No more waiting for the dreaded something to fall on her. Here it was, in the shape of a man in uniform, interrupting their Sunday.

Sarah couldn't seem to breathe. She could only watch as the two men began moving through the crowd toward her, worshippers drawing back on either side of them, the bishop in his Sunday black suit, the police officer in his gray uniform. Two authority figures, coming for her.

They stopped in front of her.

"This is Sarah Mast," Bishop Mose said. "You know everyone else, I think. Sarah, this is Chief Walker. He has something to say to you."

"I'm sorry to come here on a Sunday." The chief's voice was a low, embarrassed rumble. "Believe me, Bishop Mose, I never would do such a thing as interrupt your worship if the district attorney hadn't insisted on it. I guess he figured he wanted the whole community to know all at once."

"To know what?" Sarah discovered she could speak after all.

"Dr. Mitchell has lodged a complaint against you with the district attorney, Mrs. Mast, accusing you of practicing medicine without a license by delivering babies."

Someone around her gave a gasp. That was the only sound.

"What will happen as a result of this complaint?" The

bishop's voice was as even as if this sort of thing happened every day.

"There will be a hearing in front of a judge at the county courthouse. The judge will listen to both sides before deciding if the complaint is justified. If he decides that it is, then Mrs. Mast will be put on trial." He paused. "I know you don't hold with such things, Bishop Mose, but it would be best if Mrs. Mast had a lawyer to represent her. I can make arrangements about that, if you want."

Bishop Mose nodded gravely, his white beard moving with the motion. "That is kind of you."

"In the meantime . . ." Chief Walker held out a folded paper to Sarah. Her hand numb, she accepted it. "This is a restraining order, requiring you not to deliver any babies until this matter is settled by the court. If you break this order, you could be arrested."

Sarah stood perfectly still, the paper stiff in her fingers. This, then, was what she'd been waiting for. She knew now what it was like. It was like a mountain of snow sliding off a roof, burying her completely, wiping her from existence.

Aaron glanced out the kitchen window. "Look, it's snowing," he said, hoping to distract Molly. Ever since he'd returned from church with the news of what had happened to Sarah, she'd been unable to talk about anything else.

Molly gave a cursory glance outside. "Do you still think Sarah will stop today?"

"I don't know. Maybe." Would she? She'd said she'd come to see Molly this afternoon, but that had been before her business had come crashing down in ruins.

No, not business. Her world. He shouldn't try to minimize it.

"Tell me again what happened." Molly seemed unable to settle, moving from sink to table to stove and back again, as if driven by something he couldn't understand.

He studied her, noting the flush in her cheeks. "I will tell it yet again, even though you've heard it three times already. But only if you will sit down and try to relax."

"How can I relax?" That had obviously been the wrong thing to say. "I want Sarah to deliver this baby, right there in the room you built. I don't want to go to a hospital where no one even knows me. Who knows what they might do?"

"I understand," he said, trying to soothe her, even though the truth of it was that he didn't understand. He led her to the rocker. "Sit down, Molly, please. You're making me nervous."

That got a small smile from her. "Ach, I'm not going to have this baby today, if that's what you're thinking." She sat, but a cloud still hovered in her expression. "What right has this Dr. Mitchell to interfere with how I have my baby? Or the police? It's not their baby."

"To do him justice, I don't think Chief Walker wanted to be there any more than we wanted to see him. It sounds like he was pushed into it."

"Well, then—"

"Molly, Sarah can't disobey the court's order," he explained for what seemed like the twentieth time. "They could put her in jail if she disobeyed."

"Jail." Molly's eyes widened. "Poor Sarah. How she must feel! Aaron, you tried to comfort her, I hope."

"Ja, of course." Had he? Really? "But the women were doing a much better job of it than I could. Anna, Rachel, Leah, Ada . . . they were all supporting her."

"But some people weren't." Molly was too sharp to be fooled by half a story.

"No one spoke out against her, if that's what you're imagining. But some folks did just . . . stay back. Maybe they think it's not their problem."

"It's everyone's problem," Molly said hotly. "You told her we support her, didn't you?"

"I . . . well, there wasn't a chance." His conscience pricked him at that excuse. "You can tell her yourself when you see her." He patted her hand. "I'm sure she'll be along soon. She's not one to forget what she said she'd do, and she'll know you'll be worried."

Somehow he didn't doubt that at all. He'd grown to know Sarah Mast better in a little over a month than some people he'd known for a lifetime. He just hoped she'd come before Molly wore a hole in the floor, hard as she was rocking.

It couldn't have been a half hour before he heard a buggy in the lane. He looked out the window. "Here is Sarah now." Before Molly could move, he went to the door. "I'll go and meet her. You sit still."

He had little hope that Molly would stay still, but at least maybe she wouldn't try to come outside in the cold.

Sarah was climbing down already, her black valise in her hand. He grabbed the buggy horse.

"I'll take care of the rig. You go on in to Molly. She's been fretting herself into a state since I got home."

Sarah nodded. "There's no need for her to be upset. This will work out as God intends." She took a step toward the back door, but his outstretched hand stopped her.

She looked up at him, flakes of snow forming white stars on her black bonnet. He'd thought, in his first glimpse, that the shock and pain had disappeared from her face, but now he saw that they were still there, just hidden by the calm face Sarah presented to the world.

"I'm sorry." Her pain seemed to grab his throat, choking the words. "I'm sorry for your trouble, Sarah."

For a moment she looked at him, her clear eyes assessing the truth of his words. Then she acknowledged them with a small nod and turned away, going on into the house.

Had she believed him? Did he even believe himself? The doubts were like whirling snowflakes in his mind as he led the horse to the hitching rail.

He was sorry, of course. Sorry for the pain this caused her. But would he be sorry if she had to stop practicing? He didn't know the answer.

By the time he reached the kitchen, Sarah had shed her outer garments and was seated in a chair next to Molly, talking softly as she took a blood pressure cuff from her bag.

"I know you have questions, but just let me check on you and the boppli first, ja? That's what's most important now."

Aaron watched his sister's face as Sarah took her blood pressure and listened to her heart. Molly was visibly relaxing at Sarah's gentle touch and quiet words. Sarah had a gift—he couldn't deny that.

"Everything seems fine," Sarah said finally, folding her stethoscope and putting it back into the bag. "But you are getting upset, and you mustn't. It's bad for the baby. He or she needs a calm mammi, ja?"

Molly nodded, looking a little shamefaced. "Poor Aaron. He had to bear the brunt of my temper."

"Ach, Aaron's shoulders are strong enough to carry that," Sarah said. "But you can't get all ferhoodled about this. We will find the answers."

"But I want you to deliver my baby." Molly's blue eyes filled with tears suddenly, wrenching Aaron's heart.

"I know." Aaron knelt next to her, taking her hands in his. "But you muscht not ask Sarah to do something that will get her into trouble with the law."

"I know." Molly's fingers clutched his. "But what will we do instead?"

She was his little sister, turning to him for help and thinking he had the answers. He wished he did. "There is the doctor in town—"

"If you think I'll go to the man who's causing all this trouble for Sarah, you don't know a thing, Aaron Miller!"

"No, no, that won't do." He didn't like that idea himself.

"What about the clinic at Fostertown?" Sarah said, her voice soft. "I know it's a bit far, but you could have Ben Morgan on standby, ready to take you as soon as you go into labor. And Aaron or Nathan could stay there with you until you're ready to come home."

Molly made a visible effort to quench her tears. "Ja. I guess that is all we can do."

"If you want, I will call the clinic and make arrangements for you. Dr. Brandenmyer and his staff are fine people. They'll take care of you."

Was it wrong of him to feel secretly relieved that things had turned out this way? Molly would have his niece or nephew in a hospital setting, where the most modern of medical procedures were ready if something went wrong. He couldn't help but be relieved at that.

Sarah rose, and he stood with her. "Denke, Sarah."

She shook her head, as if it didn't merit thanks. "It's no trouble. But I must get home to Aunt Emma. She is fretting too, I'm afraid."

"She can't help worrying, I know." He walked with her to the door, holding her coat as she slipped it on. "This isn't what she wanted for you."

"No." They walked out together into the swirling snow. "But it is my responsibility, not hers. I am the one who went to Dr. Mitchell on behalf of the Englisch woman."

"Emma wouldn't fault you for that." This was hard for him to say, but he must. "She is a strong woman who always puts other people first. I have been wrong to judge her harshly all these years."

"She doesn't blame you for your feelings." Sarah put the bag into the buggy and prepared to climb up. "I'm glad if you have forgiven Aunt Emma for what happened. But that hasn't changed your mind about midwifery, has it?"

His throat clutched. "I'm sorry, Sarah." He couldn't tell her less than the truth. "But I guess it hasn't. I can't forget that if Mammi had gone to a hospital, she'd be alive today."

Chapter Seventeen

Sarah had never felt so out of place in her life. She sat erect, feet together, hands clasping each other in her lap. With her gaze lowered, she couldn't see the curious stares from the two other people waiting in the lawyer's office in Lewisburg. Or the equally curious glances from the receptionist behind the desk.

But she was aware of them, probing, wondering what an Amish woman was doing in a lawyer's office. Only the presence of Bishop Mose, sitting stolidly by her side, kept her from running away.

Gratitude filled her heart, chasing a little of the fear. Bishop Mose had arranged everything. He had contacted the lawyer the police chief recommended, he had made the appointment, and he had asked Ben Morgan to drive them today.

She let her gaze slip sideways a little. Bishop Mose sat squarely, hands planted on his knees. He looked as unmovable as an oak, and just as strong.

"Don't worry so much," he said softly, knowing, as she

did, that the others in the room wouldn't understand the dialect. "The lawyer will tell us what to do, and we will do it."

We, he'd said, and the word touched her heart. She wasn't alone.

"I do not know how to thank you for . . . all of this. Just the fact that you were willing to come with me . . ."

Her voice threatened to break, so she let the words trail off. Surely Bishop Mose knew better than anyone how great her debt was to him. By this act, he had cut off much of the criticism that would be leveled at her for seeking a lawyer's advice.

"Taking care of my people is my duty and my joy," he said. "What kind of leader would I be if I did not support you?"

"There are many who would say I got what I deserved for becoming involved with the Englisch woman and the doctor. And some who would like to see all our mothers go to a hospital." She took a breath, trying not to think of Aaron.

"All Amish do not think alike." He didn't sound perturbed about that. "All each of us can do is follow the teachings of the church and the voice of God in our hearts."

She turned that over in her mind. Did she feel confident that her actions had been in keeping with God's guidance? She thought so, but how could she be sure?

She was about to confess her doubts to Bishop Mose when the secretary stood.

"Mrs. Mast? You can go in now."

Sarah rose, feeling like a rag doll jerked upright by a child's hand. Everything she did this day was unfamiliar. Unknown. She and Bishop Mose walked into the lawyer's office.

The lawyer came forward to meet them, hand outstretched. A woman, it was—probably not much older than Sarah herself. Somehow that settled some of the butterflies dancing in her stomach.

"Mrs. Mast. Bishop. It's a pleasure to meet both of you.

I'm Sheila Downing. Come, sit down." She led them to a pair of leather chairs and sat opposite them.

Sarah managed to remove her gaze from her lap long enough to assess the woman. Had Bishop Mose known that the attorney was a woman? He must have. Maybe he thought that a woman would better understand women's feelings about having their babies.

Sheila Downing wore a skirt and blouse of a bright turquoise color, the skirt far shorter than anything an Amish woman would wear, of course. Her dark brown hair fell softly to her chin, and a glint of silver earrings showed when she turned her head.

The lawyer slid a pair of dark-rimmed glasses into place and picked up a long pad of paper. "Now, let's just go over the facts of the situation. I know a bit already from my conversation with the bishop. And I've talked with Dr. Brandenmyer at the clinic in Fostertown." She smiled. "He's a strong advocate for you, you know."

For a moment Sarah could only stare. "I . . . I know Dr. Brandenmyer, ja. But I didn't realize you would be talking to him."

"I wanted to get the medical perspective, so to speak, especially since it's the local doctor who instigated this action." She gave a crisp nod, as if congratulating herself for thinking of that. "We have to consider what our argument before the judge will be."

Sarah could feel the blood drain from her face. "I will have to go before an Englisch judge? I hoped maybe you could settle this without . . ." She let that die out, because the woman was shaking her head already.

"It doesn't work that way, I'm afraid. The only way this could be over so easily would be for you to stop practicing midwifery." There was, perhaps, a challenge in her face.

Sarah hesitated. To have it over, so quickly, but at what a cost. She couldn't give away Aunt Emma's lifetime of work so easily. She couldn't deny the gift God had given her.

"No," she said. "No, I can't do that."

She sensed approval coming from Bishop Mose. The lawyer smiled, giving a sharp nod.

"Good," Ms. Downing said. "I hoped that was what you'd say. Now, we just have to figure out our strategy. You do realize, don't you, that the Pennsylvania Department of Health doesn't certify lay midwives?"

"Ja, I know. Many states have a certification system for lay midwives, but Pennsylvania only grants recognition to certified nurse-midwives."

The lawyer looked a bit relieved, she thought, that Sarah understood the situation. "For the most part, the state government has let groups like the Amish alone when it comes to how they have their babies. But Dr. Mitchell is insisting that you're practicing medicine by delivering babies."

Sarah shook her head, still as bewildered by that as she'd been when she first heard the words. "I don't understand that. I'm not giving women prescription medicine, only herbal remedies. I'm not operating on them. Amish go to medical doctors and hospitals for that. It's the woman who has the baby. I'm just there to help her through the labor and catch the baby."

"I understand that you see it that way, but the district attorney will try to convince the judge that childbirth is a medical procedure. That's why I needed an opinion from Dr. Brandenmyer. He's highly respected and well-known for his work, and with him on our side, we have a much stronger argument."

She went on, detailing some of the arguments she would make, and Sarah realized that Ms. Downing was relishing the battle.

Sarah wasn't. All she wanted to do was go back to delivering babies. It seemed to her that the babies and mothers were being lost in all this talk of law and precedents.

"Has there ever been a case like this one in the Englisch court?" Bishop Mose seemed to be following better than she was.

"Something similar did happen a couple of years ago,"

Ms. Downing said. "Action was taken against a non-Amish lay midwife, charging that she didn't have Pennsylvania certification."

Sarah was almost afraid to ask. "How did it turn out?"

"It's not really much help to us legally, because the case was dismissed on a technicality. But it did show that the court was swayed by public opinion when a lot of people showed their support for the woman. The more local support you have, the better."

Sarah's heart sank. "I have not been here long. I'm not sure that most people in Pleasant Valley have even heard of me."

If the attorney was disappointed, she didn't let it show. "Well, we have Dr. Brandenmyer at least. That will help. Bishop, do you think any of your women would be willing to testify to Sarah's skill?"

"I couldn't ask that." Sarah's heart cringed at the thought of expecting her patients to go into an Englisch courtroom for her.

"You will not ask," Bishop Mose said. "I will do so. It's better that way."

After a moment's hesitation, Sarah nodded. Did he mean to spare her the pain of having people refuse? Or did he think women would feel they should agree if he asked them?

Neither possibility was reassuring. She thought of the babies she'd delivered here. If Dora Schmidt testified about the day Aunt Emma had her mini-stroke, that incident might do more harm than good.

And then there were the babies yet to come, and Molly's pain at having her plans for her baby's birth turned upside down.

"This order not to deliver any babies until after the hearing . . ."

Sarah hesitated, but the lawyer nodded encouragingly.

"We have a baby due soon, and the mammi is upset about going all the way to the clinic. Is it possible to get permission to deliver that one baby?" Aaron wouldn't like it, but for Molly's sake she had to try.

The lawyer leaned forward, her gaze intent on Sarah's face. "I can try to get a modification in the order. But in the meantime, you must not deliver any babies. I'm not saying they'd go that far, but they could arrest you for that. You understand, don't you? This is important, and it could prejudice the judge against you."

"I understand."

"Good." The woman sat back, looking relieved. "Well, I think that's all we can do today if you have the information I asked the bishop to have you bring?"

Sarah nodded, holding out a bulky envelope. It contained the history of her life as a midwife—her training, her work, the babies she'd delivered, information about the birthing center in Ohio. "It is all here."

"Fine." Ms. Downing took the envelope. "I'll go through all this information and begin to organize our arguments. Bishop Mose, if you'll let me know of any people who are willing to testify, that would be very helpful."

He nodded.

"I may want to come out and see your birthing rooms at some point. Take a few pictures. Is that okay?"

The bishop nodded. "So long as you do not show Sarah's face in any photos."

"Right." She stood. "That's all I need from you right now. Try not to worry about it too much. I can't guarantee that we'll win, of course, but we'll put up a good fight."

Sarah managed a smile, even though her heart ached at the words. She didn't want to fight. She just wanted to help women have their babies.

She and Bishop Mose walked in silence along the hall and down the stairs. She didn't know about him, but she felt a little dazed after the conversation with the lawyer.

As they approached the door to the street, Sarah could see through the glass panel that Ben's car waited at the curb.

"I will be glad to get home," she said as they stepped outside. "Aunt Emma will—"

She lost whatever she was about to say as a man with a camera popped up in front of her, snapping. Gasping, she turned her face away, only to find another close at hand. A woman thrust a tape recorder at her face.

"Give us a comment about this case, Mrs. Mast. Is the DA going to shut you down?"

"Look this way," someone else shouted.

For a terrifying moment she was caught between them, like a mouse cornered between two cats.

Then Bishop Mose grabbed her on one side and Ben on the other. They hustled her into the car. She held her hands in front of her face, near tears, while the two men piled into the car after her. Ben, muttering to himself, accelerated out of the parking space.

"I'm right sorry about that," he said once they were safely away. "If I'd been faster, I could have gone around to the back, but I was afraid you'd walk out while I was doing that. Ghouls," he muttered, and she understood he meant the reporters.

"I never thought of such a thing. Why are they interested in me?"

"Amish are always news, I guess," Ben said.

"Ja, especially when we butt up against Englisch laws." Bishop Mose shook his head. "I should have expected it." His voice was heavy with regret.

Was the regret for the reporters? Or for coming to her defense?

A chill went through Sarah, and it was all she could do to keep her body from shaking.

How could she go through with this? How could she possibly do it?

More snow began in midmorning the next day, drifting down as scattered flakes. Glancing out, Sarah could only think how exactly the sky matched her mood—dark, heavy, brooding.

"Looks like we're getting some snow." Talking to Aunt Emma about the weather was far better than talking about the subject that weighed on her heart. No matter how generous Aunt Emma was in her support, Sarah couldn't forget that she'd brought this trouble on them.

"Ja, I heard tell we'd get an inch or two today." Aunt Emma rocked and knitted, the click of her needles keeping pace with the squeak of the maple rocking chair.

"What are you making?" Sarah sat down across from her, picking up the mending basket. She may as well do something useful, too.

"Socks for Jonas's oldest boy. He goes through them too fast." Aunt Emma was silent for a moment. "I had a note from Jonas in the mail, wanting me to go and stay with them for a few weeks." The needles clicked. "I might do that."

Sarah's throat went tight. Aunt Emma didn't want to be here any longer. Maybe she didn't want to witness her business disappearing. Or maybe she didn't want to be associated with Sarah in all that was going on.

Sarah cleared her throat. "That might be gut."

What else could she say?

By noon the snow was piling up outside, with the wind sending drifts forming against the house. From the front window Sarah could normally see the road, but now the place where it should be was an expanse of unmarked white.

"Nothing has gone by on the road in over an hour," she said, her breath forming a cloud on the pane of glass.

Aunt Emma moved to stand next to her. "Looks more likely we're getting a couple of feet than a couple of inches." She turned. "I'll put some soup on for lunch. That'll taste gut. We're luckier than the Englisch when it comes to weather like this, I think. We don't have to worry about the electric going off."

"We'll stay warm, no matter what," Sarah agreed. She

followed Aunt Emma to the kitchen. "I'll slice some bread to go with the soup."

She was just reaching for the loaf when someone or something pounded against the back door. Exchanging a startled look with her aunt, she hurried to open it.

Benjamin stood there, covered with so much snow that she could barely make him out.

"Benjamin! Goodness, what are you doing out in this? Komm in." She ushered him into the warmth, closing the door behind him. "Get out of those wet clothes and warm up."

"I can't." He unwound his muffler, revealing a young, frightened face. "Sarah, you must komm, schnell. It's Molly. She says she's in labor, and Aaron and Nathan are away, and I can't get through to anyone to help."

"You have a phone in the shop, don't you?" Aunt Emma guided him close to the stove.

"Ja, but the lines must be down. Please, you must help."

"I'll try our phone." Sarah grabbed her coat, silent prayers on lips. *Please, dear Father, be with Molly now.*

The instant she stepped onto the porch, the wind caught her, whipping her skirt around her legs. She fought her way along the house, one hand against its sturdy wooden planks, until she reached the phone shanty.

Inside, she was sheltered from the wind with Aaron's workmanship strong and protective around her. She picked up the receiver, breath going out in a sigh of relief when she heard a dial tone.

It took three tries before the 911 operator answered, and even then, she was not encouraging. Half the county was snowbound, it seemed, and traffic at a standstill. She would alert the closest paramedics, but it might be hours before they could clear a way through.

Trying to think, Sarah fought her way back to the house. Benjamin lunged up from the chair Aunt Emma had probably forced him into. "Did you get them? Is it all right?"

"They will komm when they can, but the roads—" She gestured helplessly.

"Then you must." Benjamin started wrapping the muffler around his face again. "Hurry, Sarah. She's all alone."

Sarah looked at Aunt Emma, but it was the lawyer's voice that rang in her head. If she did this, she could go to jail. But if she didn't—

"I must go."

"Ja." Aunt Emma nodded, conviction filling her face. "I will come, too."

Sarah shook her head. "If I get into trouble for delivering Molly's baby, someone must still be here to take care of things."

She could see that sink in. Finally Aunt Emma seemed to give in. "I will get your bag. And you must not try to walk. I still have the old sleigh, and Dolly is trained to pull it. You'll stand a better chance of getting through that way."

Sarah glanced at Benjamin. Aunt Emma was right. That was their best chance.

"I'll go hitch up," Benjamin said. Grabbing his mittens, he banged out the door.

Sarah checked her bag, trying to calm her mind as she considered what she might need. Black cohosh for a stalled labor, shepherd's purse for hemorrhage, motherwort to calm the nerves, raspberry-leaf tea to help with the labor . . . all the remedies she had were there.

Aunt Emma tied a scarf around Sarah's neck, tucking it in, and then paused, her hand on Sarah's cheek. "Maybe the paramedics will get there before the baby. Maybe you'll just have to keep Molly calm and comfortable."

"Maybe." She breathed a silent prayer. "But I will do what I must. No matter the consequences."

"You will do what is right." Aunt Emma held Sarah's face in both hands. "I'm sorry if I doubted you, my Sarah. When I said that I would not have gone to Dr. Mitchell for the Englisch woman—it was my own cowardice that would have stopped me."

"No—"

"Ja," she said firmly. "But we must always do what we

know is right, no matter what the cost." She pulled Sarah into a quick, strong hug. "Da Herr sei mitt du."

The Lord be with you. They would need that, all of them.

Sarah followed Benjamin outside, turning her face away from the wind, thankful for the protection of her bonnet. Snow still fell so heavily that the shoulders of her coat were white by the time she reached the sleigh.

Dolly seemed energized by the snow. She tossed her head as if she were a filly again, eager to move. Sarah climbed in next to Benjamin, and they slid off down the lane.

Sarah tucked the blanket over their laps. The sleigh was totally open, without the protection an enclosed buggy would provide. Snow blew into her face, and the wind seemed to find every chink in the heavy clothes she wore. Benjamin must be half-frozen.

But when she looked at him, she detected a bit of a smile in his eyes. "Never drove a sleigh before," he said, maybe in explanation.

Sarah patted his hand. "Me, neither. It would be fun if we weren't so worried about Molly."

"Ja." He clucked to Dolly, urging her into a trot when they reached the surface of the road. "The snow's packed down a little on the road. Maybe we can make better time." He was still for a moment. "Will Molly be all right?" His voice cracked a little on the question.

"Molly is a strong, healthy young woman. Having a baby is a natural thing, you know. Women were having babies without even midwives for generations."

"I know." His lips pressed together, eyes narrowed against the snow. "But they weren't my sister."

"You love Molly," she said gently. "It's natural to worry, but she and her boppli are in God's hands, and He loves them, too."

"My mammi died." The words burst out of him. "I lived, but my mammi died."

That was it, of course. Aaron might think he could protect his siblings, but by not telling Benjamin the truth, he'd left the boy open to imagine the worst—to think that he was somehow responsible.

Sarah breathed a silent prayer for guidance. "What happened with your mammi was very unusual. In all the hundreds of babies Aunt Emma has delivered, that was the only time something like that went wrong." She hesitated, trying to find a way to comfort him without betraying any secrets. "Aunt Emma said that when you came, so strong and healthy, your mamm was so happy. She held you, talked to you, told you she loved you."

Aunt Emma hadn't provided details, but Sarah knew, anyway. Every baby she'd delivered had been greeted that way.

"I always thought . . . was afraid . . . that it was my fault." His voice choked. "That maybe Emma had to choose between saving me or saving my mamm."

"Ach, why would you think such a thing?" She shook his arm gently. "That's just not so. It was only afterward that something went wrong." She didn't want to give him details, fearing that would only make him worry more about Molly. "Just you remember that your mammi loved you. And loves you still."

Dolly slowed, unable to go faster despite Benjamin's urging. The snow lay deeper here, blowing across the road in a never-ending curtain of white.

Sarah glanced at Benjamin's face. He looked thoughtful, but at least not so agonized as he had a moment ago.

"Did Molly tell you how far apart her pains were?"

"Ach, ja, I was supposed to tell you. Fifteen minutes, she said."

"Well, that's not so bad. First babies can take a long time getting here. We should have plenty of time for the paramedics."

If they could make it at all, she added silently. They'd have to have a plow to lead the way, bad as it was.

"Move on, Dolly," Benjamin called to the horse. "Almost there now, and I'll have a fine warm place for you in our barn."

"There's your mailbox," Sarah said, relief flooding her. They were almost there. "Why is Aaron not at home?"

"He and Nathan went to town this morning to do some work for Bishop Mose. He'd never have gone if he'd thought the snow would get so bad."

"No, I'm sure he wouldn't." As protective as Aaron was, Molly had probably had to urge him to go. "Well, maybe by the time Aaron gets home, he'll have a brand-new niece or nephew."

"Ja." Benjamin grinned, probably thinking he'd score off his brothers if he were the first to meet the new arrival.

They pulled up to the back door. Grabbing her bag, Sarah clambered out of the sleigh. "I'll go check on Molly while you settle Dolly. Give her an extra scoop of oats for this."

She hurried to the back door, prayers rising.

Molly turned from the sink, relief filling her face. "Sarah. Thank the gut Lord you are here. I was so scared when the contractions started and only Benjamin was here." She reached out a hand, and Sarah clasped it reassuringly.

"No need to worry. No need at all." Sarah shrugged out of her wet, heavy coat. "I'm here, and the paramedics will come as soon as they can get through."

"But what if they can't make it?" Fear edged Molly's voice. "If you deliver my baby, they might put you in jail."

"If, if," Sarah chided. She guided Molly to a seat and opened her bag. "Let's not worry so much about what might happen. All you need to know is that you and the boppli are safe."

"Ja." Molly's tension eased visibly. "You are here. I knew Benjamin wouldn't let me down."

She was remembering her father, letting her mother down when her life was at stake. Sarah could think of nothing to say that would erase that memory from Molly's mind.

She checked Molly quickly. Just as she put the stethoscope down, a contraction hit. She glanced at the clock, automatically timing it.

"I didn't want to have the boppli here." Molly gasped through the contraction. "He'll remember—"

"Don't talk. Just breathe."

Aaron would remember the day his mammi died. But this was a different day. Molly would be fine. Sarah had to believe that. Molly was in God's hands.

And if she had to deliver Molly's baby, and the police came to arrest her because of it? Well, she would be in God's hands then, too.

Chapter Eighteen

Aaron's breath was coming in short gasps as he and Nathan finally started up the lane to the house. It took an effort just to pick up one foot and put it in front of the other. He glanced at his brother, and Nathan managed a grin.

"A long, cold way from the crossroads," he said.

"Ja." A very long way when you were slogging through snow above your boot tops. "Glad we're home."

Nathan, shielding his eyes from the driving snow, looked toward the barn. "Whose cutter is that, pulled up by the barn door?"

Apprehension snaked along Aaron's spine as he focused on the sleigh. "Emma's the only one I know who has a sleigh like that."

It could mean nothing. Maybe Emma had offered it to Benjamin to take a joy ride in the snow.

Or maybe not. He forced his feet into a trot, made it to the back porch, and lunged through the door.

Benjamin, standing at the stove, spun around at his entrance, relief spreading across his face. "Aaron! It is ser gut you are home."

"What's happening? Molly?" He yanked off his mittens and coat. "Where is she?"

"Upstairs. It's all right. Sarah is with her."

Aaron bent, pulling off his boots and scattering snow across the clean kitchen floor. He'd clean it up as soon as he saw for himself that Molly was fine.

"We saw the cutter. Sarah drove over?"

Benjamin was already shaking his head. "Molly is in labor. I had to go for Sarah."

Aaron could only stare at him. "You should have called the paramedics. Why didn't you—"

"I did."

Aaron barely heard Benjamin's protest as he bolted toward the stairs. Molly in labor, and he hadn't been here. And Benjamin had gotten Sarah instead of calling for help.

He rushed into the room. Molly sat in the rocking chair, Sarah beside her. His sister looked up and smiled when she saw him.

"Ach, I heard all that noise downstairs and knew it was you," Molly said.

He went to her, kneeling and taking her hand. "Benjamin said . . . is the baby really coming?"

"Definitely." Her hand tightened on his, and she gasped. She leaned forward, and Sarah began stroking her back.

"Breathe, remember." Her voice was soft. "Count the seconds. It will be over soon."

Soon. It seemed an eternity before Molly leaned back again. She let out a whoosh of air. "They're getting stronger."

Sarah nodded. "Gut. That's what we want."

"No." Aaron didn't realize he'd spoken until the word was out. He stood. "This isn't right. Benjamin should have called nine-one-one. Why didn't he?"

"He tried." Sarah stood, too, facing him. "Please, Aaron,

just calm down. Your shop phone must have been knocked out by the snow. So Benjamin walked over to get me."

His hands clenched. That telephone . . . might know it would go out the first time it was really needed.

"I'll check it again. Maybe . . ."

"There's no need. I called and asked them to send the rescue squad. They'll be here as soon as they can get through. In the meantime, I will help Molly. There's nothing else to be done."

He looked down at his little sister to find her eyes sparkling with amusement.

"Aaron doesn't want to hear that there's nothing for him to do, ain't so?"

"But . . . if we could get someone with a snowmobile. I think Jack Tyler has one. I'll go to his place."

"Jack Tyler is two miles from here. By the time you got there, it would be too late." Sarah's face was sympathetic, but her voice was firm.

"And if you think I'm getting on a snowmobile in this condition, you're ferhoodled," Molly said, her voice sharpening. She gave a little gasp. "Sarah—"

"It's all right." All Sarah's attention went immediately back to Molly. "You're doing fine, just fine. It's hard work, having a baby. He or she will be here soon." Her voice soothed, coaxed, calmed Molly through the pain.

When she finally leaned back again, Aaron could turn his attention to the problem. "There's really nothing I can do? I still think—"

Sarah stood, took his arm, and guided him firmly out of the room. Once they'd reached the hall, she let go.

"Why did you do that? I was just asking—"

"Molly needs you to be strong just now. Strong and calm. Not firing questions at her." She patted his arm as if he were a child in need of comforting.

It should make him mad. Instead, it made him smile. "I guess I am being a little crazy. That's my little sister in there. I knew how to help her with broken dolls and bumped knees. I don't know how to do this."

"Molly is fine. Believe it or not, women do know how to have babies."

"But you." He closed his hand over hers. "You are risking everything by being here. If the paramedics don't get here in time, if you—"

She put her hand gently over his lips to stop him. "Don't. I've already been through that with Molly. If they don't come, I will deliver her baby. The rest is in God's hands." She drew her hand away. "Now I must go back to Molly. And you should go and reassure your brothers."

He nodded. "Benjamin . . ."

"Benjamin did exactly what had to be done to take care of Molly." She hesitated, and he could see that there was more she had to say. "He talked a little. Aaron, Benjamin fears that he is responsible for your mamm's dying."

A hard hand seemed to close over his heart. "No. He can't."

"He does. I tried to reassure him, but he needs to hear it from you. Aaron, he needs to hear the truth."

He was still shaking his head when Molly called out, and Sarah turned and went back into the room.

She couldn't be right. That was all he could think as he went back down the stairs. Surely, if Benjamin felt that way, he'd have confided in his big brother. Wouldn't he?

Nathan and Benjamin both looked at him as he entered the kitchen, an identical question in their faces.

"Molly?" Nathan said. "Is she all right? Is it true, what Benj says?"

"Ja, she is all right. She's fine, even teasing a little between . . . when she's resting. Sarah is taking gut care of her."

Nathan grinned, bouncing back quickly as he always did. "We're going to have a little niece or nephew today. I wonder what she'll call him. Or her. Do you think she wants anything?" He turned as if to go up the stairs.

"Don't disturb them now." The words came out more

sharply than he meant, and he regretted it. He didn't want to infect the others with his own fear. "We could all stand to eat something, and Molly will need a light meal once the baby comes. Why don't you get two or three quarts of that chicken noodle soup Rachel Zook made and heat it up?"

"Ja, right, that would taste great." Nathan spun and headed for the basement steps and the shelves where extra canned goods were stored when the pantry was full. "I'll bring up the clean sheets that are hanging in the basement. They should be dry by now, and Sarah might need them."

Nathan was all right. But Benjamin—their little brother still looked at Aaron with fear in his eyes. And that meant Sarah was right. Aaron had been trying to protect Benjamin, but he'd just caused more trouble.

"She really is fine." He went to Benj, putting his hands on the boy's shoulders. "And you did exactly right, going to Sarah, taking care of Molly that way." He ruffled his hair. "Mammi would be proud of you."

Nathan stumped back up the stairs, his arms filled with quart jars. "Don't give him a swelled head," he said. He grinned at his little brother. "I have to admit it, though. You took care of things."

"I hope." Benjamin's blue eyes were still shadowed though. "Mammi—you said she'd be proud of me. Sarah said she loved me. But if I hadn't been born, maybe she'd still be here."

"That's not so." Aaron tilted the boy's chin up so that Benjamin met his eyes. "I'm telling you the truth, now. It's not on account of you that Mammi died."

Sarah was right. The truth was needed. He looked from one to the other.

"You'd better both hear this, so you'll understand. After you were born, Benjamin, something went wrong. Emma knew right away that Mammi had to go to the hospital, and she sent Daad to get help. But he never made it. He was drunk, and he never got help. And that's the truth." He took a breath, feeling as if he hadn't inhaled in a long while.

Nathan was frowning, shaking his head a little. "Why didn't you ever tell us before?"

"I didn't know. The only ones who knew were Emma and the neighbor who found him, maybe Bishop Mose, too. They thought it would only hurt us to hear it. Maybe they were right then, but now . . . well, we're all grown. We deserve to know the truth."

"Poor Mammi." Nathan's eyes filled with tears. "And poor Daadi, too, knowing he failed her."

Aaron grasped his shoulder. "You have a gut heart, Nathan."

"That's why you were so upset about the beer," Benjamin said. "It wondered me why you got so angry. You were afraid I'm like Daadi." Benjamin looked up, eyes wide and frightened. "What if I am?"

Aaron hugged him close, his heart expanding with love. "We know the answer to that already. When a crisis came, you kept your head and did the right thing in a difficult situation. You're not like Daadi. You're turning into exactly the kind of man Mammi would want you to be."

Benjamin leaned his head against Aaron's shoulder, just as he had when he'd been a toddler, leaning on his big brother, and Aaron could feel the relief that went through him.

"That's not so hard," he said. "I just thought what you would do, and I did it."

A glance out the window told Sarah that the snow still fell heavily, darkening the day. Hours had gone by, and there'd been no sign of the paramedics.

Sarah had checked the baby periodically with the fetal stethoscope and been reassured each time. Molly's brothers had been in and out, bringing soup, tea, encouragement. Molly had spent most of her time either walking slowly or rocking in the rocking chair through the contractions.

Molly turned her head restlessly against the chair back in the aftermath of a contraction. "It's hard."

"Ja, it is. The hardest work you'll ever do." Sarah took Molly's arm. "Let's move you to the bed for a bit. Maybe you'll be more comfortable there."

Molly nodded, and together they crossed the few feet to the bed. Sarah arranged pillows around her. "Some women find it easiest to rest on their side between contractions, supported by pillows. Why don't we try that?"

Molly had slept in this bed as a child, had looked out the window at the old oak tree now covered with snow. She would be gaining comfort and reassurance from the surroundings, far different from an impersonal hospital room.

Once Molly was settled, Sarah massaged in a small, steady circle on Molly's lower back. Sarah's hand and arm had begun to ache from the constant movement, but the massage eased Molly's discomfort.

"That's right. Let your body do the work. Think about the contraction opening a door to let your baby into the world."

"What if I'm not doing this right? What if I'm too tired?" Molly's voice caught on a note of self-doubt.

Sarah had heard it so many times—the doubt that crept in when the goal was nearly reached. Every first-time mother seemed to hit that point.

"You're doing wonderful gut, Molly. Just exactly right." She picked up the cup of raspberry tea Nathan had brewed at her direction and held it to Molly's lips. "Drink a little more of this. It will help with the contractions."

"The contractions are so fast." Molly sipped and then caught her breath as another one grew.

"Breathe, Molly, breathe easy." Sarah set the tea aside. "Feel yourself float right up to the top of the contraction. Just go with it and picture your baby pushing his way out into the world." Some women seemed helped by that image, so she always used it.

Molly nodded, but her eyes were round with apprehension. She was tiring, her concentration slipping. Sarah couldn't let her focus on fear, or labor would turn from exhausting work to pain.

"Why don't we call Aaron in to help?" She knew all the reasons why that wasn't wise, and one compelling reason why it was. Molly needed someone to lean on right now. Her husband couldn't be here, but her big brother could.

"He shouldn't . . . He can't . . ." Molly was obviously thinking of all those reasons against bringing Aaron into the room. Then she bit her lip, tears welling in her eyes. "I need Aaron. Tell him. Tell him I need my big brother."

Sarah went quickly to the door. She could hear movement downstairs and knew that Aaron wouldn't be far away.

"Aaron, Molly wants you with her. Will you komm?"

She didn't wait for an answer. She knew already what it would be. Aaron would never deny his siblings what they needed out of his own fear. That was the kind of man he was—strong, reliable, self-sacrificing.

By the time she'd returned to Molly, Aaron was there, hurrying into the room, his face drawn. "Molly? Are you all right?"

"Molly's fine," Sarah said. She touched his arm, willing him to take his cue from her. "But it will soon be time for her to push, and she needs someone strong to lean on. She needs her big brother."

Deftly she rearranged the pillows, spreading a sheet over Molly and easing her into a better position for pushing.

"Now, you will sit against the headboard here, and Molly will lean back against you." She looked up, her gaze meeting his, and nodded in reassurance. "It's all right. You can do this."

He didn't answer. He just slid into the position she'd indicated, letting Molly rest against him.

Denke, Father.

She coached Molly, talking gently, calmly, encouraging her on with the job. All her focus had to be on Molly and the baby as Molly moved into the next stage of labor. She was just as wrapped up in the task as Molly was.

"You're going to push this baby out now. He or she is

ready to come. Just take a breath when the contraction starts and push down."

Molly nodded. She clutched Aaron's arms and pushed.

"Gut, gut job." Sarah massaged with oil, easing the passageway for the baby.

Intent as she was, she couldn't help glancing at Aaron now and then. She saw the moment when the fear began to fade from his eyes. Soon he picked up on her words, speaking to Molly in a gentle, encouraging way.

"That's it, Molly. You can do it. You could always do anything you set your mind on. Even when you were a tiny girl. Remember when you climbed to the top of the oak tree? No one thought you could do it, but you did." His arms reddened where Molly gripped them, but his voice stayed calm.

Molly gave a watery chuckle. "You taught me."

"I did. Maybe I'll get to teach my little niece or nephew."

Finally, after what Molly must think was a lifetime of pushing, the baby crowned. "Stop pushing now, Molly," Sarah said. "Just breathe nice and easy for a moment. The baby is coming out, and I need to ease the way." She couldn't help holding her own breath at this point. "Okay, now push."

Molly groaned with the effort, and the baby's head slipped through.

"One more push. You can do it." On her words the baby slid out into her waiting hands, wet and wiggling and full of life. "It's a boy. You and Jacob have a son, Molly." The baby's cry punctuated her words.

Sarah held him for just a second, heart filled with prayers of thanks. And then she put him in Molly's arms.

This was the moment—that precious moment when the new mother looked at her baby, cradling him close against her, murmuring words of love that only he could hear. This made anything worthwhile, even the cost she might have to pay for her actions.

Aaron bent close, his face filled with awe, and dropped

a kiss on his sister's head. Then he touched the baby's tiny hand with his large one, so gently. He looked up, meeting Sarah's gaze, and joy filled her heart to overflowing.

Perhaps there would never be anything more between her and Aaron, but they had shared this wondrous moment together.

Sarah stirred the pot of chicken soup on the stove, inhaling its comforting aroma as it warmed. Molly's brothers were upstairs with her, staring in wonderment at the new arrival. She'd give them a little time together while she prepared a light meal for Molly.

And she'd had a sudden need to get away from Aaron. That experience of working together to birth Molly's baby had been too intense, and her feelings for him were so raw that she feared giving herself away with every look, with every word.

A step sounded behind her. She didn't need to look to know it was Aaron who stood there.

"This will be ready soon." She stirred, not turning toward him. "Molly probably won't want much, she's still so excited, but she should eat something."

"Ja, she should. She worked hard."

He moved closer—so close Sarah could feel the warmth of him. She yearned to lean back, to feel his arms close around her. But she couldn't.

"Does she need me?" She half turned, wooden spoon in her hand.

He shook his head. "I wanted to ask if I should chase the boys out. I don't want her to tire herself."

"She's running on sheer joy, I think. When I take her meal up, I'll have them leave. Then I think she will settle down and sleep for a bit."

"She's fretting over not being able to let Jacob know right away, but there's nothing we can do about that." He gestured toward the window and the still-swirling snow. "It might be slacking off a little, but it's going to be a record-breaker for sure."

He'd moved a little toward the window as he spoke, and Sarah seemed able to breathe again.

"No way of getting through to the rescue squad, either," she said. "At least . . . well, I could take the sleigh back to Aunt Emma's and see if the phone is still working."

"Someone should, but not you. Molly needs you here. I'll send Nathan and Benjamin, and they must go soon, before it gets dark. They can tell Emma you're staying here."

She must have lifted her eyebrows a little at that, because he smiled.

"I'm being too bossy, ain't so? That's what Molly would say, but you are too polite. I mean, will you stay, please, Sarah? Our cousin Katie is to come and help out, but she lives clear over in Columbia County, and with this weather, it's hard to say when she'll get here."

"Ja, of course I'll stay to help Molly." Her brothers, well-intentioned though they might be, wouldn't have the least idea how to care for a new mammi and a newborn boppli. "As long as I can." She tried to keep her voice from quavering.

Aaron took a hasty step toward her. "You are thinking of the law? Ja, of course you are. But there's no reason why the police have to know about this. We must tell the truth if asked, but we don't have to volunteer it."

"Ach, Aaron, you know Pleasant Valley better than that. With the best intentions in the world, folks can't keep a secret. And there are some who'd like fine to see the midwife practice closed. Someone will tell."

"Sarah, you must not come to harm for what you've done today." He clasped both her hands in his. "That would not be right. You didn't want to break the rules. I can't let you be hurt because you helped my sister."

His hands were tight on hers, and she could feel the beat of his pulse. It was like an engine, driving hers, too, so that her heart raced with his.

She looked up at him, knowing she must be giving away

her feelings but unable to stop. "It . . . it is gut of you to care about my troubles, but—"

"Not just your troubles, Sarah." He let go of her hands, but only so that he could cradle her face between his palms. "I care about you. Since the moment I saw you standing alone at the bus station, I've known that there was something between us. I love you, Sarah. I must keep you safe."

Her eyes filled with tears she didn't want to shed. "Aaron, I . . ." And then she said no more, as his arms went around her and his lips found hers.

The world seemed to spin around her, and then to narrow down to the circle of Aaron's arms. She heard his breath, listened to the steady beat of his heart. He drew her close into his arms.

"Ach, Sarah," he murmured. "I want a future with you. Tell me that's what you want, too."

"Ja." She whispered the word, drawing back so that she could see his face. There must be no mistake in what she was about to say. "Aaron, there is something you must know before we can talk of the future. I think . . . I fear that I cannot have children. If I can't—"

He put his palm gently over her lips. "If you can't, then that is a sorrow we will bear together."

She searched his face for any shadow of doubt. There was no trace of condemnation in his eyes—only love.

"If you are sure . . ."

"I am." He smiled. "Besides, we'll have plenty of nieces and nephews to love."

She could let herself believe, and she smiled in response. "Better not mention that to Molly for a few days, at least."

He nodded, sobering. "About that—we will make the lawyers understand. You called the paramedics. It was no one's fault they couldn't get here. It was an emergency."

Hope flickered faintly. "Maybe they will not blame me."

"Any sensible person would know you couldn't risk Molly and the baby dying from lack of care when you were right here." He stroked her cheek. "They'll understand you couldn't do anything else, and you'll agree to close the practice and this trouble will all be over. You'll be safe."

His words sank in slowly. He just assumed that she would bend to the law and give up the midwife practice.

Her heart seemed to chill. Her husband's love had been conditional on her having a baby. It looked as if Aaron's love was conditional, too . . . on her giving up the midwife practice.

She took a step back, and his arms dropped. Maybe he knew already what she would say.

"I can't do that, Aaron. I have to do what is right."

"Sarah, don't. You don't have to fight this. I'm trying to protect you."

Of course. That was what Aaron did. But he couldn't protect her this time.

"I know." Her heart was heavy in her chest. "I know you mean it for the best, Aaron, but I can't do that. Being a midwife is a gift from God. I can't give it up without a fight."

"Isn't our love a gift from God, too?" He stepped back, not attempting to touch her, and she was grateful for that.

"Ja." Her voice broke. "A very precious one. But not if I can only have it by giving up what I think is right."

His face closed. He couldn't or wouldn't understand, and she had no more words to explain it to him.

"I will tell the authorities that you saved Molly and the baby by being here. I hope that will be enough."

She nodded, fighting to hang on to whatever was left of her composure. "Denke, Aaron," she whispered.

Love was over between them before it had a chance.

Chapter Nineteen

Sarah wasn't sure so unlikely a group had ever gathered in Aunt Emma's living room. She and Aunt Emma sat side by side, facing Bishop Mose and the woman lawyer. Her heart filled with gratitude for her aunt's presence, but she couldn't help thinking about the person whose support she longed for.

She hadn't seen Aaron in two days . . . not since she'd come home once the blocked roads had been cleared and Molly's cousin had arrived to help. She probably wouldn't be seeing him anytime soon. It was too painful.

"Well, let's get the worst alternative out of the way first," the attorney said briskly. "Sarah is not going to jail."

Sarah let out a breath, so relieved that she was dizzy with it. Aunt Emma squeezed her hand, and Bishop Mose murmured his thanksgiving.

"What happened? I thought . . . the police chief said—" She'd tried to resign herself to face arrest, sure that would follow her disobedience.

"Your friend Aaron Miller was on my doorstep the moment the roads were cleared, I think." The woman smiled. "He was very convincing. Said that if you hadn't acted when you did, his sister and her baby might well have died. Is that true?"

"No one could say that for sure." She couldn't say less than the truth. "Molly is a healthy young woman. She might have delivered without help, but I am glad she didn't have to."

"It's clear to anyone with a grain of common sense that you did the right thing," Bishop Mose said, his tone putting him clearly on Sarah's side. "Bad as that storm was, who knows when help would have gotten there? Not in time, ain't so?"

She nodded. She'd been half-afraid that the bishop would take her to task for disobedience, but it was obvious he hadn't considered such a thing.

"That was the convincing argument for the judge," Ms. Downing said. "I checked with the emergency response office and confirmed that you had called before you went anywhere near Molly Peachey. And I had a statement from the dispatcher."

Her smile broadened.

"He pointed out that he had three vehicle accidents, four suspected heart attacks, a kidney dialysis patient needing care, and no way to get his rescue trucks anywhere. In his words, 'Women have been having babies since the beginning of time without paramedics there.' I repeated that to the judge, and I think it made an impression."

"Ja, it's true." Aunt Emma seemed to lose her awe of the attorney as she spoke. "Sarah has probably delivered far more healthy babies than that young doctor, too."

"Another good point." The attorney scribbled a note on the pad in her lap. "In any event, common sense won the day. There will be no arrest, but the hearing has been moved up." She paused. "It's on Friday."

"This Friday?" Sarah managed to get the words out without sounding as panicky as she felt.

The woman nodded. "So we have to move along." She pulled a camera from her bag. "As I said, I'd like some photos of your birthing rooms, to show that you have a competent operation here."

"Ja, fine." Sarah rose. "It's this way." She couldn't prevent a flicker of fear as she led Ms. Downing to the first of the birthing rooms. Would they ever be delivering another baby here?

"Very nice." The lawyer glanced around, snapping pictures.

Sarah stepped carefully out of the line of her shots. Bishop Mose and Aunt Emma had stayed behind, and she could hear the soft murmur of their voices.

"Will you tell me something?" she asked.

"If I can." Ms. Downing looked at her expectantly.

"Why did you want to come here? I'm sure you don't visit all of your clients in their homes."

"Well, no." She hesitated, as if framing her answer. "You see, I've never represented an Amish client before. Never known all that much about the Amish, in fact. It seemed to me I should see for myself."

"That is only right. You had no way of knowing I was telling you the truth about what we do here."

Her lips twitched. "I didn't really doubt you, Sarah, not when Bishop Mose brought you in. He's pretty impressive. Somehow you can't believe he'd ever do anything but what's right."

"Ja." She had to blink back tears. "He is a gut man."

"And it's obvious this isn't some hole-in-the-wall operation." Her gesture took in the birthing room.

"It is modeled after the birthing center where I worked in Ohio," Sarah said. "We had a much bigger operation there and a local doctor who worked with us."

Sheila Downing nodded. "I've already spoken with him. He's not able to travel here for the hearing, but he is sending a statement of his support, both for midwifery in general and for you in particular."

"That is gut of him." She paused, trying not to give in to the fear that was her constant companion these days.

"Do we have a chance?"

Ms. Downing leaned against the foot of the bed. "Remember, this is just a hearing to determine whether there's a case to go to trial. The judge could rule that there isn't. That would be best from our point of view."

"Do you think that's what will happen?"

"Honestly, it's impossible to say. The law is pretty murky, it seems to me. If the judge feels that way, he'll be looking for a reason to dismiss the charges. My job is to give him a tool to do that."

Sarah nodded. "I understand, I think."

"You know, that's what your friend asked me, too. I gave him the same answer."

"My friend?" Her mind was blank.

"Aaron Miller. You have a strong advocate in him."

Sarah turned away, not wanting the woman to see her face. "He is grateful that I helped his sister."

But not grateful enough to think her practice worth fighting for. No matter how much she appreciated what Aaron had done in going to the attorney, she couldn't forget that.

Aaron walked the shoveled path from the shop to the house, consciously trying to force a smile onto his face. Molly was sharp as a whip at reading his moods, and it wouldn't do to have her guess his feelings.

He'd been trying to keep Sarah out of his thoughts—trying and failing. He'd offered Sarah his love, a life together, and she'd turned him down for a fight she couldn't win.

He was right. He had to believe that. So why did he feel so wrong?

He glanced up as he approached the steps. Molly stood in the open doorway, holding Baby Jacob in her arms.

"Ach, Molly, what are you doing?" He took the steps

quickly, caught her arm, and ushered her back into the warm kitchen. "You should not be going out into the cold. Or the boppli, either."

"I have to talk to you." Molly's eyes were suspiciously bright, as if she hovered on the brink of tears.

Sarah had warned him that Molly might be more easily upset these days. He should be comforting and reassuring. But why did every thought have to lead back to Sarah?

"Komm, now." He shed his coat, hanging it in the back hall. "You don't want to catch a cold and greet Jacob with a red nose, do you?"

Molly's husband should arrive tomorrow, if all went well, and none too soon. She'd been missing him.

"I'm fine, and so is little Jacob. But I have to talk to you."

"Well, I am here, so you can talk. Where is Katie?"

Why isn't she keeping you from worrying? That was what he wanted to say, but he supposed that was an unreasonable expectation, even for their determined cousin.

"Katie is upstairs, changing the bed. She doesn't have to be coddling me every minute, you know." Little Jacob wiggled in her arms, making small sounds, and she bounced him gently. "Anna was here."

"Ja, I saw her buggy." He lifted the towel that covered the basket on the counter. "Looks like she brought schnitz pies. Better make sure Benjamin doesn't get his hands on them before supper. You know how he is about dried apples."

"She also brought news. Sarah's hearing in front of the judge is on Friday. Friday!" Her voice rose. "Did you know that?"

His heart winced. "I heard."

"Why didn't you tell me?" Her fingers dug into his arm. "We must do something."

Calm and reassuring, he reminded himself. "Komm, sit down." He detached her fingers from his arm and tried to lead her to the rocking chair.

She dug in her heels, refusing to be moved. "Stop talking to me as if I'm a six-year-old."

Obviously he wasn't so gut at the calming and reassuring. "I'm sorry."

A tear spilled over onto her cheek. "No, I'm sorry. But, Aaron, this is serious. Poor Sarah."

"Ja." His voice was flat. "I know it is serious." It was what he'd tried to prevent. If Sarah had listened to him . . .

"We have to do something," Molly insisted. "We must help Sarah."

He caught her hand, holding it firmly in his. "You must calm down. That is what Sarah would be saying right now."

"I will calm down when you tell me there is something we can do to help Sarah."

"Molly . . ." She was pummeling his already sore heart. "I have already done what I can. I don't see what else we can do."

"Anna says she is going to the hearing, to show Sarah her support. I should go, too."

"No, that you must not do. You're not ready to go so far." He glanced over her shoulder. "Here is Katie, and I know she will agree with me."

Katie looked from him to Molly's tear-stained face. "And what is it that I will agree with, Aaron?"

A man could never take Katie's acceptance of his opinion for granted. Maybe that was why Katie was still unmarried at twenty-five.

"Molly wants to go clear to Lewisburg on Friday to go to a hearing in the Englisch court."

"Ja, the midwife. I heard about it." Katie looked thoughtful. "I would like to go, too. But Aaron is right. It is too much for you." She put her arm around Molly. "We must think of the baby first. That is what your midwife would say, ain't so?"

Molly nodded, and Aaron could breathe again.

"I'm sure Aaron will go in your place," Katie added.

Much as he appreciated Katie's help with Molly, she had hit upon the one thing he couldn't do. How could he sit in an Englisch court and watch Sarah's pain, unable to help her?

"I think perhaps Sarah would rather I didn't go."

He found himself pinned by two pairs of eyes.

"Ach, Aaron, that is nonsense and you know it," Molly said. "Do you think I am blind? Sarah cares for you. And you care for her, too. You must help her."

He seemed to freeze. "There is nothing I can do." The words choked him. There was nothing.

"Don't say that." Molly's eyes sparked. "Aaron, I thought sure you were over your feelings about midwives."

"I don't—"

She thrust the baby toward him, and his arms curved automatically to take little Jacob. "Look at him," Molly demanded. "We owe his safe arrival to Sarah. I had the birth I wanted thanks to Sarah. Don't you see?"

He looked down at the soft, warm bundle in his arms. Jacob stretched, yawning. He stared up at Aaron with the wide, unswerving gaze of a newborn. His milky blue eyes seemed focused on Aaron's face, as if he already knew his onkel and had known him from the moment he entered the world.

For an instant Aaron was back in the upstairs room, looking at Sarah, sharing the joy of the baby's birth. His heart seemed to twist in his chest, almost as if it were cracking open to let something out. Or maybe to let something in.

That moment . . . how could he think that was wrong, for their Molly to have her babe there, in the room that had always been hers, with those she loved helping her? With the gaze of his tiny nephew on his face, how could he set himself up to judge how women should have their babies?

"Ja." He said the word softly, tears choking his voice. He put Jacob gently back into his mammi's arms. "Ja. I must help Sarah. And I think I know how it might be done."

Sarah took a last look around the birthing rooms, unable to stop herself even though it hurt. She'd had such high hopes when she'd come here to Pleasant Valley, and opening the birthing rooms had been a confirmation of those hopes.

Now . . . was it all to end today? She grasped the footboard of the bed, closing her eyes.

Father, guide me. I hope I am doing the right thing. I hope I am honoring the gift You gave me. If I am to suffer for that, grant me the courage You gave the martyrs of old.

"Sarah," Aunt Emma called. "I see Ben's car coming down the lane. Are you ready?"

She must be ready. She fastened her coat and tied her bonnet strings, then picked up her gloves and walked out of the birthing room, closing the door behind her.

She could hear the car now, too, coming to a stop by the front porch. She crossed the living room and found Aunt Emma in the hall, also wearing her outdoor clothes.

"Aunt Emma? What are you doing?"

"I am going with you." It was the tone her aunt used when she didn't want an argument.

Still, Sarah had to try. "You shouldn't. I mean, I know that Jonas doesn't want you to go, and I'll be fine on my own." Alone. Her heart was heavy in her chest.

"There is no point in arguing, because I am going. My son should know by now that he can't tell me what to do."

"I'm sure he didn't mean it like that. He's only trying to protect you." Once again her cousin had succeeded in putting his mother's back up.

Aunt Emma clasped her hand. "If they accuse you, they accuse me, too. Komm. We must go."

There was no argument left to make. She followed Aunt Emma outside to where Ben waited beside the car.

"Morning, ladies." He held the door open, his breath coming out in a frosty plume. "We'll get there in good time, leaving now. And don't you worry, Sarah. You're going to be fine."

She would like to be sure of that. "Denke, Ben."

She slid onto the seat next to her aunt. Ben closed the

door, climbed in, and turned the car carefully between the snow banks that lined the lane. They were on their way.

She tried to think of all the things the lawyer had told her, but her mind seemed curiously empty. They passed the pond where she and Aaron had joined in rescuing Louise. There was the Miller house, a spiral of smoke from the chimney the only sign of life.

"Don't grieve too much." Aunt Emma's hand clasped hers. "If Aaron cannot open his heart for you, then it is not meant to be."

Sarah nodded. She knew that, but somehow knowing didn't lessen the pain.

The road unwound before them, faster than seemed possible, with familiar farms and shops scrolling by on either side. Pleasant Valley slept in the quiet of winter under its blanket of snow. In moments they were driving down the main street of town. She had been here such a short time, but already Pleasant Valley had begun to feel like home. She didn't want to say good-bye.

They passed Bishop Mose's harness shop, and she turned her head to look. The shop seemed to be closed. She'd hoped Bishop Mose would turn up to go with them today, but he hadn't. Still, since the shop was closed, that might mean he would meet them in Lewisburg.

"You remember all the things the lawyer said you should say?" Aunt Emma asked.

Sarah took a deep breath, trying to organize her thoughts. "I think so. I'm as ready as I can be. We must hope that is enough."

"Ja. The rest is in God's hands."

She nodded, breathing a silent prayer. Whatever happened today, she would accept it as God's will.

Traffic became heavier as they approached Lewisburg, with several buses that seemed out of place on the tree-lined streets.

"Busier than usual," Ben said. "I might have trouble

parking, so I'll let you off in front of the courthouse and then go find a place to park."

"That will be fine," Aunt Emma said, pulling on her gloves. She sounded perfectly composed. Whatever might happen, it seemed she was ready.

Sarah reached inside herself, seeking that calm. It was in God's hands.

They turned the corner, and the courthouse loomed in front of them, large and imposing. But that was not what made Sarah catch her breath.

The steps of the building, the sidewalk in front, even the street itself—all were crowded with people. Not just people. Amish. Mennonite. Others.

"Sarah, look." Aunt Emma's voice filled with wonder. "Look. The People. They are here to support you."

She shook her head, hardly able to believe it. But it seemed to be true. Black-garbed Amish stood silently. Some of the Mennonites, distinguished by the women's print dresses, held signs. Scattered among them were Englisch, too, with more signs . . . signs supporting her, supporting midwives, declaring a woman's right to choose how her baby would be born. Beyond the crowd she glimpsed people with cameras, but the press of the crowd kept them back.

Ben slid out, grinning, and opened the door. To judge by the expression on his face, he had known about this.

She got out, turning to help Aunt Emma, but Bishop Mose was already there, assisting her. Then he straightened, nodding gravely to Sarah.

"We are ready," he said.

"Ja." They walked together through a path people made for them. Murmurs of support reached her, smiles of encouragement. She still could hardly take it in.

They passed a reporter at the courthouse door talking into a microphone. " . . . in an unprecedented show of silent support, Amish, Mennonites, and others gathered at the courthouse . . ."

The door cut off the woman's words, and they were inside. Bishop Mose guided them quickly down an echoing hallway. "Ms. Downing is waiting for us in the hearing room. Wait until you see."

A uniformed officer held the door open for them, and they passed through. Sarah's breath caught. Whatever she had imagined, it wasn't this.

The entire room was filled with people in Amish dress, sitting in rows as still and expectant as if they were at worship. Familiar faces turned to greet her as she walked down the aisle . . . the whole Beiler family was there, and the Fishers, the Schmidt family, and so many more.

"We had to hire several buses to bring everyone who wanted to come. We have been waiting at the doors since seven, so we could be here in the room when you arrived," Bishop Mose said quietly, as if it were the most normal thing in the world.

Sarah's heart was so full she couldn't speak. If she had wondered whether she was accepted in Pleasant Valley, she had her answer now.

Ms. Downing stood to greet them, clearly excited. "Can you believe this? The news crews are all over it, and the DA has been looking sicker and sicker all morning. This is not the kind of publicity any elected official wants."

Sarah nodded, tried to smile, but there was only one question on her mind right now. She turned to Bishop Mose.

"How," she asked, "did you do this?"

"I wish I had thought of it," he said. "It was all Aaron's idea. He started organizing people, and then Anna and her Englisch friend got involved, and the people from the clinic. Everyone wanted to help, it seemed."

She heard it all, but her mind had snagged on one name. Aaron. Aaron had done it.

Chapter Twenty

The lawyer drew Sarah to a seat behind a long table. Stomach lurching, Sarah sat down. The hearing was beginning, then. Even with the community solidly behind her, would she be able to do what she should?

Bishop Mose bent over her. "We are all praying," he said simply. He turned, moving into the row of seats behind the table, where a place had apparently been saved for him.

"Okay?" Sheila Downing gave her a questioning look.

Sarah glanced to the front of the room, to the high carved seat flanked by flags where the judge would sit. She swallowed hard.

We are praying for you.

The fear subsided. "I am all right."

"Good." The attorney slid papers from her briefcase onto the shining surface of the table. "We don't have much time," she went on, her voice low. "You understand, don't you, why this demonstration of support is important?"

"It means I am not alone."

The woman seemed faintly surprised. "Well, yes. More importantly, both the district attorney and the judge are aware of it. The DA is already wondering why he let himself in for this battle. They're both elected officials, after all."

"I see." At least, she was trying to. "How can that make a difference in determining what is right and what is wrong?"

The lawyer paused for a moment. "It shouldn't, but in a courtroom, sometimes it does. Trust me, this is a good thing."

They could agree on that, at least, if not on the reason why.

A door opened at the front of the room. The judge came in, imposing in his black robe. He took a step or two, glanced toward the room, and his stride checked. Then he mounted the platform to his seat.

After a few formalities, most of which Sarah didn't understand, the judge leaned forward, seeming to look directly at her over the tops of his glasses. Sarah steeled herself to meet his gaze.

Oddly enough, she didn't find it as frightening as she'd expected. The judge must be about Bishop Mose's age, and he had the same calm, the same air of weighing facts carefully before he made a decision.

He cleared his throat. "Let's make a few things clear, shall we? Mrs. Mast is not on trial here. This is a hearing, held to determine whether there is a case for trial or not."

Sarah gave a small nod, not sure whether he was speaking to her or to the mass of Amish behind her.

"So we're going to keep this simple and, I trust, brief." He looked from Ms. Downing to the district attorney, as if in warning. "I will hear statements from each of you, as well as any experts who can shed light on the subject." He glanced around the crowded room. "That's all. Mr. Hoagland, you may proceed."

Sarah tried to concentrate on what came next, but she failed to follow most of it. The attorney seemed to be speaking in a different language most of the time. He mainly seemed to be saying that since lay midwives weren't registered by the Pennsylvania Department of Health, it was a crime for them to help women have their babies.

When he called on Dr. Mitchell, she began to wish she didn't understand as much as she did. The district attorney led him through a series of questions that seemed meant to establish his important credentials. And, in contrast, she supposed, to her lack of them.

"Now, Dr. Mitchell, will you tell us exactly why you are opposed to the practice of lay midwives like Mrs. Stoltzfus and Mrs. Mast?"

"Certainly." Dr. Mitchell adjusted his glasses, seeming to avoid looking toward the crowded courtroom. "It's really very simple. Childbirth is a medical procedure. In my opinion, it requires the attendance of a licensed physician and should take place in a hospital, where full medical facilities are available. Only in such a way can we ensure the health and safety of mother and baby."

"Now, Dr. Mitchell, some might think that your only interest is in protecting your own turf." Mr. Hoagland's tone made it clear that the suggestion was ridiculous.

"Of course that's not true," Dr. Mitchell said, so quickly it seemed he'd known what the attorney would say. "Believe me, my practice would be much more financially successful if I didn't deliver babies at all, what with the high cost of malpractice insurance. But I see it as my duty to the community."

There was more in that vein, and Sarah had to admit to a growing sense that the man really believed what he said. Dr. Mitchell was convinced that his position was the only correct one, and nothing would sway him.

Soon it was Ms. Downing's turn to ask questions of Dr. Mitchell. She stood a few feet away from him, smiling gently. "Dr. Mitchell, how many babies have you delivered since you came to Pleasant Valley?"

The question seemed to startle him, but surely it was a logical one. "I'm not sure, exactly. I don't have my records with me."

"An approximate number will do," Ms. Downing said.

He shrugged. "Perhaps . . . about ten, I suppose."

"And before you came here, were you in practice elsewhere as an obstetrician?"

"No." He snapped off the word. "I'm a general practitioner, but I'm fully qualified to deliver babies. In a high-risk case, I can always refer a patient to a specialist in the city."

"So, ten babies, more or less. And how many in total?"

Dr. Mitchell seemed to grind his teeth, his face reddening. "About twenty."

"I see. And do you know how many babies Mrs. Mast has delivered?"

"I have no idea, nor do I care."

Ms. Downing smiled. "Would you be surprised that her records indicate she has assisted at the births of over two hundred babies?"

He clamped his mouth shut, clearly not prepared to answer.

Dr. Mitchell was followed by a woman from the Department of Health. As Sarah listened to the questions and answers, she began to realize that the woman was treading carefully, perhaps not wanting to offend either side. But she made it clear that lay midwives like Sarah were not licensed by the state, which seemed damaging enough, despite the point Ms. Downing made in her questions that many states did certify and license lay midwives.

When the woman from the Department of Health had stepped down, it seemed to be Ms. Downing's turn. As she rose from her chair and walked forward with an air of confidence, Sarah found herself relaxing. She was in good hands—she felt it.

Dr. Brandenmyer gave Sarah a reassuring smile as he came forward. His testimony was brief and to the point, supporting the invaluable role that midwives played in helping women who wanted a midwife-assisted home birth.

"Would you want to have someone like Sarah Mast on your staff, Dr. Brandenmyer?"

He smiled. "I'd be honored to. She has an excellent record, and I have seen for myself her empathy and caring for pregnant women. A midwife with her training and experience would be certified in any of a number of states."

Once Dr. Brandenmyer stepped down, Ms. Downing presented the letter from the doctor Sarah had worked with in Ohio, along with further testimony as to the qualifications of a midwife. The district attorney asked very few questions, and Sarah began to think Ms. Downing had been right that perhaps he regretted listening to Dr. Mitchell.

Ms. Downing addressed the judge. "Your Honor, this case clearly comes down to a disagreement over whether childbirth is the natural function of a healthy body or a medical procedure. Obviously, we believe—"

The judge cut her off with a raised hand. Then he gestured the two attorneys to come forward, leaning over to talk with them in tones so low Sarah couldn't hear. A cold hand seemed to grip the back of her neck. Had he already decided against her so quickly? If she had to go to trial . . .

Ms. Downing came quickly back to her, bending over to whisper. "Everyone wants this to go away, quickly and quietly. I just have to give the judge a legal hook on which to hang that."

Sarah was beginning to understand, she thought. "Can you do that?"

"I think so." The lawyer patted her hand and turned back to face the judge. "Your Honor, the fact that the Pennsylvania Department of Health does not certify lay midwives doesn't mean that such a role does not exist. Furthermore, any interference in the way the Amish choose to give birth might be interpreted as interfering with their civil rights under the Constitution. Therefore, I respectfully submit that this court is not the proper venue for a decision as to the role of midwives in childbirth."

The judge gave a brisk nod and turned to the district attorney. "Mr. Hoagland?"

"We agree, Your Honor." It seemed he couldn't say the words fast enough.

"I'm inclined to agree as well. I see no point in wasting the court's time with this matter. The case against midwife Sarah Mast is dismissed." He banged his gavel with a look of relief on his face. And then he was gone.

A murmur went through the courtroom. Sarah felt dazed. "Is it over?"

Grinning, Ms. Downing hugged her. "It's over," she said. "It's over."

"Praise God," Bishop Mose said.

People began to surge forward, thanking the attorney, crowding around Sarah.

Sarah released herself from Anna's hug, scanning the faces around her. All dear, familiar faces, but not the one she longed to see.

And then she spotted him. Aaron stood at the back of the room, looking at her. She met his gaze. She wanted to talk to him, to thank him, to tell him . . .

"Komm." Bishop Mose took her arm. "It is time to go home."

Aaron leaned against the back porch railing at Emma's house, not quite sure why he was still here. The house had been crowded with folks ever since the return from Lewisburg. He had a feeling that most of them were still vaguely astonished at themselves for having taken on an Englisch court and won in such a way.

People came and went, but he waited. There'd been no chance to talk with Sarah yet, and he must do that. And maybe he would have his wish. Sarah came into the kitchen, glanced through the window, and saw him. A moment later she stepped onto the porch, wrapping a shawl around her.

"Aren't you cold out here all alone, Aaron?"

He shrugged. "It's not bad. Too crowded in there for my taste."

"Ja." She gave a little sigh and leaned against the railing next to him. "I love all of them, and I am so grateful for their support. But you are the one I must talk with."

Her words were an echo of his thoughts, and he turned slightly so that he faced her. "Maybe that is why I'm standing out here."

She tilted her head, looking into his face. "I owe you so much gratitude for what you did that I don't know how to begin to say—"

"Then don't," he said. "I'm not here for thanks, Sarah. I'm here to say . . ." He hesitated, trying to find the right words. "I was wrong. That's all. If I were like that lawyer, maybe I could dress it up in fancier language, but that's the truth of it. I was wrong."

Her gaze searched his face. "You have a right to believe what you will, Aaron. If you don't feel that midwifery is acceptable—"

"Then I would be like Dr. Mitchell, speaking out of ignorance. Thinking I knew what was best for everyone."

A smile curved the corner of her lips. "Some people might believe that."

Warmth spread through him at the sight of that smile. "My sister and brothers, you mean. I'm trying to be a bit better about that. I don't want to tell them what to do, only to help them find the best way."

"Even if that is different from your way?"

"Ja. But maybe it isn't." He couldn't help it—he had to take her hands in his. "Sarah, when I saw what it meant to Molly, having her baby in familiar surroundings, when I saw how you encouraged her and helped her . . . well, I began to understand the value of what you do. How important it is that a woman like Molly could have her baby the way she wanted to."

Wariness still guarded Sarah's eyes. "You didn't want me to fight for it."

"No." He looked down at her hands, clasped in his. "I didn't, but it wasn't because I thought you were wrong. I feared you'd be hurt. And I thought you could give it up and still be happy."

"Do you still think that?" The question was hardly more than a whisper.

"No." He lifted her hands to his lips, looking at her with all the love he felt clear in his eyes. "Sarah, your skills are a part of you. A precious gift from God. You could no more give that up for me than I could give up loving my sister and brothers. No one should ever ask that in the name of love."

"Aaron . . ."

His lips brushed her hands. "I love you, Sarah, and your gift is part of you, so I love that, too. Will you be my wife?"

"Are you sure?" She put her palm against his cheek, looking gravely into his eyes.

"I am certain sure."

The last of the doubt disappeared from her eyes, leaving them as clear as glass. "I love you, Aaron. Nothing would make me happier."

He bent his head to kiss her, joy flooding his heart and filling him with peace.

Epilogue

The trees, covered with the pale yellow-green of early spring, arched over the picnic tables set up in Anna and Samuel's backyard, and the flowerbeds along the house were bright with sunny yellow daffodils and deep purple hyacinths. It was an off Sunday, and Anna had invited several families for a picnic lunch and to meet Rachel's new baby.

Sarah sat in a lawn chair in a circle of women, small children playing at their feet. A stray breeze sent a shower of cherry blossoms from the tree over their heads, and Anna's small daughter laughed, reaching up to try to catch them.

Anna smiled, watching her, and smoothed her hand over the bump under her apron. "I hope she'll be so happy when she has a new little brother or sister."

"Never doubt that," Sarah said. "Your little Grace has a loving heart to match her name."

"She does," Anna said softly. "There was a time when I couldn't have believed we'd be as happy and settled as we are today." Her gaze seemed instinctively to seek out Samuel, who was deep in conversation with Aaron as they crossed the yard from the paddock.

"It won't be long until Sarah is putting a new boppli in your arms," Molly said, cuddling little Jacob, who cooed up at her. "Then your happiness will be doubled."

"Until they reach their teen years," Leah said, smiling. "Our Matthew has always been so level-headed and serious, but these days it seems he'd forget his head if it were not securely attached."

Soft laughter seemed to circle them, and Sarah looked at their warm, familiar faces with a surge of gratitude for the providence that had brought her to Pleasant Valley. She'd hoped for a new life when she came here, and God had made that life fuller than she could have imagined.

"Your turn to hold Rachel's little son." Leah leaned across to put the baby in her arms. "Of course you've already met him."

"Ja, I have that." She smiled, stroking the soft fuzz on the baby's head. "He came out crying, and a better pair of lungs I've never heard. Rachel may have her hands full with this one."

"At least my other three are big enough to help with their baby bruder." Rachel's gentle face curved in a smile. "And Gideon would gladly do everything but nurse him if he didn't have to go to work."

Women and babies . . . For a moment Sarah's heart ached with the familiar longing to have a baby of her own. She felt a touch on her shoulder and knew it was Aaron even before she looked up at him.

"Are men banned from this circle?" he asked, glancing around.

"Not if you're willing to talk about babies and child-raising," Anna said, rising. "But I must bring out some snacks for the children, and I'm certain sure someone will be ready for another dessert."

Murmuring something about helping, Leah followed her sister toward the house.

"I have driven them away," Aaron said, smiling down at Sarah. "I didn't mean to. So, this is Rachel and Gideon's little one." He touched the small hand that was curved against Sarah's dress. "He's so tiny."

"They grow so fast." She stroked the baby's soft hair. "He is actually bigger than Molly's boppli was at this age." Her voice choked unexpectedly with tears. "I wish . . ." she said softly.

"I know." His fingers tightened on her shoulder, and his voice was low under the chatter of the others. "Whether we have a child of our own or not is in God's hands, and we will accept that and love each other just as much."

She put her hand over his, too moved to speak.

"Never forget that you already have babies, Sarah. You bring them into the world. How can they not be a part of you?"

The hurt seemed to smooth out of her heart as she held Aaron's hand and looked down at the infant in her arms. Aaron was right. God had truly blessed her, and she must never forget that.

Glossary of Pennsylvania Dutch Words and Phrases

ach. oh; used as an exclamation
agasinish. stubborn; self-willed
ain't so. A phrase commonly used at the end of a sentence to invite agreement.
alter. old man
anymore. Used as a substitute for "nowadays."
Ausbund. Amish hymnal. Used in the worship services, it contains traditional hymns, words only, to be sung without accompaniment. Many of the hymns date from the sixteenth century.
befuddled. mixed up
blabbermaul. talkative one
blaid. bashful
boppli. baby
bruder. brother
bu. boy
buwe. boys
daadi. daddy
Da Herr sei mit du. The Lord be with you.

denke. thanks (or *danki*)
Englischer. one who is not Plain
ferhoodled. upset; distracted
ferleicht. perhaps
frau. wife
fress. eat
gross. big
grossdaadi. grandfather
grossdaadi haus. An addition to the farmhouse, built for the grandparents to live in once they've "retired" from actively running the farm.
grossmutter. grandmother
gut. good
hatt. hard; difficult
haus. house
hinnersich. backward
ich. I
ja. yes
kapp. Prayer covering, worn in obedience to the Biblical injunction that women should pray with their heads covered. Kapps are made of Swiss organdy and are white. (In some Amish communities, unmarried girls thirteen and older wear black kapps during worship service.)
kinder. kids (or *kinner*)
komm. come
komm schnell. come quick
Leit. the people; the Amish
lippy. sassy
maidal. old maid; spinster
mamm. mother
middaagesse. lunch
mind. remember
onkel. uncle
Ordnung. The agreed-upon rules by which the Amish community lives. When new practices become an issue, they are discussed at length among the leadership. The decision for or against innovation is generally made on

the basis of maintaining the home and family as separate from the world. For instance, a telephone might be necessary in a shop in order to conduct business but would be banned from the home because it would intrude on family time.

Pennsylvania Dutch. The language is actually German in origin and is primarily a spoken language. Most Amish write in English, which results in many variations in spelling when the dialect is put into writing! The language probably originated in the south of Germany but is common also among the Swiss Mennonite and French Huguenot immigrants to Pennsylvania. The language was brought to America prior to the Revolution and is still in use today. High German is used for Scripture and church documents, while English is the language of commerce.

rumspringa. Running-around time. The late teen years when Amish youth taste some aspects of the outside world before deciding to be baptized into the church.

schnickelfritz. mischievous child

ser gut. very good

tastes like more. delicious

Was ist letz? What's the matter?

Wie bist du heit. how are you; said in greeting

wilkom. welcome

Wo bist du? Where are you?

Recipes

Grandma's Noodles

1 whole egg
3 egg yolks
1 to 2 cups flour
3 cups chicken broth

Beat together the whole egg and yolks. Add flour until a stiff dough forms. Turn out onto a well-floured board and let rest for 15 minutes. Using flour as needed and a large breadboard, roll the dough out to a paper-thin sheet. Cover with tea towels and let dry for several hours. Cut the sheet of dough into quarters, then roll up each quarter and slice very thinly. Shake out the rounds of dough into noodles. Add to boiling chicken broth and simmer for 20 minutes, stirring to avoid sticking. Delicious served with fried chicken or over mashed potatoes. Makes 6 to 8 servings.

Snickerdoodles

½ cup butter or margarine, softened
¾ cup sugar
1 egg
1½ cups flour
1 teaspoon baking powder
1 teaspoon baking soda
½ teaspoon ground nutmeg
¼ teaspoon salt
2 tablespoons sugar, for rolling
2 teaspoons cinnamon, for rolling

Cream together butter or margarine and sugar. Add egg and beat until fluffy. In a separate bowl, stir together flour, baking powder, baking soda, nutmeg, and salt. Blend into creamed mixture to make a stiff dough.

Mix the 2 tablespoons sugar and cinnamon together in a small bowl. Shape the dough into balls the size of walnuts. Roll cookie balls in the cinnamon sugar. Place on greased cookie sheet and flatten with a fork. Bake in a preheated oven at 400 degrees for 10 to 12 minutes or until very lightly browned. Remove to cooling rack, cool, and enjoy! Makes about 3 dozen small cookies.

Vegetable Beef Soup

1½ pounds chuck roast with bone
2 large onions, chopped
3 stalks celery, chopped
4 tablespoons salt
¼ cup barley
2 large carrots, diced
½ head of cabbage, chopped
1 cup potatoes, diced
1 turnip, chopped
1 parsnip, chopped
2 boxes frozen mixed vegetables
2 (32-ounce) cans whole or chopped tomatoes, undrained

Place meat, bone, onion, celery, and salt in large pot with two quarts water and boil for 4 hours. Remove the fat and bone. Add barley and cook for 1 hour longer. Add carrots and simmer for 30 minutes. Add cabbage, potatoes, turnip, and parsnip, and simmer another 30 minutes. Add frozen mixed vegetables and tomatoes and continue to simmer for 3 hours. Cool and skim off fat. Add more water as desired to thin the soup. Extra soup can be frozen or canned to preserve it. Makes about 6 quarts.

Dear Reader,

I hope you've enjoyed meeting the people of Pleasant Valley. Sarah's Gift *is the fourth book in my Pleasant Valley series, and I've loved the chance to revisit and see what's been happening to the characters I've created. Although the place doesn't actually exist, it seems very real to me, as it is based on the Amish settlements here in my area of central Pennsylvania.*

Sarah Mast is, I hope, a tribute to all those who have suffered for their determination to give women the sort of birthing experience they want, and her aunt is modeled after the strong women of my own family, especially my dear grandmother Mattie Dovenberger.

I would love to hear your thoughts about my book. If you'd care to write to me, I'd be happy to reply with a signed bookmark or bookplate and my brochure of Pennsylvania Dutch recipes. You can find me on the Web at www.martaperry.com, e-mail me at marta@martaperry.com, or write to me in care of Berkley Publicity Department, Penguin Group (USA) Inc., 375 Hudson Street, New York, NY 10014.

Blessings,
Marta Perry

Read on for an excerpt from

Katie's Way

Pleasant Valley

BOOK FIVE

by Marta Perry

Fast-paced chatter in Pennsylvania Dutch, followed by a ripple of women's laughter, floated through the archway from what used to be a hardware store. Caleb Brand forced himself to focus on the rocking chair he was waxing, trying to ignore the commotion.

He didn't like change. This building, with its two connected shops, had been a male enclave for years. Now all that was different, because Bishop Mose had decided to rent the other side to Katie Miller for a quilt shop.

Caleb gritted his teeth and rubbed a little harder, trying to concentrate on the grain of the hickory. Rocking chairs were among his best sellers, and this one had turned out to his satisfaction. He'd never let anything leave his shop that he wouldn't be happy to have in his own home.

Another peal of female laughter. How many women were over there anyway, helping to set up for the opening tomorrow? It sounded like half the sisters in the church district.

There was no reason why Katie Miller, newly komm to

Pleasant Valley from Columbia County, shouldn't open a quilt shop. He wished her well. Just not next door to him.

The bell on his own front door jingled, and he looked up. Bishop Mose, his white beard fluttering in the mild May breeze that swept down the main street of the village, ducked into the shop.

"Bishop Mose." Caleb half rose, showing the man where he was behind the counter at the rear of the showroom.

"Ach, Caleb, I thought you'd be tucked away in your workshop at this hour." The bishop, his years seeming to sit lightly on him, wound his way through the handmade wooden furniture that filled the room.

"Nobody's here to help out today, so I have to mind the shop." Caleb replaced the lid on the furniture wax, tapping it down tight. "Can I do something for you today?"

"Ach, no." The bishop's blue eyes, wise with a lifetime of service to the Amish of Pleasant Valley, crinkled a little. "Chust thought I should see for myself how you're dealing with your new neighbor."

Caleb glanced down at the rocker to avoid meeting the bishop's gaze. "Fine. Everything's fine, I think."

Maybe he didn't understand why Bishop Mose had seen fit to install a quilt shop next to him, but he wouldn't complain. He'd never forget that when it seemed every person in the valley had turned against him, Bishop Mose had accepted his word.

It was eight years since then, and Caleb supposed folks still talked. But thanks to Bishop Mose, he had his place here.

In the brief silence between them, the sound of women's voices came through clearly, talking about how best to display some quilts, it seemed.

"That's gut," Bishop Mose said. "I thought maybe it would be a bother to you, having a quilt shop next door instead of a hardware store."

Caleb caressed a curved spindle of the rocker absently, the wood warm and smooth under his hand. Could he drop a hint in the bishop's ear?

"Well, I did think a hardware store was a better fit with my shop." He said the words as cautiously as if he were walking on eggs. "We shared more of the same customers, ain't so?"

"You don't think the folks who buy Katie's quilts will be interested in your fine rocking chairs and chests?" Bishop Mose lifted white eyebrows.

Another burst of laughter scraped at Caleb's nerves. "No. I don't think a bunch of quilting women are likely to want what—"

He stopped, a little too late, he supposed. Katie Miller stood in the archway, and he didn't doubt she'd heard him.

He cleared his throat, trying to think what to say, but she beat him to it.

"Ach, Bishop Mose, I thought I heard your voice." The warm smile she directed toward the bishop probably didn't include Caleb. "Would you like to see what we've done with the shop?"

"We would like nothing better." He reached across the counter to clap Caleb's shoulder. "Komm, Caleb. We'll have a look at your new neighbor, ain't so?"

Caleb hesitated, glancing at Katie. Her blue eyes were guarded, it seemed to him, and her strong jaw set. Katie Miller looked like a determined woman, one bent on doing things her way.

Which was maybe how she'd reached her midtwenties without marrying, unusual for an Amish woman. And at the moment, her way most likely didn't include showing him her shop.

But in the next instant, her expression had melted into a smile. She smoothed back a strand of light brown hair under the white kapp on the back of her head and nodded. "Komm. I'd like fine to show you how the shop looks now."

With the bishop's hand on his shoulder, Caleb couldn't very well pull away. He walked through the archway, feeling as if he were moving into a foreign land.

It looked that way, too. Harvey Schmidt's barrels of

nails and spools of wire were long gone, of course. The shop had been stripped down to the bare shelves during Harvey's closing sale. But now—

The walls and shelves had been painted white, as had the counters. Against the white, every color possible glowed in bolts of fabric and spools of thread. It looked like a huge flower bed in full bloom.

And that was saying nothing of the quilts. Several quilts were draped on a four-poster maple bed that had been placed in the center of the space. Another quilt, in shades of blue and yellow and white, sagged between Molly, Katie's cousin—and the reason Katie had come to the valley in the first place—and Sarah Mast, Pleasant Valley's midwife. Both were up on chairs, obviously trying to hang the quilt from a rod that Harvey had used to support coils of rope.

"That looks like a dangerous thing to be doing." Bishop Mose was quick to steady the chair on which Molly teetered. "Especially for a new mammi."

Dimples appeared in Molly's cheeks. "Ach, you sound just like my Jacob. Anyone would think I was made of glass, to hear him. After all, our little boy is nearly three months old now."

"Ja, well, komm down anyway," Katie said, and went quickly to grasp the quilt from them. "This I'll put on top of the quilts on the bed, so that I can turn each one back when someone wants to see them. I have some quilted table runners that can hang from the rod instead."

Molly and Sarah climbed down, looking a little relieved, Caleb thought.

"We'll take care of it. You have guests to show around," Sarah said.

Katie surrendered the quilt to Sarah and spread her arms wide in a gesture that took in the whole of the small shop. "Here it is, as you can see." Another smile blossomed on her face, touching her eyes and bringing a glow to her cheeks.

Happiness. Hope. They radiated from Katie like heat from a stove. Caleb couldn't help but be touched.

But that didn't change anything, he reminded himself. Having the woman's business right next door was going to be a nuisance, at the very least.

And if she'd heard what folks said about him, he could only wonder why she'd want to be here at all.